FRACTURED FABLES

Praise for

A SPINDLE SPLINTERED

An NPR Best Book of 2021

A Locus Best Book and Editor Favorite of 2021

Shortlisted for the Hugo, Locus,
and British Fantasy Awards!

"A vivid, subversive, and feminist reimagining of 'Sleeping Beauty,' where implacable destiny is no match for courage, sisterhood, stubbornness, and a good working knowledge of fairy tales."

—Katherine Arden, bestselling author of the Winternight trilogy

"An exceptional heroine, smart writing, and a winning plot."

—Nancy Pearl

"It's funny, sharp, queer, and deeply loves its source material. . . . This novella pushes against the hopelessness of inevitability; it dares us to believe in sympathetic magic; it tells us we're connected through story. It might dent your heart a little, but it's good fun."

—NPR

"Like *Into the Spider-Verse* for Disney princesses, *A Spindle Splintered* is a delightful mash-up featuring Alix E. Harrow's trademark beautiful prose and whip-smart characters."

—Mike Chen, author of *Here and Now and Then*

"A wonderfully imaginative and queer-as-hell tale for those who wish to be the authors of their own stories."

—Kalynn Bayron, author of *Cinderella is Dead*

"This is a self-aware, empowered riff on 'Sleeping Beauty' that manages to be thrilling, funny, smart, and sweet."

—Sarah Pinsker, Nebula Award–winning author of *A Song for a New Day*

"Alix Harrow takes traditional fairy tales, turns them inside out, then upside down, and uses them to kick ass. Brava!"

—Ellen Klages, Nebula and World Fantasy Award–winning author of *The Green Glass Sea* and *Passing Strange*

"Harrow creates a lush and magical world with well-developed characters who are easy to love and root for."

—*School Library Journal* (starred review)

"Themes of female friendship, female strength, and female independence leave good feels behind, not to mention some laugh-out-loud bits. . . . This fairy tale–superhero movie mash-up is pure entertainment."

—*Kirkus Reviews*

"Bestselling author Harrow revives and rejuvenates the Sleeping Beauty fairy tale with a feminist twist in her latest. . . . Harrow uses her excellent skill as a storyteller to give agency back to the passive princess."

—*Booklist*

"Accompanied by Arthur Rackham's original illustrations, this quick read is a must for fairy-tale readers."

—*BuzzFeed*, Best Books of October List

PRAISE FOR

A MIRROR MENDED

A HUGO AND LOCUS AWARD FINALIST

A FINALIST FOR THE SIBA SOUTHERN BOOK PRIZE!

"A lively, engaging fairy-tale retelling perfect for devouring in a single sitting."

—*Kirkus Reviews*

"Series fans and lovers of fractured fairy tales will find plenty to hold their attention."

—*Publishers Weekly*

"Readers who love stories that twist narratives into knots will fall for Harrow's fractured fairy tale." —*Library Journal*

"Zinnia is a wonderfully unique figure in the long tradition of biblio-fantasy: a reluctant heroine whose superpower doesn't derive from spindles or mirrors, but from skillfully deconstructing the very stories she's in."

—*Locus*

Books by Alix E. Harrow

FRACTURED FABLES

A Spindle Splintered

A Mirror Mended

The Ten Thousand Doors of January

The Once and Future Witches

Starling House

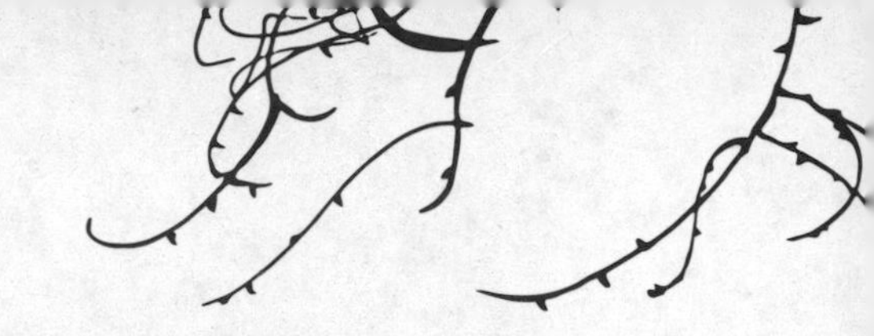

FRACTURED FABLES

COLLECTING

A SPINDLE SPLINTERED

A MIRROR MENDED

Alix E. Harrow

TOR PUBLISHING GROUP
NEW YORK

Many silhouette illustrations by Arthur Rackham set throughout this book were unavoidably harmed, fractured, and splintered during the design process. Can you spot the changes?

This is a work of fiction. All of the characters, organizations, and events portrayed in these novellas are either products of the author's imagination or are used fictitiously.

FRACTURED FABLES

Interior illustrations by Arthur Rackham and Michael Rogers

Designed by Gregory Collins

A Tordotcom Book
Published by Tom Doherty Associates / Tor Publishing Group
120 Broadway
New York, NY 10271

www.tor.com

The Library of Congress Cataloging-in-Publication Data is available upon request.

ISBN 978-1-250-90575-8 (paperback)
ISBN 978-1-250-32681-2 (ebook)

Our books may be purchased in bulk for promotional, educational, or business use. Please contact your local bookseller or the Macmillan Corporate and Premium Sales Department at 1-800-221-7945, extension 5442, or by email at MacmillanSpecialMarkets@macmillan.com.

First Edition: 2024

Printed in the United States of America

0 9 8 7 6 5 4 3 2 1

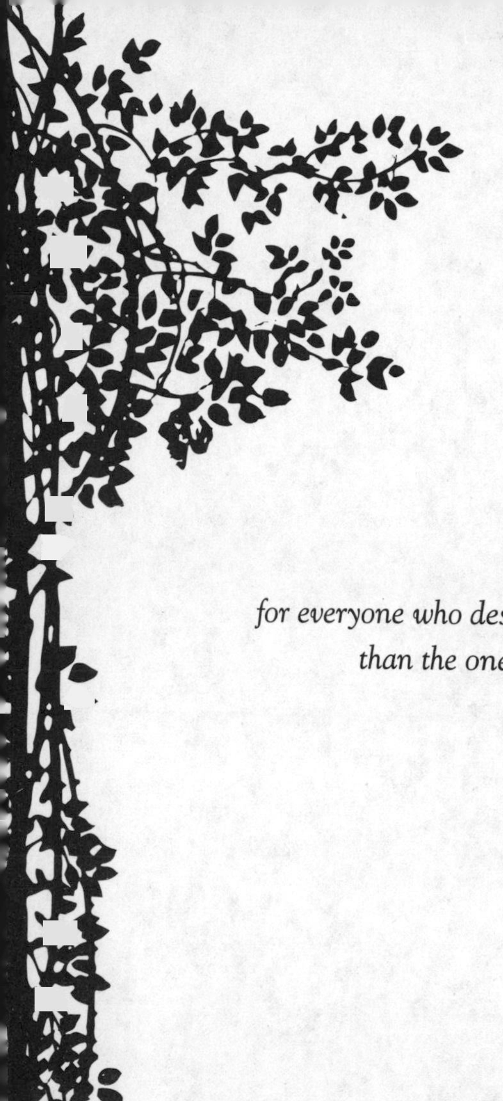

for everyone who deserves a better story
than the one they have

INTRODUCTION

I can't usually identify the moment an idea arrived. But this one came to me in the parking lot of the Cinemark Theatre in Richmond, Kentucky, on a December afternoon in 2018, about eight minutes after leaving a matinee of *Spider-Man: Into the Spider-Verse*.

(Forgive me if you've heard me tell this story before; in my defense, that's sort of the theme of this essay.)

Spider-Verse was and remains the best superhero movie I've ever seen, because it understands how many superhero movies I've already seen. It knows how many times I've seen Peter Parker bitten by the spider and Uncle Ben shot, how many different actors I've seen under the mask. It's self-aware, but not snide; subversive, but not shrill. It doesn't ignore all its previous iterations, or despise them—it gives them speaking lines.

And it's just so *fun*. Every frame is saturated with a sort of gleeful, giddy mischief. You can almost hear the creators cackling to themselves.

(Please imagine this as a monologue delivered to my husband. He is listening, but he is also guiding me gently toward the car, because I have forgotten where I parked.)

It wasn't that I'd been a huge comic-book kid, honestly. If anything, I'd been a fairy-tale kid. I grew up on Little Golden Book versions of Disney movies, followed by my mom's leather-bound book of Grimms' fairy tales, the one with full-page illustrations protected by filmy, translucent sheets of wax paper, followed in turn by the sudden and delightful explosion of young adult fairy-tale retellings: Levine, Yolen, Marillier, McKinley.

At that point, my two remaining neurons collided, and I said, "I want to Spider-Verse a fairy tale."

My husband said that sounded great and asked if my seat belt was buckled (it was not).

Of course, fairy-tale retellings have been done before. A fairy tale is a retelling almost by definition: a story that has been told before and will be told again, over and over, for a purpose that shifts according to time and place.

The Grimms retold them to help construct a unified national identity for the nascent German state (and to make money). The Victorians retold them to instill specific gender and class values in their children, and to lay claim to a broader white European heritage (and to make money). Disney put fairy tales on the screen almost exclusively to make money, which worked because the Victorian project had been so successful that by 1937 every midwestern American kid knew Snow White's name, and because she so perfectly embodied the purity, perseverance, and passivity of the ideal American girl.

I'm making it sound like fairy-tale retellings are inherently hegemonic, but by now they've been thoroughly subverted, revised, reinvented, reclaimed, deconstructed and reconstructed, canceled and resurrected. The princesses have rescued themselves, the witches have been redeemed, the princes have been introduced to the concept of consent. A feminist fairy-tale retelling is no longer "necessary" or "long-overdue," thank God; it's just Tuesday.

And yet: we're still not done with them. We keep circling back, like fictional murderers to the scene of the crime. I think when we want to make sense of the new, we reach for the oldest tools. I think our favorite songs are the ones we've heard before; I think we like stories best when they echo.

That's what A *Spindle Splintered* and A *Mirror Mended* are about, really: the stories we keep telling and the echoes between them. I hope it reminds you of books you've read before but doesn't bore you; I hope you know the ending but are still surprised.

I hope you can hear me, faintly, cackling to myself on every page.

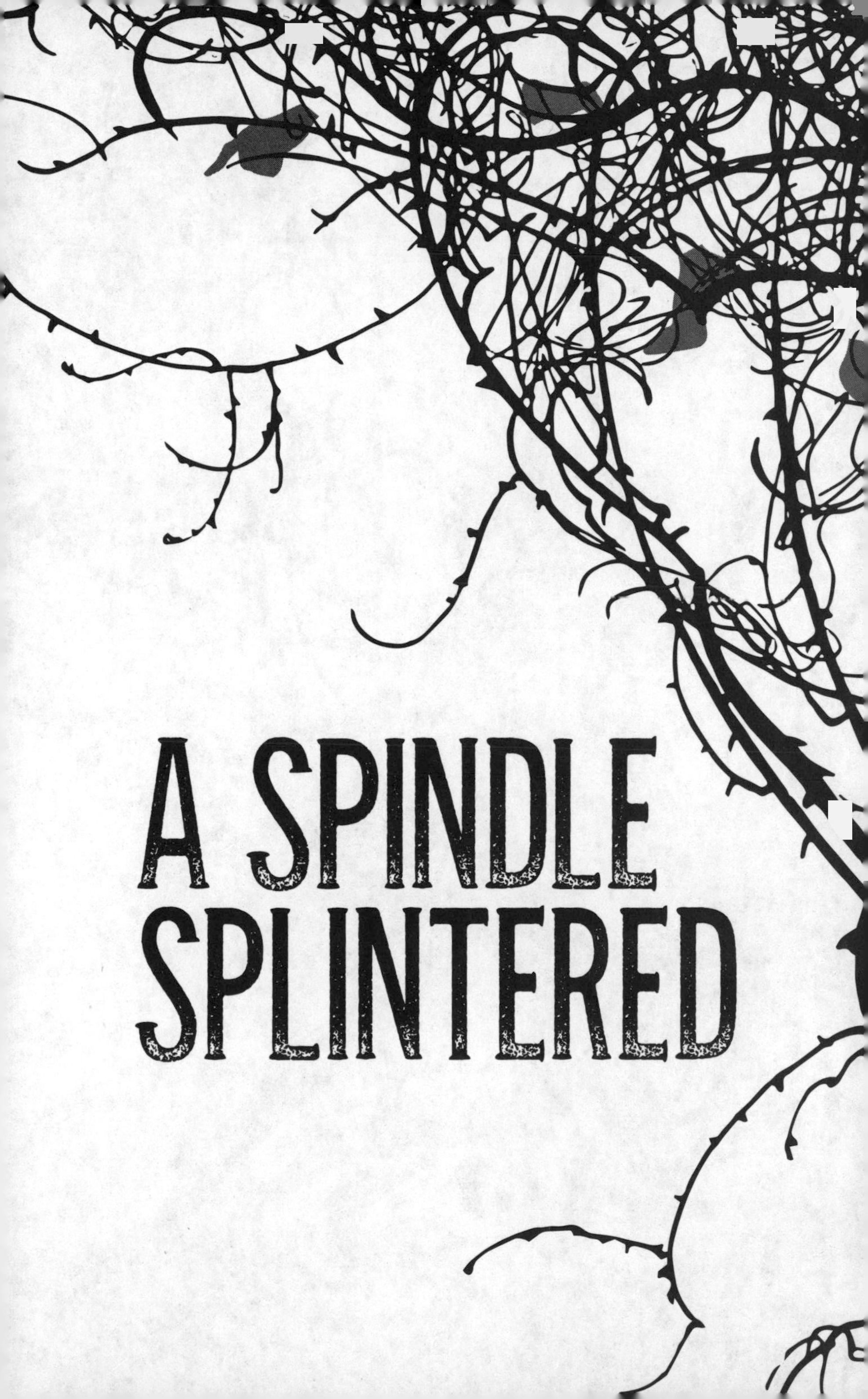
A SPINDLE
SPLINTERED

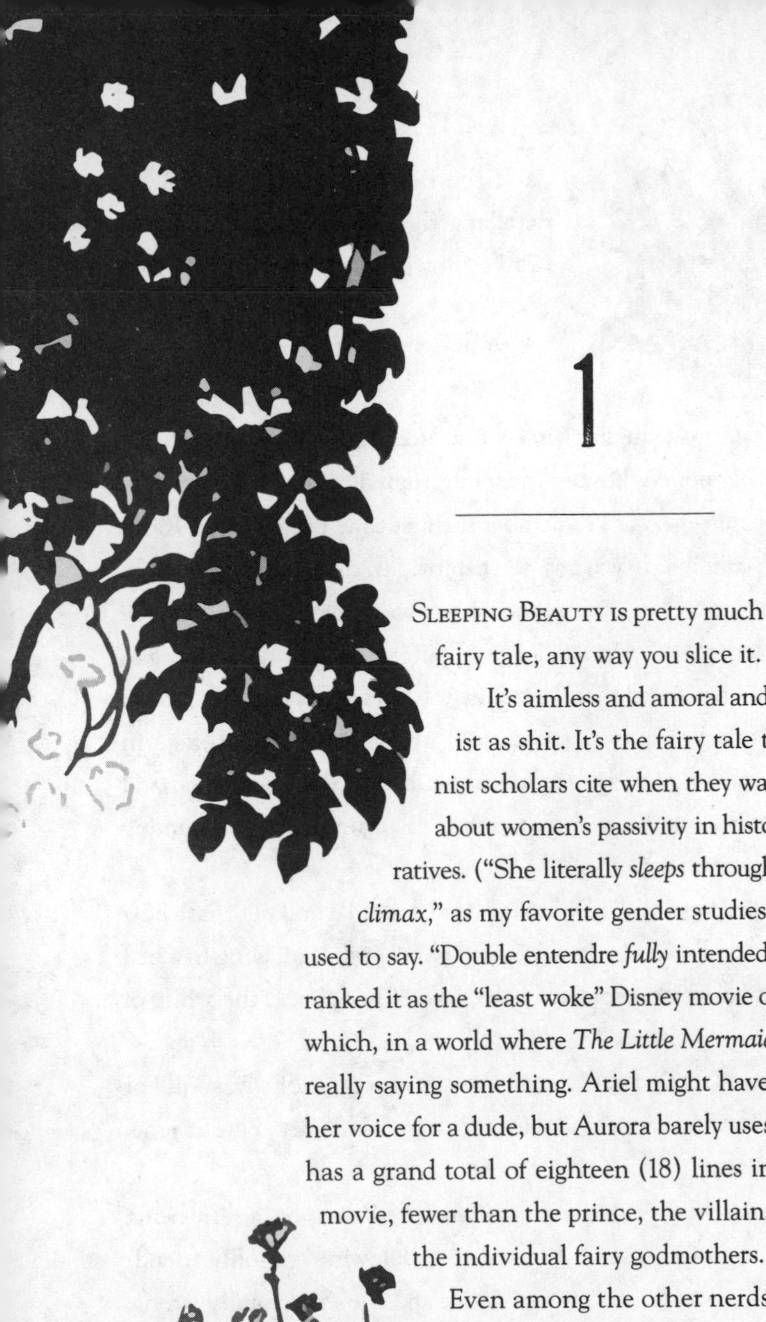

1

Sleeping Beauty is pretty much the worst fairy tale, any way you slice it.

It's aimless and amoral and chauvinist as shit. It's the fairy tale that feminist scholars cite when they want to talk about women's passivity in historical narratives. ("She literally *sleeps* through her own *climax*," as my favorite gender studies professor used to say. "Double entendre *fully* intended."). *Jezebel* ranked it as the "least woke" Disney movie of all time, which, in a world where *The Little Mermaid* exists, is really saying something. Ariel might have given up her voice for a dude, but Aurora barely uses hers: she has a grand total of eighteen (18) lines in her own movie, fewer than the prince, the villain, or any of the individual fairy godmothers.

Even among the other nerds who majored in folklore, Sleeping Beauty is nobody's favorite. Romantic girls like Beauty

and the Beast; vanilla girls like Cinderella; goth girls like Snow White. Only dying girls like Sleeping Beauty.

❁ ❁ ❁

I DON'T REMEMBER the first time I saw *Sleeping Beauty*—probably in some waiting room or hospital bed, interrupted by blipping machines and chirpy nurses—but I remember the first time I saw Arthur Rackham's illustrations. It was my sixth birthday, after cake but before my evening pills. The second-to-last gift was a cloth-bound copy of Grimms' fairy tales from Dad. I was flipping through it (pretending to be a little more excited than I actually was because even at six I knew my parents needed a lot of protecting) when I saw her: a woman in palest watercolor lying artfully across her bed. Eyes closed, one hand dangling white and limp, throat arched. Black-ink shadows looming like crows around her.

She looked beautiful. She looked dead. Later I'd find out that's how every Sleeping Beauty looks—hot and blond and dead, lying in a bed that might be a bier. I touched the curve of her cheek, the white of her palm, half hypnotized.

But I wasn't really a goner until I turned the page. She was still hot and blond but no longer dead. Her eyes were wide open, blue as June, defiantly alive.

And it was like—I don't know. A beacon being lit, a flint being struck in my chest. Charm (Charmaine Baldwin, best/only friend) says Sleeping Beauty was my first crush and she's not totally wrong, but it was more than that. It was like looking into a mirror and seeing my face reflected brighter and better. It was my own shitty story made mythic and grand and beautiful. A princess cursed at birth. A sleep that never ends. A dying girl who refused to die.

Objectively, I'm aware our stories aren't that similar. Wicked fairies are thin on the ground in rural Ohio, and I'm not suffering from a curse so much as fatal teratogenic damage caused by corporate malfeasance. If you drew a Venn diagram between me and Briar Rose, the overlap would be: (1) doomed to die young, (2) hot, in a fragile, consumptive way, (3) named after flowers. (I mean, look: I have a folklore degree. I'm aware that Sleeping Beauty's name has ranged from Talia to Aurora to Zellandine (do *not* google that last one), but the Grimms called her Briar Rose and my name is Zinnia Gray, so just let me have this one, alright?). I'm not even blond.

After that birthday I was pretty obsessed. It's one of the rules for dying girls: if you like something, like it *hard,* because you don't have a lot of time to waste. So I had Sleeping Beauty bedsheets and Sleeping Beauty toothpaste and Sleeping Beauty Barbies. My bookshelves filled with Grimm and Lang and then McKinley and Levine and Yolen. I read every retelling and every picture book; I bought a DVD set of the original *Alvin and the Chipmunks* run just to watch episode 85B, "The Legend of Sleeping Brittany," which was just as awful as every other chipmunk-related piece of media. By the time I was twelve, I'd seen a thousand beauties prick their fingers on a thousand spindles, a thousand castles swallowed by a thousand rose hedges. I still wanted more.

I graduated high school two years early—another one of the rules for dying girls is *move fast*—and went straight into the Department of Folk Studies and Anthropology at Ohio University. Seven semesters later I had an impractical degree, a two-hundred-page thesis on representations of disability and chronic illness in European folklore, and less than a year left to live.

Dad would cry if he heard me say that. Mom would invent some urgent task in her flower beds, tending things that weren't going to die on her. Charm would roll her eyes and tell me to quit being such a little bitch about it (it takes a particular kind of tough to pick the dying girl to be your best friend).

All of them would remind me that I don't know exactly how long I've got, that Generalized Roseville Malady is still largely unstudied, that new treatments are being tested as we speak, etc., etc., but the fact is that nobody with GRM has made it to twenty-two.

Today is my twenty-first birthday.

My relatives are all over for dinner and my grandma is drinking like a fish, if fish drank scotch, and my worst aunt is badgering Dad about crystals and alternative therapies. My cheeks hurt from fake-smiling and my poor parents are doing their very best to keep the

celebration from feeling like a wake and I have never been more relieved in my short, doomed life to feel the buzz of my phone on my hip. It's Charm, of course: happy birthday!!

And then: meet me at the tower, princess.

* * *

TOWERS, LIKE WICKED fairies, are pretty rare in Ohio. We mostly have pole barns and Jesus-y billboards and endless squares of soybeans.

Roseville has a tower, though. There's an old state penitentiary out on Route 32, abandoned in the '60s or '70s. Most of it is hulking brick buildings with smashed-out windows and mediocre graffiti, obviously haunted, but there's an old watchtower standing on one corner. It should be exactly as creepy as the rest of the place, poisoned by decades of human misery and institutional injustice, but instead it looks . . . lost. Out of time and place, like a landlocked lighthouse. Like a fairy tale tower somehow washed up on the shores of the real world.

It's where I always planned to die, in my morbid preteen phase. I imagined I would dramatically rip the IVs from my veins and limp down the county road, suffocating in my own treacherous proteins, collapsing Gothic-ly and attractively just as I reached the highest room. My hair would fan into a black halo around the bloodless white of my face and whoever found me would be forced to pause and sigh at the sheer picturesque tragedy of the thing. Eat your heart out, Rackham.

God, middle schoolers are intense. I no longer plan to make anyone discover my wasted body, because I'm not a monster, but I still visit the tower sometimes. It's where I went after high school to ditch track practice and get high with Charm; it's where I made out for the first time (also with Charm, before I instituted dying girl rule number #3); it's where I go when I can't stand to be in my own house, my own skin, for another second.

I switch off the headlights and coast the last quarter mile down Route 32, because the old penitentiary is technically private property upon which trespassers will be shot, and park in the grass. I pop my eight o'clock handful of pills and make my way down the rutted lane that leads to the old watchtower.

I'm not surprised to see the orange flicker of light in the windows.

I figure Charm dragged a few of our friends—her friends, if we're being honest—out here for a party, rather than hosting it in the hazardous waste zone she calls an apartment. I bet she brought red plastic cups and a half keg because she wants me to have a legit twenty-first-birthday experience, completely ignoring the fact that alcohol interferes with at least three of my meds, because that's the kind of friend she is.

But when I step through the tower door, it doesn't smell like beer and weed and mildew. It smells luxuriant, heady, so sweet I feel like an old-timey cartoon character hooked by the nostrils.

I waft up the staircase. There are murmuring voices above me, faint strains of very un-Charm-like music growing louder. The highest room in the tower has always been empty except for the detritus left by time and teenagers: windblown leaves, beer tabs, cicada shells, a condom or two. It's not empty tonight. There are strings of pearled lights crisscrossing the ceiling and long swaths of blushing fabric draped over the windows; a dozen or so people wearing the kind of gauzy fairy wings that come from the year-round Halloween store at the mall; roses absolutely *everywhere*, bursting from buckets and mason jars and Carlo Rossi jugs. And in the very center of the room, looking dusty and rickety and somehow grand: a spinning wheel.

That's when I recognize the song that's playing: "Once Upon a Dream." The main theme from Disney's *Sleeping Beauty*, a waltzing melody stolen straight from Tchaikovsky's ballet.

I am way, way too old for a Sleeping Beauty–themed birthday. I can't stop smiling. "Oh, *Charm*, you *didn't*."

"I one hundred percent did." Charm passes her PBR to the girl beside her and flings herself at me. She does a little heel-pop when I hug her, like an actress in a black-and-white movie except with more tattoos and piercings. "Happy birthday, baby, from your fairy godmothers." She waggles her wings at me—blue, because Merryweather is her favorite character—and mashes a plastic princess crown onto my head.

Our friends (her friends) clap and hoot and pass me warmish beer. Someone switches the music, thank God, and for a few hours I pretend I'm just like them. Young and thoughtless and happy, poised at the first chapter of my story instead of the last.

Charm keeps it going as long as she can. She forces everyone into a game of Disney trivia that appears to have no rules except that I always win; she passes around pink-and-blue frosted cupcakes in a plastic Walmart clamshell; she plucks petals from the roses and flings them at me whenever my smile threatens to sag. Everybody seems to enjoy themselves.

For a while.

But there's only so long you can hang out with the dying girl and her best friend without mortality coming to tap her knucklebones at your window. By eleven, somebody gets drunk enough to ask me, "So like, what are you doing this fall?" and a chill slinks into the room. It coils around our ankles and shivers down our spines and suddenly the roses smell like a funeral and nobody is meeting my eyes.

I consider lying. Pretending I have some internship or job or adventure lined up like the rest of them, when really I have nothing planned but a finite number of family game nights, during which my parents will stare tenderly at me across the dining room table and I will slowly suffocate under the terrible weight of their love.

"You know." I shrug. "Just playing out the clock." I try to make it jokey, but I can tell there's too much acid in my voice.

After that, Charm's friends slither out of the tower in cowardly twos and threes until it's just us, like it usually is. Like it won't be for too much longer. Her friends took their speaker with them, so the tower is silent except for the gentle rush of wind against the windows, the crack and hiss of another beer being opened.

Charm resettles her fairy wings and looks over at me with a dangerous softening around her eyes, mouth half open, and I have a terrible premonition that she's about to say something unforgivably sincere, like *I love you* or *I'll miss you*.

I flick my chin at the spinning wheel. "Dare you to prick your finger."

Charm tosses a bleached slice of hair out of her eyes, softness vanishing. "You're the princess, hon." She winks. "But I'll kiss you after." Her voice is saucy but unserious, which is a relief. Dying girl rule #3 is *no romance,* because my entire life is one long trolley problem and I don't want to put any more bodies on the tracks. (I've spent enough time in therapy to know that this isn't "a healthy attitude toward attachment," but I personally feel that accepting my own imminent mortality is enough work without also having a healthy attitude about it.)

"You know it wasn't originally a spinning wheel in the story?" I offer, because alcohol transforms me into a chatty Wikipedia page. "In the original version—I mean, if oral traditions had original versions, which they don't—she pricks her finger on a piece of flax. The Grimms used the word *spindel*, or spindle, but the wheel itself wasn't commonly used in Europe until the mid-sixteenth . . . why are your eyes closed?"

"I'm praying for your amyloidosis to flare up and end my pain."

"Okay, fuck you?"

"Do you have any idea how hard it is to fit a spinning wheel in the trunk of a Corolla? Just prick your finger already! It's almost midnight."

"That's Cinderella, dumbass." But I lurch obediently to my feet,

discovering from the delicate spin of the windows that I'm slightly drunker than I'd guessed. I curtsy to Charm, wobble only a little, and touch my finger to the spindle's end.

Nothing happens, naturally. Why would it? It's just a dusty antique in an abandoned watchtower, not nearly sharp enough to draw blood, and I'm just a dying girl with bad luck and a boring life. Neither of us is anything special.

I look down at the iron spike of the spindle, slightly cross-eyed. For no reason I think of the girl in that Rackham illustration, blond and tragic. I think how it must have felt to grow up in the shadow of a curse, how much she must have hated the story she was handed. How in the end all her hate didn't matter because she still reached her finger for that spindle, powerless to stop the cruel gears of her own narrative—

Distantly, I hear Charm say, "Jesus, Zin," and I become aware that I'm pressing my finger into the spindle's end, burying the point in the soft meat of my skin. I look down to see a single red tear welling at the end of it.

And then something happens, after all.

THE ROOM VANISHES around me. The world smears sideways behind my eyelids, blurring into an infinity of colors. I figure I'm dead.

It's a pretty solid bet: Generalized Roseville Malady has a lot of symptoms and side effects, but the most noticeable one is sudden death. I don't want to go into all the jargon—Charm is the science nerd, bio and chem double major, headed for a prestigious internship at Pfizer—but essentially, my ribosomes are ticking time bombs. They're supposed to fold my proteins into clever little origami shapes, which they've been doing, mostly, but one day they're going to go haywire and start churning out garbage. My organs will fill up with mutant proteins, murderous fleets of malformed paper cranes, and I'll drown in my own fucked-up biological destiny.

I figure that day is today. It occurs to me what a twisted sense of humor the universe has, to kill me in the highest tower in the land just as

I pricked my finger on a spindle's end. I wonder if I look hot, sprawled limp and lifeless among the roses. I wonder if that will be the very last thing I wonder.

But my vision isn't going dark. The world is still rushing past me, colors and sounds and flashing by like riffled pages. I assume at first this is the life-flashing-before-my-eyes thing, but it seems longer and stranger than the twenty-one years I've lived.

And the faces I see don't belong to me. They belong to a thousand other girls reaching out toward a thousand spinning wheels or spindles or splinters. Other sleeping beauties, in other stories? I want to stop them, shout some kind of warning—*stop, you boneheads!*

One of them seems to hear me. She looks up at me with eyes that are an impossible shade of cerulean, her face framed by locks of literal gold, her finger hovering a centimeter above the spindle's end. Her lips frame a single word: "*Help.*"

The world stops smearing.

I am still on my feet. Still slightly drunk. Still touching a throbbing finger to something sharp. But everything else is different: the spinning wheel before me is polished smooth with use, the bobbin wound with flaxen thread, the distaff gleaming wickedly. The water-stained plywood of the floor has been replaced by smooth flagstones, the rickety windows by narrow, glassless slits. A cool wind slinks through them, smelling of midnight and magic.

I look up, reeling, and meet those ridiculous eyes again. They belong to a girl so gorgeous she veers from the beautiful toward the unnerving. Nobody outside a fashion magazine has skin without pores or lips the color of actual rose petals. Nobody outside a Ren faire wears dresses with pleats and girdles and trailing sleeves.

"Oh!" she says, and even her voice is fucking musical. "From whence have you come?"

I want to assure her that none of this is real. That she and her tower are hallucinations produced by the last desperate misfires of my synapses. That her usage of *whence* was grammatically suspect at best, anachronistic at worst.

I manage a single wheezy, "Holy *shit*," before my vision goes black.

❁ ❁ ❁

I WAKE UP in bed. Not mine; mine is a twin mattress with faded Disney sheets that I grew out of years ago but don't see the point in replacing. This bed is an absurd, canopied affair of white silk and soft down. It's the sort of bed that only exists in period romances and fairy tales, because actual medieval beds were a lot smellier and lumpier; the sort of bed where a princess might sleep comfortably for a hundred years.

I part the canopy with one finger and find a room that matches the bed: dark stone and rich rugs, tapestries and carved-oak chests. I blink into the cheery morning light for several seconds, half expecting a songbird to alight on the windowsill and break into an upbeat chorus, before sinking calmly back against the pillows.

This is the point in your standard fantasy adventure where the heroine would give herself a good hard pinch to determine whether or not she's dreaming. But I can hear the labored thump of my heart in my ears, feel the slightly hungover scratchiness of my eyeballs: I'm not sleeping. I'm not hallucinating. Unless the afterlife is even more profoundly wacky than most major religions have so far posited, I'm not dead. Which means—

I can't seem to finish the thought. It

sends a giddy, hysterical thrill up my spine and a nameless rush of something behind my ribcage.

My phone hums in my jean pocket. I fish it out to find roughly eight hundred texts from Charm. Most of them are variations of wtf wtf WTF where are you interspersed with threats upon my person (if this is some kind of sick joke I swear to jesus I will kill you before the grm does) and pleas for a response (hey your parents are calling me now and idk what to say so if you're alive NOW'S THE TIME BITCH).

I start to type back an apology then pause, wondering about data rates between Ohio and wherever the hell I am and how *exactly* I have cell signal, before that wild hysteria bubbles over. I write sorry babe. got spider-verse-ed into a fairy tale.

As I hit send, I feel that unfamiliar rushing in my chest again, and it turns out it has a name, after all. Oh, *hell.* You'd think twenty-one years under a life sentence would be enough to squash all the hope out of me, but here I am, lying in a bed that doesn't belong to me, filled with the desperate, foolish hope that maybe my story is about to change.

The phone buzzes in my palm: is this a joke to you

Followed by: i thought you were dead/abducted!!! what the HELL zin???

I'm tapping out a longer explanation when that impossible girl with the impossible hair sweeps aside the canopy and carols, "Oh, you're awake! Thank goodness!"

I squint at her—this slender golden princess limned in dawn light, her cheeks flushed and her eyes shining—and slowly raise my phone, take her picture, and send it to Charm with the caption not joking.

"Are you well?" the princess asks earnestly. "Should I call for a healer?"

I ignore her, choosing instead to watch Charm's

little typing bubble appear and disappear several times. It's worth mentioning at this juncture that Charm is profoundly, disastrously gay, and suffers from a diagnosable hero complex. Willowy princess-types with slender wrists and visible collarbones are essentially her kryptonite.

The bubble reappears. who is thjat

*that

I grin up at the princess, who now has two tiny lines marring her perfect brow. "What's your name?" I ask.

She tilts her chin very slightly upward. "I am Princess Primrose of Perceforest. And who are *you*?" I detect a hint of haughtiness in that *you*, as if she barely restrained herself from adding *peasant* after it.

"Zinnia Gray of, uh, Ohio." My eyes return to my phone. Princess

Mothereffing Primrose, apparently, I type. dude, where did you get that spinning wheel??

pam's corner closet & more. Pam's is the nearest flea market to our old high school and an extremely unlikely place to purchase an accursed or enchanted object. It's mostly just used vacuums and Beanie Babies perched on moldy piles of *National Geographics*.

"Lady Zinnia." The princess's voice is less musical when she's annoyed. "If I could but beg your attention for a moment. I would very much like to know how you came to be in the tower with me last night."

I slide the phone into my hoodie pocket and scooch upright in bed, legs crossed. "Is there coffee in this universe? No? Okay, just sit down." From Primrose's expression, I suspect she's not accustomed to being invited to sit on her own bed by sickly, short-haired interdimensional travelers in unwashed jeans. "Please," I add.

Primrose perches at the foot of the bed, her posture painfully upright.

"How about we start with you. What exactly were you doing in that tower room?" I'm seventy-five, maybe eighty percent sure I already know.

She draws a measured breath, and for the first time I catch a gleam of something raw beneath the porcelain-doll perfection of her face. "I—don't know. It was my first-and-twentieth birthday yesterday." Of course it was. "And I went to sleep very late. My dreams were strange, unsettled, full of a green light that called my name . . . And then I woke in a room I'd never seen before! Far from my bed, reaching for that strange object."

"You mean the spinning wheel?"

Her pale face grows two shades paler, and the raw thing in her eyes swims closer to the surface: a desperate, lonely terror. "I thought it must be," she breathes. "I'd never seen one 'til last evening."

"Because, I assume, your father ordered them all destroyed?" Standard Perrault stuff, repeated by the Grimms a hundred years later and canonized by Disney in the '50s.

Primrose stares at me for a long second, then nods.

"Mother says he spent months riding the countryside, holding bonfires in every village. He was trying to save me." I can hear the weariness in her voice, the exhaustion of being unsavable. Dad used to spend hours on the phone with specialists and experimental labs and miserly insurance companies, mortgaging the house in his search for a cure that doesn't exist, trying so hard to save me that he nearly lost me. He stopped only when I begged.

"Hold on a second." I slide my phone back out and start to text Dad, wimp out, and write Charm instead. can you tell mom & dad I'm not dead pls?

already done, she writes back, because she is, and I cannot stress this enough, the best.

"Okay, continue."

The princess appears to brace herself for a grand speech. "I am cursed, you see. Twelve fairies were invited to my christening feast. But a thirteenth fairy arrived, uninvited!" I don't think I've ever heard a person speak with so many implied exclamation points. It's exhausting. "A most wicked creature who placed a curse upon me—"

"To prick your finger on your twenty-first birthday and fall down dead? That sound right?"

Primrose deflates slightly. "An enchanted sleep."

"Lucky you."

"You think it *lucky* to be cursed to sleep for a century—"

"Yeah, I do." It comes out harsher than

I mean it to. I swallow hard. "I'm sorry. Look. I'm—cursed, too. Last night was my twenty-first birthday. I was in my own world, minding my own business. I pricked my finger on a spindle as a joke, and all of a sudden I was here. In an honest-to-Jesus *castle* with an honest-to-Jesus *princess*. And historically inaccurate furnishings."

The lines have reappeared between Primrose's brows. "Was it a wicked fairy that cursed you, as well?"

I consider trying to explain that my world doesn't have curses or fairies. That my fate was determined by lax environmental regulations and soulless energy executives and plain old bad luck. "Sure, yeah," I say instead. "Except I'm going to die, not sleep, and there's nothing anybody can do to save me." But hope flutters in my chest again. I'm in a land of magic and miracles now, not ribosomes and proteins. Who knows what is or isn't possible?

"I'm sorry," says the princess, and I can tell she means it. Most people don't know what to do when you tell them you're dying. They flinch or look away or step back, as if bad luck is contagious, or they go all maudlin and grip your hands and tell you how brave you are. Primrose just looks at me, steady and sorry, like she knows exactly how much it sucks, and neither pities nor admires me for it.

I feel snot gathering in my throat and cough it away. "It's not a big deal, it's fine," I lie. I can tell that she knows it's a lie, because she's spent roughly twenty-one years telling herself the same one, but she doesn't call me on it.

"Well. Thank you, however you came to be here. I've never met anyone else . . ." *Cursed,* I think, but she says, "Like me." She gives me a furtive, hungry look that causes me to suspect the life of a cursed princess is several degrees lonelier than the life of a dying girl.

Primrose clears her throat. "And thank you for saving me from my curse. At least for now." She looks toward her bedroom door, eyes flashing eerie green. "I still feel it calling to me. I haven't slept all night for fear I will wake in that tower room, reaching toward that wheel. Perhaps if I destroy it—my father would surely burn it if he knew—"

"No!" Panic makes my voice overloud. "I mean, please don't. I'm pretty sure that thing is my only ticket out of here. It must be a portal or something, a match to the one back home." A sly little voice whispers, *Are you sure you want to go home?* I elect to ignore it.

Primrose looks doubtful. "But what if it sends you into an enchanted sleep, as it would me?"

"Maybe. I don't know the rules, man." I run my fingers through the greasy tangle of my hair. "I'm just saying don't set it on fire yet. Give me a second to think."

Primrose opens her mouth to respond, but a light tap comes at the door. A voice calls, "Your Majesty. Your father requests your presence in the throne room."

I watch the pale bob of her throat as the princess swallows. "Of course. A moment, only." She spins back to me. "I have to go. Stay hidden until my return." It's an order, casually issued, as if she can't imagine anyone disobeying her.

I bow my head as she sweeps from the room.

I scroll through the ten or fifteen messages I've missed from Charm (are you okay tho? are there pharmacies in fairyland??) and type back: I only have 35% battery so I'm turning this off in case of emergencies. xoxo ummmm this IS an emergency. why are you not freaking out. why are you not trying to come back.

I start to type because but can't decide what comes next. Because I don't want to, at least not yet. Because I've fallen out of my own story and into one that might have a happy ending. Because this is my last chance to have a real adventure, to escape, to do more than play out the clock.

In the end I just write i'll come back. cross my heart, before turning my phone off. Then I wallow my way out of Primrose's ridiculous bed, steal a gown from her wardrobe, and slip out the door after her.

3

When I was eleven, I used my Make-A-Wish Foundation wish to spend a night in the Disney castle and get the full princess experience. It was a total letdown. I think I waited too long: eleven is old enough to see the cracks in the plaster, to sense the pity behind the megawatt smiles of the staff. It was like trying to play with my Barbies a year after I'd outgrown them, perfectly remembering how it used to feel but unable to feel it again.

Primrose's castle is about a thousand times better. The stone is smooth and cool beneath my tennis shoes and the torch brackets smell of oil and char. My dress isn't polyester and plastic; it hangs heavy on my shoulders, literal pounds of burgundy velvet and gold thread. I try to walk like Primrose, a glide so delicate it suggests my feet touch the earth only by happenstance.

I pass a pair of women who I think might be actual chambermaids and they pause to stare, mouths slightly open. Maybe it's my haircut or my shoes, or the fact that I couldn't figure out the laces and strings in the back of the dress and left it gaping open like one of those terrible paper hospital gowns. Whatever. Surely they're used to inbred nobility with eccentric habits of dress.

I wave cheerily at them and they fall into belated curtsies. "Which way to the throne room?"

One of the maids points wordlessly down the hall. I attempt a regal nod in return, which causes one of them to giggle and the other to elbow her.

The throne room looks exactly like you might expect a throne room to look: a long hall with vaulted ceilings and high windows. There are honest-to-God *knights* stationed along the walls, surrounding a small crowd of people who look like lost extras from the set of *A Knight's Tale*, all puffed sleeves and sweeping trains. A ruby-red carpet splits the room, leading to a man and woman sitting on golden chairs.

Primrose looks nothing like her parents. I guess when twelve fairies bless you with hotness, you lose some of the family quirks. The queen has ordinary brown hair, a too-long nose, and an expression of permanent weariness; the king is roundish and baldish and alcoholic-looking. Standing beside them, Primrose looks like one of those Renaissance angels descended among mortals, softly glowing. I touch my own chin—the tiny, too-sharp chin I got straight from Mom—and almost like it for the first time in my life.

Primrose's eyes flick up at my movement. They widen very slightly.

I give her a cheery shrug.

Before she can either banish me or die of embarrassment, the king taps his ringed knuckle against the arm of his throne. The court falls quiet. "It is my very great pleasure to announce that the curse laid upon our fair princess has failed! She is one-and-twenty years old, and yet untouched by that wicked promise!" His accent is vaguely English, the way medieval accents are in movies, and his voice booms exactly like a king's should. When the clapping and hurrah-ing dies down, he continues, "And it is my even greater pleasure to announce my daughter's betrothal!" I guess exclamation points are inheritable. "To none other than the good Prince Harold of Glennwald!"

It's only then that I notice the person standing on the other side of the thrones: a twenty-something man wearing a tunic and an expression of criminal smugness. He's handsome, in that generic, Captain America–ish way that does absolutely nothing for me, and I can tell from the briefest glance at Primrose that I'm not alone. She's smiling, but there's a falseness to it that reminds me of those Disneyland actresses when I was eleven.

That smile jars me, like a little shock of static or a missed step on the stairs. I know this story really, really well: after the curse is broken, Prince Charming marries the princess and they live happily ever after, the end. But this version has slid sideways somehow, like a listing ship. The curse isn't quite broken, the prince isn't quite charming, and that's not a happily ever after I see swimming in the princess's eyes.

The king has been speechifying for some time about his hopes for their blessed union and Prince Harold's many virtues. "—a true son to us, who has tirelessly striven to end the curse for years now, even tracking the fairy to her lair, though she fled before his might." I squint at Harold, all jawline and puffed pride; surely even an off-brand discount-store Maleficent could take him if she wanted to. "That their marriage may be delayed no longer, Princess Primrose and her betrothed will speak their vows in three days hence!"

There's a final swell of applause as Primrose and Harold step before the thrones and clasp hands. Primrose's hand looks limp and boneless in his, like a small, skinned animal.

I lurk at the back of the crowd for a while after that, smiling and nodding and collecting odd looks, before a voice hisses, "What do you think you are *doing*?"

I spin to face Primrose and sweep her my most absurd curtsy. "Why, Your Majesty, may I not celebrate your engagement?" Oh God, now I'm doing the fake British accent thing.

She barely seems to hear me, her face still gritted in that plastic smile, her pupils wide and hunted. "Your hair, your shoes . . . you look *deranged*. If anyone sees you—my father's court does not take kindly to the uncanny!"

Her hand clamps around my bicep and steers me into a side hall. "Return to my rooms and wait for me." I cross my arms and give her my best *make me* glare. "Please," she adds, looking at me with those enormous eyes of hers, "I beg of you."

I'm at least three-quarters straight, but her lashes are very long and very golden and I'm not made of stone. I nod. She closes her eyes as if summoning some inner strength before swishing back into the throne room with her smile shining like a shield.

I get lost two or three times on the way back up,

startling a pair of amorous knights in a broom closet and briefly alarming a cook. By the time I climb all nine hundred stairs I can hear my pulse a little too loudly in my own ears, feel my lungs pressing too hard against my ribs. I think of my morning handful of pills back in Ohio and the last round of X-rays that showed the chambers of my heart shrinking, my lungs congested. I hadn't showed them to Charm.

Primrose's room is warm and sunshiny and quiet. I shrug out of the burgundy velvet gown and curl in her window in my socks and hoodie, staring out at the countryside like a girl in a Mucha ad, thinking about curses and fairies and stories gone sideways. Thinking that I should probably go find that magic spindle and prick my finger and peace out of this entire medieval hallucination.

Instead, I wait. I watch the slow creep of shadows and the lazy dance of dust motes in the air. The sun is squatting fat and red on the horizon by the time Primrose returns.

She's still stunning, but I must be getting used to it, because I can see past the shine to the weary set of her mouth, the grim line of her spine. She sets a silver platter

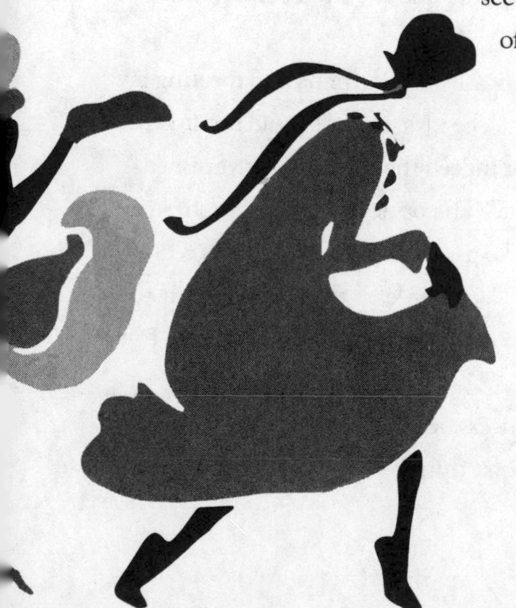

of heaped food on the seat beside me and collapses back onto her bed, vanishing behind the canopy with a dramatic sigh.

I take three enormous bites of something that I recognize from *The Great British Bake-Off* as a hand-raised pie. "So." I swallow. "Harold seems nice."

"Yes." Her voice is muffled, as if she's facedown in a pillow.

"Good-looking, if you're into cleft chins."

"Quite."

"And yet I can't help but detect a tad of reluctance on your part."

There's a short sigh from behind the canopy. "He's—it's—fine. I'm fine." It's a lie but I let it stand because she did the same for me, and sometimes lies are lifeboats.

The sheets rustle as Primrose rolls over. "Anyway, it hardly matters. None of them understand that the curse is still . . . waiting. Calling to me. Eventually I'll have to sleep, and I fear I will wake again only as my finger pricks the spindle's end."

I struggle not to roll my eyes at this excessive drama. "Okay, but like, just let me zap myself back to Ohio and then you can set it on fire or whatever. Boom, curse dodged."

Primrose sits up slowly, brushing aside the curtains and meeting my eyes. "I searched for it, after supper," she says softly. "I could not find the spinning wheel, nor the room, nor indeed the tower. It has vanished."

I think: *oh, shit*. I say, "Oh, shit." The princess doesn't flinch, so either they don't have swears in Fake-ass Medieval Fairy Land or Primrose isn't as proper as she seems. "Well, at least there's Harold. If you fall into an enchanted sleep, nine out of ten doctors recommend true love's kiss—"

"Harold is not my true love. I *assure* you." Her lips are thin and pale, twisted with revulsion. "I don't think—I don't know that there's any escaping it."

"No. There is, there has to be." I'm standing for some reason, my fingers curled into useless fists. I remind myself that this isn't my problem or business or story. That I should be sitting at home with my parents for whatever time I have left, like I promised I would, rather than gallivanting through the multiverse without my meds.

"Look. Both of us should have died or been cursed or whatever last night, on our twenty-first birthdays. But something messed it up. Our lines got crossed." I picture that listing ship again, or maybe a train leaping off its tracks and hurtling into the unknown. "It feels like we have a chance to make it come out different. To do something." I haven't wanted to "do something" since I was sixteen, packing my backpack and planning my escape.

The princess sighs a long, defeated sigh, but I can see a foolish flicker of hope in her eyes. "Like what?"

"Like . . ." The idea leaps from my skull fully formed, armored and Athenian and deeply stupid. I love it. "Like taking matters into our own hands." I feel a slightly demented smile stretching my face. "Where's this wicked fairy, exactly?"

4

THE THING ABOUT bad ideas is that they're contagious. I watch mine infect the princess, her expression sliding from bafflement to horror to frozen fascination.

"Her lair lies through the Forbidden Moor," she says slowly. "At the peak of Mount Vordred."

"Yeah, that sounds about right. How long would it take to get there? By, uh, horse or whatever?"

"It took Prince Harold three days of swift riding."

Her answer initiates a complex series of calculations involving the number of missed pills over the amount of preexisting protein buildup, magnified by physical exertion and divided by the number of days I have left. If I were a machine, all my warning lights would be blinking. I ignore them.

"We'll need supplies and food and stuff. Do you have anything more . . . rugged to wear?"

Primrose is watching me as if I'm a grisly car accident or a public marriage proposal: gruesome but mesmerizing. "It won't work, you know."

I'm already rooting through her wardrobe, looking for something free of ruffles, lace, pleats, bows, satin, ribbons, or pearls and not finding it. I wish briefly but passionately that I'd been zapped into a different storyline, maybe one of those '90s girl power fairy tale retellings with a rebellious princess who wears trousers and hates sewing. (I know they promoted a reductive vision of women's agency that privileged traditionally male-coded forms of power, but let's not pretend girls with swords don't get shit done.)

Primrose tries again. "She is powerful and cruel, and terribly ancient. Some say she has lived seven mortal lives!" I try not to let my pulse leap or my hands shake, to remind myself that hope is for suckers. "She evaded my father's men for one-and-twenty years. Even when Prince Harold—"

"Harold does not strike me as a Perceforest's best and brightest."

"But neither are we, surely!"

I spin to face her, arms full of satin ruffles. "So what's your plan? Stay here and wait for the curse to catch you, like you did for the first twenty-one years of your life? Close your eyes and go to sleep and let the world go on without you?" My voice is an angry hiss, but I don't know which of us I'm angry at.

Primrose's face is a waxy green color, her lips pressed white. I step closer. "In my world there's nothing I can do to save myself. No curse to break, no fairy to defeat. But it's different here. You can do something other than stand around and wait." I riffle through my mental box of inspirational quotes and come up with a Dylan Thomas line that I actually know from *Interstellar*. "Do not go gentle into that good night, princess. I beg of you."

She must be susceptible to begging too, because she stares at me for another breathless second before inclining her head infinitesimally. "Alright."

I clap my palms together. "Swell. Now do you happen to have a magic sword or anything? An enchanted amulet? A shield imbued with special powers?"

I'm mostly joking, but Primrose wrings her hands, thumbs rubbing hard along slender wrists. "Well." She kneels and reaches beneath the soft down of her mattress, emerging with something that gleams cruelly in the reddening dusk. "There's this."

It's a long, narrow knife, sharp as glass and black as sin. It looks out of place among the feather pillows and ball gowns of Primrose's world, as if it belongs to some other, darker story.

"Where the *hell* did you get that?"

Primrose holds the knife flat on her palms. "A traveling magician sold it to me when I was sixteen. He swore to me that a single cut was enough to end a life." She says it flatly, matter-of-factly, but her eyes have gone hollow and her face is waxy again and suddenly I don't feel jokey at all. Suddenly I wonder why a princess would sleep with a poison blade beneath her bed, why she would purchase it in the first place.

I picture myself at sixteen, a scarecrow of a girl stuffed with hormones and hunger instead of straw, so sick of dying I would do anything to live. I ran very different calculations in those days, comparing the Greyhound bus schedule to the number of hours before my parents would report me missing, multiplying hoarded pills by the number of days I would have on the run. I figured I could make it to Chicago before the cops were even looking for me, and from there I could go—anywhere. Do anything. Steal a few months or years for myself rather than feeding them all to my parents and their broken hearts.

Except I told Charm before I ran, and she instantly told Dad. He came up to my room looking like—I try not to remember it, actually. His face was a snapshot of my own death, a time-lapse video of the devastation I would leave behind me. We made a deal that night: if I promised not to run away, he promised to stop trying so hard to keep me.

A week later I took the SAT and dropped out of high school with my parents' blessing. Dad paid my application fee and I enrolled at Ohio University that fall. I loved it. The food was bad and my roommate was a nightmare who kept trying to sell me essential oils, but it was the first time I'd felt like a real adult. Like someone who owned their future, who belonged to no one but herself.

That feeling had been trickling away all summer as I folded myself back into the teenage-shaped hole I left behind at my parents, but what would I have done without that brief escape? What if I'd been trapped with no future and no friends, like Primrose? Perhaps I would have turned toward a darker, uglier kind of escape.

I take the knife from Primrose very, very carefully. "How . . . helpful. I'll carry this, okay?" I wrap it in the least expensive-looking skirt I can find. "So. Which way to the stables?"

"What—you mean now? *Tonight?*"

Apparently Primrose never learned dying girl rule #1: *move fast.* "Yes, dummy. How long do you think you can go without sleep?"

❁ ❁ ❁

IN THE FOLLOWING hour, several things become clear to me.

First, that Primrose isn't quite as helpless and damsel-in-distress-ish as I thought. Rather than sneaking through the castle and making off with a pair of horses by moonlight, she simply informs the stable hands that she and her ladies are going for a dawn ride through the countryside and would like two horses saddled and waiting with a picnic packed for six, please and thank you. "They won't miss us for hours, this way," she says calmly.

Second, that I do not technically "know" how to ride a "horse," to quote an unnecessarily shocked princess. "But how do you travel in your land? Surely you do not walk?" I consider explaining about internal combustion engines and state highways and asking if she'd like to try driving a stick shift with a sketchy second gear. I shrug instead.

Third, that one cannot learn to ride a horse in five minutes, at least not well enough to be trusted on a midnight journey to the Forbidden Moor.

I wind up perched behind the princess on a pile of folded blankets, clinging desperately to her traveling cloak and thinking that Charm would give a year of her life to be cozied up behind Primrose as she galloped into the night on a daring half-cocked rescue mission.

Even I can admit it's pretty cool. The air is clean and sharp and the stars reel above us like ciphers or hieroglyphs, stories written in a language I don't know. The trees are dark Arthur Rackham-ish tangles on either side of the road, reaching for us with wicked fingers while the night birds sing strange songs. My lungs ache and my legs are numb and I know Dad would have a stroke if he could see me, but he can't, and for tonight at least my life is my own, to waste or squander or give to someone else, no matter how little of it might be left.

We stop twice that night. The first time in a grove of tall pines, silver-blue in the moonlight, where the horse's hooves are silenced by soft needles. I don't so much dismount as fall sideways, barely managing to keep my phone uncrushed in my back pocket. The princess makes a graceful, sweeping gesture that somehow ends with her standing beside her horse, cloak pooled elegantly around her slippered feet. Her shoulders are a bowed line.

I don't generally do a lot of worrying about other people, except for Charm and my parents, but even I can see she's tired. "We could sleep here if you like." I poke the deep-piled pine needles. "It's nice and squashy."

Primrose shakes her head. "I'd like to be further from the castle before I sleep." There's a green gleam in her eyes as she looks back the way we came.

We ride on.

The next time we stop is beneath a gnarled hawthorn, where the earth is bare and knotted with roots. Primrose's dismount looks much more like mine this time, her legs stiff, her hands clumsy. I half catch her in my arms, thinking only briefly how heroic I look before settling her between the least lumpy roots. By the time I tuck our extra clothes and blankets around her, she's asleep.

Which is just as well, because that way she can't comment on my intelligence or life skills as I wrangle the saddle off the horse and loop her reins around a low branch. The princess's horse must be a patient soul, because she merely gives me a long-suffering ear flick rather than stomping me into jelly.

I pull my arms inside my hoodie sleeves and hunch against the warm leather of the saddle, looking up at stars through the crosshatched branches and doubting very much that I'll be able to sleep.

I must be wrong, because I wake abruptly, my legs stiff and damp, dew-soaked. The sky is the profound, reproachful black of four in the morning and someone is moving nearby.

It's Primrose, standing, her head tilted oddly to one side, her eyes wide open. There's a sickly shine to them, like the reflection of something poisonous.

"Princess?" She doesn't seem to hear me. She takes a step deeper into the woods, then another, as if there's an invisible thread tugging her deeper into a labyrinth. "Primrose!"

I heave upright and stumble toward her, grabbing her shoulders and shaking hard. "Jesus, *wake up*!" She does. I feel the weird tension slide out of her body, her arms un-tensing beneath my hands. I release her.

"Lady Zinnia?" She looks back at me with eyes that are vague and sleep-soft, perfectly blue once more. "What—oh. Dear."

I swallow the stale taste of fear. "Yeah." It's one thing to read about dark enchantments and fairy curses; it's quite another to watch them take hold of a woman's will and march her like a porcelain puppet toward her own doom. The glossy sheen of this place is wearing thin, like paint peeling to reveal black mold running beneath it.

I shrug at her with my hands shoved deep in my jean pockets. "I'll keep watch, if you want to get a little more sleep."

She worries at her lower lip with teeth that are too white in the dark. She nods and curls back among the hawthorn roots, arms wrapped tight around herself, hair spilling over her cloak.

I watch in silence until her body uncoils and her fingers unclench. Afterward I find myself squinting into the spaces between trees, looking for a hint of green or the shine of a spindle's end, getting steadily more spooked by the cool touch of wind down my neck and the soft scuttling sounds of night creatures in the woods. I decide it's a good time to check my phone.

There are several dozen more texts from Charm, mostly threats upon my person should I fail to return; a handful from Dad, their tone genial listing toward worried; one from the Roseville Public Library informing me that I now owe them $15.75 in fines and/or my firstborn child.

A few hours ago it had seemed like a perfectly fine idea to go have a little adventure, face down a fairy, rescue a princess (and maybe, somehow, myself), and zap back home like Bilbo strolling back into the Shire. But now—huddled in the cold dark with a cursed princess and a tightness in my chest that's either terror or impending death—I'm feeling more like Frodo, whose story was full of danger. Who never did get to return home, or at least not for long.

I text Charm. going to face Maleficent and break curse, should be home in three days.

She texts back so fast I feel a hot stab of guilt, knowing she's sleeping with her ringer on. how are you getting home??

portkey?

there's no such thing as portkeys asshole. A brief pause. and i thought we agreed never to mention joanne or her works ever again

I consider asking her how she would explain interdimensional travel into overlapping fictional narratives, but Charm probably has at least three solid theories she would like to discuss. At length. With slides. So instead I lean over to take another picture of Primrose. Even on my mediocre camera, blurred and dim, she's luminous. Her face glows white out of the gloom, a sleeping beauty by way of Rembrandt.

A slight pause before she replies: do not attempt to distract me with your hot imaginary friend. I repeat: there's no such thing as portkeys

says who

says physics

hon, I respond patiently, I am currently on a quest to find and defeat a wicked fairy. pretty sure the laws of physics no longer apply

the laws of physics always apply, that's why we call them laws

There's a long gap while her texting bubble appears and disappears.

give her hell from me, babe

I can almost hear the rasp of Charm's voice as she says it, the sudden sincerity that no one expects from a girl with a giant Golden Age Superman tattoo on her shoulder. There's no reason to choke up over it, so I don't. I send her another xoxo and power the phone off before the battery can dip below 20 percent.

After that I sit with my arms around my shins and my cheek on my knees, watching the dawn paint the princess in silver and shadow and wondering what it would feel like to sleep and keep sleeping. Better than dying, I guess, but Jesus—what a shitty story the two of us were given. I don't know about the moral arc of the universe, but our arcs sure as hell don't bend toward justice.

Unless we change them. Unless we grab our narratives by the ear

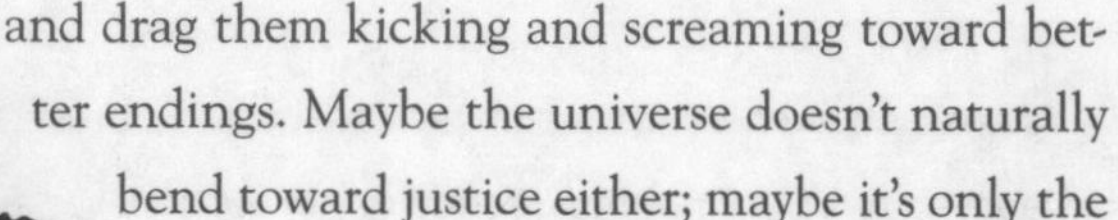

and drag them kicking and screaming toward better endings. Maybe the universe doesn't naturally bend toward justice either; maybe it's only the weight of hands and hearts pulling it true, inch by stubborn inch.

❊ ❊ ❊

"So, WHY IS the moor forbidden?" I'm aiming for nonchalant, but my voice sounds tense in my ears. "Are there flying monkeys? Rodents of Unusual Size?"

"What?"

"Just checking."

It's the morning of the third day and we've abandoned the road, picking our way over scrubby hills and wind-scoured stone. The sun is grayish and reluctant here, as if it's shining through greasy paper, and the trees are stunted and crabbed.

Primrose has pulled the horse to a stop before a pair of tall, jagged stones. They aren't carved with strange symbols or glowing or anything, but there's something deliberate about the angle of them, like they aren't there by accident.

The princess makes her graceful dismount and touches her palm to the sharp edge of one of the stones. "It's forbidden because my father wishes to protect his people, and the moor is dangerous if you don't know the way."

"Do we know the way?"

"Harold told me. In some detail." The flatness of her tone suggests that Harold is one of those men whose conversations are more like long, boastful speeches. "I listened well."

Without the slightest change of expression, without even drawing a breath, Primrose drags her palm hard across the edge. When she draws back the stone shines slick and dark with blood.

"*Jesus*, Primrose, what are you doing?"

She doesn't answer, but merely lifts her hand to the sky, palm up. I watch her blood run down her wrist, red as roses, red as riding hoods. I was so sure I'd landed in one of those soft, G-rated fairy tales, stripped of medieval horrors; I can feel it shifting beneath my feet, twisting toward the kind of tale where prices are paid and blood is spilled.

A shape wings toward us across the moor, ragged and black. It lands on the standing stone in a rush of feathers, and for the first time in my life I fully appreciate the difference between a crow and a raven. This bird is huge and wild-looking, clearly built for midnights dreary rather than McDonald's parking lots.

It dips forward and laps at Primrose's palm with a thick tongue and this, I find, is a little much. "Okay, what the *fuck*?"

"We'll leave Buttercup behind and continue on foot," Primrose says evenly. "Walk close behind me, and do not stray to either side." The raven launches back into the air, cutting a curving path through the smeary sky, and lands on a low branch a quarter mile ahead. Primrose follows it, stepping between the standing stones with her bloodied palm held tight to her chest. I follow them both, muttering about antibiotics and blood poisoning and tetanus, feeling the cold knock of the knife against my ribs, hoping to God all this nonsense is worth it.

❁ ❁ ❁

BY NIGHTFALL, A mist has risen. I'm tired and hungry and my muscles are shuddering from three days without supplements or steroids.

Primrose isn't much better; the curse has woken her at midnight for each of the last three nights, the pull growing stronger each time. I'm not sure she slept at all last night, but merely curled beneath her cloak with her eyes screwed shut, fighting the silent call of her spell.

The damn bird leads us in circles and loops, twisting and doubling back so many times I come very close to stomping off on a path of my own making, screw magic—but the shadows fall strangely across the moor. I keep thinking I see dark shapes creeping beside us, furred and clawed, gone as soon as I turn to look.

I stay behind Primrose. We keep following the raven.

I don't know if it's the mist or something more, but the mountains arrive all at once: black teeth erupting before us, crooked and sharp. A rough road coils up from the moor, biting into the mountainside and ending in a structure so ruinously Gothic, so bleak and desperate, it can only belong to one person in this story.

"Should we approach by the main road?" Primrose whispers. "Or go around, perhaps sneak in and take her by surprise?"

At some point I suppose I should stop being surprised when the princess is more than a doe-eyed maiden, ready to faint prettily at the first sign of danger. I'm always annoyed when people are surprised that I have a personality beyond my disease, as if they expect me to be nothing but brave smiles and blood-spotted handkerchiefs.

I watch the raven spiral up the mountain. It soars through a narrow slit at the top of the tallest tower of the castle. "Oh, I think we can probably just knock on the front door, like civilized folk." Even before I finish speaking the window pulses with a faint, greenish light. "She already knows we're coming."

5

THE PATH UP the mountain doesn't take as long as it ought to. We've barely rounded the first turn in the road when we find ourselves standing at the foot of the castle. Up close it's even more unsettling: the battlements jagged and uneven, the stones stained, the windows staring like a thousand lidless eyes. All its angles seem subtly wrong, off-putting in no way I can name. I want to laugh at it; I want to run from it. I mentally compose a text to Charm instead: it's Magic Kingdom for goths. Gormenghast by Escher.

I swallow hard. My fist is raised to knock at the doors—which are exactly as tall and ornate and ghastly as you're imagining—when they swing silently inward. There's nothing but formless dark beyond them.

"Well." I glance sideways at Primrose. She's pale but unflinching, jaw tight. "Shall we?"

She nods once, her chin high, and offers me her arm. It's only once I take it that I feel her trembling.

We're barely a half step inside when a voice cracks from the walls, shrieking like bats from the eaves, everywhere at once. "Who dares enter here?"

I open my mouth to answer but Primrose beats me to it, stepping forward with her chest thrown out and her voice pitched loud, and for the first time it occurs to me that princesses grow up to be queens. "It is I, Princess Primrose of Perceforest, and the Lady Zinnia of Ohio." She turns back to me and hisses low, "Draw out the blade. Ready yourself. I will distract her."

It's a good plan. It might even work.

Except I didn't come here to kill a fairy, because I'm not a prince or a knight or a hero. I'm not Charm, who would charge a dozen dragons for me if only she knew where they lived. I'm just a dying girl, and the last rule for dying girls, the one we never say out loud, is *try not to die*.

I slide the knife from my hoodie and unwind the soft satin. I hold it aloft, showing it clearly to our unseen enemy, then toss it casually to the ground. It throws sparks as it slides across the flagstones.

"Lady Zinnia! What are you—"

I ignore Primrose. "Excuse me?" I call into the shadows. "Miss Maleficent?"

There is a long, frigid silence. Green light flares at the end of the hall, a sickly torch held in a hard-knuckled hand. The light falls across a slender wrist, a black hood, a dramatic sweep of robes. I'm distantly disappointed that she isn't wearing a horned cowl.

"That is not my name." This time the voice comes only from the black hood, a low growl instead of a shriek.

"My bad." I raise both hands, empty of weapons. "I was hoping you had a second to chat." I wait. "I will take your frozen silence for a yes.

We come to beg a favor from you." There's an indrawn breath beside me, then Primrose's voice repeating the word *beg* as if it's foreign and rather filthy.

"You want the enchantment lifted, I suppose." I don't know if I'm imagining the bitter irony in the fairy's voice.

I clear my throat. "Two curses, actually. You're familiar with Primrose's situation, I think, but not mine. I was . . . similarly cursed, in a land far from here. I come to you now in the hope that you—in all your infinite wisdom and limitless power, who have unlocked the secrets of life eternal"—I am aware that I'm laying it on thick and don't care, dignity is for people with more time than me—"might free us both from our misfortunes. I have no jewels or treasures to offer you, save one." I practiced this speech for the past two nights while I kept watch over the sleeping Primrose. I lift my face to that green torchlight and pull my features into an expression of deepest sacrifice. "My firstborn child."

Primrose gasps again. "Zinnia, you cannot! I forbid it!"

"Chill," I tell her through slightly gritted teeth. I don't feel like explaining to her that (a) multiple doctors have informed me that my ovaries are toast and (b) I do not want and have never wanted kids, having spent my life trying to save my parents from the trolley problem of my death. Hard pass.

The hooded figure at the end of the hall takes a step, another, and then somehow she's standing directly before us, the raven perched on her shoulder and her eyes gleaming like poison through the shadows. Her gaze falls first on Primrose. "Even if I could break the spell I laid on you one-and-twenty years ago, I would not." The princess stares back, her face gone hard and cold, stark-shadowed in the torchlight.

I'm not sure I would turn my back to anyone who looked at me like that, but the fairy doesn't seem to give it much thought. "And you . . ." She takes a step toward me and snatches my hand, snake-fast. I recoil, but she holds it firm, flipping it palm up to inspect the pattern of lines and veins. She mutters as she looks, tracing a yellowed nail along one or two of the routes as if my palm is a poorly labeled map.

"Mm." She releases my hand more slowly, almost gently. Her voice, when she speaks, is even rougher. "Keep your unborn child."

"But—"

"I can't save you, girl." Her voice is a slap, harsh and hard, but there's a note of mourning behind it.

"Oh." I rub my palm hard with my thumb, blink against the nothing-at-all stinging my eyes. "Okay." I was prepared for this, really I was. Sick kids learn to calibrate their expectations early, to negotiate with their shitty luck again and again. "Okay. How about a trade? I'm basically a princess back in Ohio. Let me take Primrose's place. I'll prick my finger and fall into your enchanted sleep, and she goes free." Maybe I'll zap back into my own world stuck in some magical cryogenic stasis; maybe a handsome prince will wake me and I'll be cured. Either way, sleeping has to be better than straight-up dying. Strangers tend to imagine that sick people are looking for ways to die with dignity, but mostly we're looking for ways to live.

The fairy's eyes flash beneath her hood. "You think to save yourself."

"And her." I nod at Primrose. "I'm not a monster."

The hood shakes back and forth. "The enchantment cannot be shared or stolen or tricked. You cannot take her place." She gestures at Primrose with her torch. "She has evaded my terms, but only briefly. There is no escaping fate."

There's a sudden movement behind the fairy. I see rose lips snarling, white knuckles around a black blade. The torch clangs to the castle floor and the fairy's head is hauled back, a knife hovering a hairsbreadth above her throat. "Oh no, fairy?" Primrose pants into her ear. The princess's eyes are green in the torchlight, burning with twenty-one years of bitter rage.

I can see the fairy's face clearly for the first time. I don't know what I was expecting—glamorous eyeliner and devastating cheekbones, perhaps, or a gnarled crone with snaggled teeth—but she's just a woman. Silvery blond, plainish and oldish and weary.

"Kill me if you like, child. It won't save you." That mournful sound has returned to her voice and her eyes are welling with some deep, grim sympathy. Shouldn't she be cackling and cursing? Shouldn't the pair of us be turned into toads or ravens? I feel the story stumbling again, another wrong note in a song I know well.

"I'm sorry." The fairy whispers it, and I think dizzily that she means it.

Primrose makes a strangled, raging, weeping sound in her throat. The knifepoint trembles. "*Sorry*? You who ruined my life and stole my future? Who cursed me?"

"I did not curse you, girl." The fairy sighs the words, long and tired, and Primrose can't seem to speak through her fury.

The fairy reaches two fingers up to the blade at her throat and suddenly it's not a blade at all but merely a feather, glossy and black. It falls from Primrose's fingers. Her eyes follow it—the feather that was once her only weapon, her way out, secret and cruel—as it slips silently, harmlessly, to the floor.

The fairy turns to face the princess. She touches the perfect arch of her cheekbone, very gently. "I *blessed* you."

❁ ❁ ❁

PRIMROSE HAS AN expression on her face that I recognize vaguely from middle school plays, when one kid said the wrong line and the other was left in baffled, sweaty limbo.

"What?" Primrose asks, with admirable calm.

"It was meant to be a blessing. It still is, by my reckoning."

A flicker of that bitter fury returns to the princess's face. "How is a century of sleep a blessing, exactly?"

"There are worse things than sleep," the fairy answers softly, and she may be the villain, but she's not wrong. "Stay a moment, and I will explain. Would you like some tea?"

The middle-school-play expression returns to Primrose's face, and probably mine. Both of us glance helplessly around at the hall, full of twisted black columns and bare stone. No place has ever looked less likely to provide a cup of tea.

"Oh!" The fairy taps her forehead. "Apologies. Let me just—"

She snaps her fingers twice. The walls quiver around us like a reflection in rippling water, and then—

We aren't in a castle anymore.

The three of us are standing in a smallish room with hardwood floors and deep-piled rugs. Everything is pleasantly domestic, bordering on cozy: there's a scarred kitchen table set with three teacups; neatly banked coals in a stone fireplace; shelves of clay jars and blue glass bottles bearing tidy cursive labels. The ghoulish green torchlight has been replaced by the honeyed glow of beeswax candles.

The fairy herself is no longer draped in black robes, but wearing a grease-spotted apron over a plain cotton skirt. A small, bright-eyed blackbird perches on her shoulder where the raven once stood.

For a second I think Primrose might fall into an actual swoon. I position myself to catch her, wondering distantly who's going to catch me because I'm one surprise away from a swoon myself. The wrong note I heard before has become an entirely wrong tune, dancing us toward God knows where.

"Forgive my little illusion," says the fairy. "I find a sufficiently menacing first impression discourages most visitors."

Primrose replies with a faint *oh*. I drift a little dazedly over to the nearest window. We're still on a mountainside, but it appears to be a much gentler mountain than the craggy peak that confronted us through the mist. I see the pale heads of wildflowers swaying in the moonlight, hear the green shushing of grass stalks in the breeze. The moor below looks more like a meadow now, all gentle curves and grassy knolls.

"So all that was just . . . an aesthetic?" Honestly, I admire her commitment. "The castle. The raven. The *blood sacrifice*—"

The fairy flinches at the word *blood*. "Oh!" She bustles to a shelf and returns to the table with an armful of clanking bottles and a length of plain cloth. "Sit, please."

Primrose sits, looking like an actor still waiting in vain for someone to give her a line. The fairy points to her hand, curled and crusted with dried blood, and Primrose blinks a little dreamily before laying it on the table between them. The fairy mutters and dabs at the cut—a raw line that strikes like red lightning across her palm—plasters it with honey, and wraps it in clean white cotton. She pats it twice when she's finished.

Primrose stares at her own hand on the table as if it's a sea creature or an alien, wildly out of place. "I don't understand." Her musical voice is ragged around the edges.

"I know. But I don't know where to begin." The fairy stares at the princess with eyes that are gentle and wry and very, very blue. I squint at her hair. Was it true gold once, before it was silver?

I take the third seat at the table and lean across it, hands clasped. "How about you start with your name?" I have a wild suspicion that I already know it.

The fairy chews at her lower lip—palest pink, like the fragile teacup roses Mom grows along the drive—before whispering, "Zellandine."

Oh, hell. I hear a small, pained sound leave my mouth. I glance at Primrose and know from the polite puzzlement of her face that she doesn't recognize the name. "She's one of us," I explain. But I'm lying; her story is far worse than ours.

"You know my tale, then?"

I was hoping until that moment that I was wrong, that Zellandine's story went differently in this world. But I can tell from the look in her eyes—a scarred-over grief, healed but still haunted—that it didn't.

I want to tell her I'm sorry, to take her hand and congratulate her for surviving. Instead I give her a stiff nod. For someone who's spent her entire life being comforted, I'm pretty shit at it.

"Were you cursed as well, then?" Primrose asks, reaching gamely for her familiar lines.

Zellandine stands abruptly. She pokes at the coals in the hearth and swings an iron pot low above them, her back turned to us. "Before there were curses—before there were fairies or roses or even spindles—there was just a sleeping girl."

Even with my Sleeping Beauty obsession, I didn't read Zellandine's version until the fifth week of FOLK 344—Dr. Bastille's Fairy Tales and Identity course. I guess it's such an ugly story that we prefer to leave it untold, moldering in the unswept corners of our past like something gone to rot in the back of the pantry.

"I was born with a disorder of the heart." Zellandine speaks to the steady heat of the coals. "If I overexerted myself or if I suffered a shock, I might fall into a faint from which no one could rouse me for a spell. It was no great matter when I was a child. But by the time I was older . . ."

She trails away and I look sideways at Primrose to see if she understands what's coming, hears the dark promise in that ellipsis. Apparently a princess's life is not so sheltered that she doesn't know what sorts of things might befall a woman who can't cry out, can't run. Her fingers curl around the white line of her bandage. "Surely your father protected you, or your mother."

"I was a maid in a king's castle, far beyond my family's protection." In the version we read in Dr. Bastille's class, a translation from medieval French, Zellandine is a princess who falls into an endless sleep when her finger is pierced by a splinter of flax. I wonder how many tiny variations there are of the same story, how many different beauties are sleeping in how many different worlds.

Zellandine lifts the pot from the fire with a fold of her apron and fills our teacups. I've read enough fantasy books and spy novels to know better than to drink anything offered to me by an enemy, especially if it smells sweet and inviting, like bruised lavender, but I no longer think Zellandine is our enemy. I curl my fingers around the cup and let the heat of it soak through skin and tendon, right down to the bone.

"Soon enough I caught the eye of the king's son. I was careful and quiet; I was sure never to tend his rooms when he was present. But one day he returned unexpectedly while I was shoveling the ashes from his hearth. He startled me when he spoke my name, and my heart betrayed me. The last thing I remember is the crack of my skull against the stones." Zellandine is seated again at the table but she still isn't looking at us. "When I woke, I was in a bed far grander than any I'd seen before. So wide my hands couldn't find the edges, so soft I felt I was drowning, suffocated by silk." Her nostrils flare wide, white-rimmed. "I can still smell it, if I'm not careful. Lye from the castle laundry, rose oil from his skin."

Right now you're thinking: *this isn't how the story goes.* You might not have a degree in this shit but you've seen enough Disney movies and picture books to know there's supposed to be a handsome prince and true love and a kiss, which can't be consensual because unconscious people can't consent, but at least it breaks the curse and the princess wakes up.

But in the very oldest versions of this story—before the Grimms, before Perrault—the prince does far worse than kiss her, and the princess never wakes up.

I make myself keep listening to Zellandine, unflinching. I always hate it when people flinch from me, as if my wounds are weapons.

"I did not tend the prince's hearth after that. I hoped—if I were quiet and careful enough—I might be safe. That it might be over." Zellandine's fingers spread against the softness of her own stomach. "Soon it became clear that it wasn't."

In that oldest story the still-sleeping princess gives birth nine months after the prince visits her in the tower. Her hungry child suckles at her fingertips and removes the splinter of flax, and only then does she wake from her poisoned sleep.

I felt sick the first time I read it, betrayed by a story that I loved, that *belonged* to me. I slouched into class the next day, arms crossed and hoodie pulled up, scowling while Dr. Bastille lectured about women's bodies and women's choices in premodern Europe, about history translated into mythology and passivity into power. "You are accustomed to thinking of fairy tales as make-believe." Dr. Bastille looked straight at me as she said it, her face somehow both searing and compassionate. "But they have only ever been mirrors."

I reread the story when I got home, sitting cross-legged on my rose-patterned sheets, and felt a terrible, grown-up sort of melancholy descending over me. I used to see Sleeping Beauty as my wildest, most aspirational fantasy—a dying girl who didn't die, a tragedy turned into a romance. But suddenly I saw her as my mere reflection: a girl with a shitty story. A girl whose choices were stolen from her.

Zellandine has fallen silent, staring at the table with her face folded tight. I take a sip of my flowery tea. "What happened to the baby?"

She looks up at me and her mouth twists. "There was no baby. I followed whispers and rumors and found a wisewoman in the mountains who knew the spell I needed. I chose a different story for myself, a better one." The memory of that choice softens her face, settling like sunlight across her features. "I stayed with the wisewoman, after. She taught me everything she knew, and I taught myself more.

I gathered power around myself until I could turn blades into feathers and huts into castles, could read the past in tea leaves and the future in the stars."

It shouldn't be possible to look intimidating sipping tea in a stained apron, but Zellandine's eyes are rich and knowing and her smile is full of secrets. The smile dims a little when she continues. "Some of the things I read there . . . I saw my own story played out over and over. A thousand different girls with a thousand terrible fates. I began to interfere, where and when I could." I feel a strange flick of shame as she says it; it seems that some dying girls follow different rules and dedicate themselves to saving others, rather than themselves.

"A witch, they called me, or a wicked fairy. I didn't care." Zellandine turns the rich blue of her gaze to Primrose for the first time in a long while. "I still don't, if it saves even a single girl from the future she was given."

Primrose can't seem to look away, to move. "What fate did you see for me?" Her voice is the ghost of a whisper.

The blackbird on the fairy's shoulder tilts its head to consider Primrose with one ink-drop eye. Zellandine strokes a finger down its breast. "Surely you can guess, princess."

Primrose stares at her with brittle defiance.

"Without my curse, you would be wed by now," says the fairy, ever so gently. "How well would your marriage bed suit you, do you think?"

The princess is still silent, but I watch the defiance crack and crumble around her shoulders. It leaves her face pale and exposed, and I understand from the anguished twist of her lips that it's not only Prince Harold that she objects to, but princes in general, along with knights and kings and probably even handsome farm boys.

Zellandine continues in the same gentle, devastating voice. "I saw a marriage you did not want to a husband you could not love, who would not care whether you loved him or not. I saw a slow suffocation in fine sheets, and a woman so desperate to escape her story she might end it herself."

Primrose lifts her teacup and sets it quickly back down, her hands trembling so hard that tea sloshes over the rim. I want to pat her shoulder or touch her arm, but I don't. God, I wish Charm were here; she'd have the princess weeping therapeutically into her shoulder within seconds.

"You could have—" Primrose pauses and I watch her throat bob, like she's swallowing something barbed. "You could have done something else. Warned me or protected me, stolen me away—"

"I've tried that. I've built towers for girls and kept them locked away. I've chased them into the deep woods and left seven good men to guard them. I've turned their husbands into beasts and bears, set their suitors impossible tasks. I've done it all, and sometimes it has worked. But it's difficult to disappear a princess. There tend to be wars and hunts and stories that end with witches dancing in hot iron shoes. So I did what I could. I gave you a blessing disguised as a curse, an enchantment that would prevent your engagement and marriage. I gave you one-and-twenty years to walk the earth on your own terms, unpursued by man—"

"Oh, hardly that." Primrose's voice is beyond bitter, almost savage. It occurs to me that I got it wrong, and that the knife beneath her pillow might not have been intended for her own flesh at all. I thought she was an Aurora, empty and flat as cardboard, but she was just a girl doing her best to survive in a cruel world, like the rest of us.

"—followed by a century to sleep protected by a hedge of thorns so high no man could reach you. I gave you the hope that when you wake you will be forgotten, no longer a princess but merely a woman, and freer for it. The hope that the world might grow kinder while you sleep."

Zellandine, who is neither selfish nor a coward, reaches her hand toward Primrose's. "I'm sorry if it isn't enough. It's all I could give, and there's no changing it now."

Primrose stands before the fairy's fingers can find hers, chair scraping across the floorboards, hands curled into fists. "I can't—I need—" She reels for the door and staggers out into the velveteen night before I can do more than say her name.

The door swings stupidly behind her, swaying in the breeze. I sit watching it for a while, my tea freezing and my heart aching, before Zellandine observes, "The heaviest burdens are those you bear alone."

I transfer my blank stare to her and she adds, a little less mystically and more acerbically, "Go talk to her, girl." I do as I'm told.

6

SHE'S SITTING AMONG the pale-petaled wildflowers, her arms wrapped around her knees and her eyes fixed on the eastern horizon. Her face makes me think of those eerie Renaissance paintings of Death and the Maiden, youthful beauties dancing with alabaster skeletons.

"Hey," I offer, feebly. She doesn't answer.

I sit carefully beside her and run my fingertips over the white satin flowers. When I was a girl, I used to pull daisy petals one by one and play my own macabre version of *he loves me/he loves me not*. It went *I live/I die*, and I would keep playing until I ended on an *I live*.

"I heard you speak to me, that night. When I almost touched the spindle." She sounds distant and dreamy, as if she's talking in her sleep.

I twist at a flower stem. "I called you a bonehead."

"You told me not to do it. And it was like a spark falling into my mind, catching me on fire. I asked for your help because it was the first time I thought anyone *could* help me, that I might truly have a choice. That my own will might matter." She's staring at the horizon, where the gray promise of dawn is gathering. "I'd almost begun to believe it."

My lungs feel tight and I don't know if it's the amyloidosis or the heartbreak. "Yeah. Yeah, me too." I'd half convinced myself that I'd found a loophole, a workaround, a way out of my bullshit story. I thought the two of us together might change the rules. But even in a world of magic and miracles, both of us remain damned. I clear my throat. "I'm sorry."

Primrose shakes her head, hair rippling silver in the starlight. "Don't be. These three days have been the best of my life." I think of the long days of riding and the haunted nights among the hawthorn roots, of a raven's tongue lapping at her blood, and try not to reflect too deeply on what this says about the princess's quality of life.

"So. What now?"

She lifts her shoulder in a gesture that might be called a shrug in a less graceful person. "Return to my father's castle and bid my parents farewell. Then I suppose I prick my finger on the spindle's end, the way I was always going to. Perhaps you might do the same, and return home." She doesn't sound sad or angry; she sounds like a woman resigned to her fate. This time I'm sure the tightness in my chest is coming from my heart.

Primrose stands and offers me her hand. She tries to make herself smile and doesn't quite manage it. "Maybe we'll both wake up in a better world."

The fairy packs us seedy bread and salted meat and twelve shining apples before we leave. She takes our hands in hers and rubs her thumb across the crisscrossed lines of our palms. "Come visit me, after," she tells us, which displays what my grandmother would call *a lot of damn gall,* given that she knows we're riding toward certain death/a century-long sleep.

We cross the gentle green meadow that was once the Forbidden Moor, following a blackbird that was once a raven. I look back just before we pass through the standing stones. Instead of that ruinous castle there's only a stone hut leaning into the mountainside, sunbaked and sweet and just a little lonely. As we step between the stones the hut vanishes, hidden by greasy coils of mist and miles of gloómy moor once more. The blackbird becomes a raven again, all curved talons and ragged feathers. He watches us leave with a bright black eye.

❁ ❁ ❁

THE FIRST NIGHT we take shelter on the leeward side of a low bluff and I make a very passable fire (shoutout to Mom for making me stay in Girl Scouts through third grade). I feel like I'm getting good at this whole medieval camping thing, but Primrose can't seem to sleep. She rustles and thrashes beneath her cloak for hours before sighing and sitting up. She warms her hands by the dying coals, the fairy's bandage glowing orange across her palm. "You ought to sleep, Lady Zinnia. I can't."

Her eyes are puffy and red with exhaustion. "I won't let you wander off," I tell her. "Just so you know."

She doesn't look at me when she answers. "The curse is getting stronger. I think it's been denied long enough, and now it wants me very badly, and I must fight it all the time. I don't know if you'd be able to stop me." I can't tell if her eyes are green or blue in the dimness. Her voice gets smaller. "I wanted to see my mother once more, before the end."

We don't stop much after that. Primrose sleeps only in stolen snatches and wakes with haunted eyes. Her face goes hollow and grayish, her skin stretched like wet paper over the hard bones of her cheeks. By the third day I'm not so much clinging to her as I am holding her desperately upright.

Her head lolls forward, her hands slack on the reins.

"Hey, princess. I was wondering—who inherits the throne once you fall asleep?" I absolutely do not care about the inheritance laws of a fairy tale kingdom I'm about to zap myself out of, but I figure it's the kind of thing a princess might care about.

Her head jerks upright. "What? Oh. I believe the crown will pass to my Uncle Charles, as I have no brothers or sisters." I wonder exactly when the exclamation points left her sentences, and wish absurdly that I could restore them.

"I don't have any siblings either," I offer, sounding like an extremely boring first date. "I always wanted a little sister, but . . ." Mom and Dad said they only ever wanted one kid, but I'm pretty sure they're lying. I think they wanted to spare me from a younger sibling who would inevitably outgrow me, a 2.0 version of myself with all the bugs and fatalities worked out, but honestly I wish they'd had a second kid to pour their hearts into. "Anyway. At least I had Charm."

"Charm?" Primrose says it like a noun rather than a name.

"Haven't I mentioned her? Here." I fish my phone from my hoodie and power it on (18%). I curve my arm around the princess so she can see my lock screen: Charm simultaneously blowing me a kiss and flipping me off. It's summer and she's wearing a black tank top to show off what she refers to as her "lady-killers" (biceps) and her "job-killers" (tattoos).

Primrose looks at Charm's face for a length of time that confirms my suspicions about her. She straightens in the saddle, shutting her mouth with an almost audible click of teeth. "A friend of yours?"

"The very best." The only, really. "We met in second grade when she decked a kid for asking if my parents let me pick out my own casket. She got sent to the principal's office and I played sick so I could go sit with her in the hall. She's stuck with me ever since, despite my . . . curse." Or, if I'm being honest with myself, *because* of it.

Charm's parents already had three kids when they saw a '90s *Frontline* special about homeless youth in Russia. They "rescued" Charm from a St. Petersburg orphanage six months later and never let her forget it. Every time she misbehaved they told her to be grateful she wasn't begging on the streets; every Christmas her dad jokes that they already got her the American Dream, so what else could she want?

It gave Charm a gigantic chip on her shoulder, biweekly counseling sessions at school, and a lifelong desire to be a hero. To be the one doing the saving, rather than being saved. There's a reason she has a tattoo on her shoulder of an adopted foreign baby who grew up to save the world again and again.

I figure the GRM made me the ultimate challenge, an unrescuable damsel. Charm used to spend hours and hours with her brother's chemistry set and a stack of *Encyclopedia Britannicas*—as if a third grader was going to discover the cure to an incurable genetic disorder—until she grew out of it and gave up. At least it wasn't a complete waste of time: she blew the top off the science section of the ACT and got her pick of internships at fancy biotech companies when she graduated. (I was pushing for this tiny start-up that was trying to clone organs on the cheap, but she went with Pfizer, an objectively terrible pharmaceutical giant, for reasons I genuinely cannot fathom).

She's texted me twenty or thirty times since I last checked my phone: theories and questions and ultimatums; secondhand worries from my folks who are apparently growing concerned that my "sleepover" is now six days long; a bunch of screenshots from sites about physics and the multiverse and the infinity of alternate realities that lie one atop the other, like pages in a book.

I think about replying but can't think of anything to say. I power the phone off before I can do anything embarrassing, like cry.

"Perhaps when you return to your world, you and Charm might find your fairy and defeat her together," Primrose says. "I—I could not have faced Zellandine without you."

I shrug against her back, feeling a little guilty. I hadn't gone for her sake, after all. "Didn't do much good."

"No. Although . . ." Primrose's weary shoulders straighten a little. "Although I feel stronger than I did before, knowing the truth. It's the difference between being dragged to the gallows blindfolded and walking with your head held high and eyes wide open. It's the lesser of two evils, I suppose."

God, that's bleak. She deserves so much more than the gallows, more than this tight-laced world of towers and thorns and lesser evils. I remind myself how much I dislike being cried over and try very hard not to cry over Primrose.

"Perhaps your curse will prove more negotiable than mine. Perhaps—"

"It's not . . ." I didn't really plan on explaining teratogenic damage to a medieval princess whose medical knowledge probably involves bloodletting and wandering uteri, but it's still half a day's ride to the castle and I can't stand the note of stubborn hope in her voice. "It's not a curse, exactly, and there's no wicked fairy."

We ride, and I talk. I talk about natural gas extraction and MAL-09, the chemical compound that contaminated the tap water in Roseville in the late '90s, which had been tested and approved on adult men—but not pregnant women. I talk about placental barriers and genetic damage and the forty-six infants who were born with fucked-up ribosomes in the greater Roseville area. I talk about the years and years of legal battles, the fines that didn't matter and the settlement that put me through college. I'm sure at least three-quarters of it is soaring straight over Primrose's head, but she listens with an intensity that I find weirdly flattering. In my world, everybody already knows about Generalized Roseville Malady. They've seen the five-episode documentary on Netflix and argued with conspiracy theorists on Facebook and to them I'm just another headline, not a story in my own right.

"Some of the other GRM kids formed a group—Roseville's Children—that's done a lot of activism stuff. They marched on the state capitol, did some sit-ins in Washington. They always get a lot of press, but nothing ever seems to change. Mom and Dad took me to the monthly meetings when I was a kid, but . . ." I trail away. I stopped going to the Roseville's Children meetings at sixteen, when I decided I didn't want to spend my remaining years chanting slogans and wearing cheesy T-shirts. Now I feel another squirm of guilt, thinking of all the sleeping beauties I hadn't even tried to save. There are fewer of us than there used to be.

"Anyway. I'm on a ton of steroids and meds to try to delay the protein buildup, but my last X-rays weren't great. The phrase 'weeks, not months' was used." I aim for a casual tone, but I hear Primrose's gasp of horror.

"I'm sorry," she says eventually, and there isn't really anything else to say.

We ride on—we dying girls, we sorry girls, gallows-bound—until the fairy tale spires of Perceforest Castle rise through the trees, gilded by the setting sun.

❁ ❁ ❁

THE GROOM NEARLY faints when we turn up in the stables, smelly and tired and road-grimed. There follows a long period of shouting and running about, while the groom fetches a better-dressed groom who fetches an even better-dressed fellow, who sweeps the pair of us into the castle and up to the king's council room.

The atmosphere reminds me of a hospital waiting room, cold and airless, thick with worry. The king and queen are seated across from Prince Harold, muttering over a map of the kingdom. They fall silent at the sight of the princess.

There follows a medieval version of the classic "young lady, where have you been, we were worried sick" speech. There are a few more "whences" and "wherefores," but it covers the same territory. I do my best to melt into a tapestry while the king thunders and the prince tries not to look disappointed that he doesn't get to ride out in daring rescue of anyone and the queen stares wearily at the table.

No one seems particularly interested in Primrose's explanation—although to be fair, "I went for a morning picnic and got lost in the woods" is pretty weak sauce. It seems more important for them to stress how terrified they were and how precious and fragile she is. "For one-and-twenty years I have sought only to protect you," the king says mournfully. "How could you risk yourself in this manner? Did you think nothing of our love for you?"

In that moment he reminds me of Charm's parents, or maybe my own: a person whose love is a burdensome thing, a weight dragging always at your ankles.

Primrose listens with a glassy, passive expression that tells me she's heard it many times before, has grown so used to the shackles around her legs that she barely feels them.

I make a small, involuntary sound somewhere between disgust and empathy. Prince Harold looks up. "And who is this?" His voice cuts through the king's speech. "She is not one of your ladies, I would swear it, and she is dressed most curiously."

It takes physical effort not to flip him off.

The princess's expression remains glassy, opaque. "This is the Lady Zinnia. I met her on my journey, and I am indebted to her for her courage against the perils we faced."

"There need not have *been* any perils if you'd stayed where you belong!" The king launches into another long speech about duty, family, fatherhood, honor, womanly virtues, and the obedience owed to one's elders and monarchs, but Prince Harold's eyes remain on me. His face is too lumpishly handsome to pull off *canny*, but there's a suspicious set to his mouth that I dislike.

Whatever. Soon enough I'll be home and his fiancée will be asleep, and none of his suspicions will matter.

Eventually the king blusters himself into silence and tells his daughter they'll discuss her punishment in the morning.

"Of course, Father," Primrose says placidly. Her eyes cut to her mother and for a moment the glass cracks. Her lips twist, her mouth half opens, but all she says is, "Good night, Mother." The queen dips her head in a low, almost apologetic nod that makes me wonder if her love might not be quite so burdensome.

The two of us are escorted up to her rooms by a bustling flock of maids and ladies. The princess is fed and fussed over, pampered and cooed at, bathed and dressed in a nightgown so stiff with embroidery it can't possibly be comfortable. It's nearly midnight before they leave us alone.

Primrose climbs into that enormous, ridiculous bed, half swallowed by eiderdown and shadow. "You—you'll follow me, when I go?"

"Yeah." I consider the window seat or the carved chairs, then peel out of my hoodie and tennis shoes and crawl in bed after the princess. She doesn't move or speak, but I catch the wet gleam of her eyes in the dark, the silent slide of tears. I pretend I'm Charm, who knows how to comfort someone who can't be comforted. "Hey, it's okay, alright? I'll walk with you, every step. You won't be alone." We might not be able to fix our bullshit stories, but surely we can be less lonely inside them, here at the end. "Just go to sleep. I'm right here."

Her hand reaches into the space between us and I place my palm over it. We fall asleep curled toward one another like a pair of parentheses, like bookends on either side of the same shitty book.

❁ ❁ ❁

THE CURSE COMES for her in the fathomless black after midnight, but long before dawn. I wake to find the princess sitting up, her eyes open and vacant, foxfire green. She climbs out of bed like a sleepwalker, full of terrible, invisible purpose, and I pad behind her on bare feet.

The castle corridors are twistier and colder than I remember, with every torch doused and every door closed. The wind whips through narrow slits in the stone, tangling Primrose's hair and raising goosebumps on my arms as we wind down one corridor and up another, through a plain door I bet a million bucks didn't exist until just now. Behind it are stairs that spiral endlessly upward, lit by a sourceless, sickly light.

I don't need to tell you what happens next. You know how the story goes: the princess climbs the tower. The spinning wheel waits. She reaches one long, tapered finger toward it, her eyes faraway and faintly troubled, as if she's dreaming an unpleasant dream from which she can't wake.

The only difference is me. A second princess, crownless and greasy-haired, desperately in need of modern medicine and clean laundry, quietly crying in the shadows behind her. "Goodnight, princess," I whisper. She hesitates, the frown lines on her face deepening briefly before the fairy's enchantment smooths them away.

Her finger is an inch from the spindle's end when I hear a sound I've never heard in real life, but which I recognize from an adolescence spent rewatching *Lord of the Rings*: a sword being drawn from a scabbard. Then comes the ringing of boots on stairs, the drag of cloaks on stone, and armored men pour into the tower room.

A broad hand closes around Primrose's arm and hauls her backward. A silver blade crashes down on the spinning wheel and I flinch from flying splinters. I lower my arms to see a square-jawed man standing triumphantly above the shattered wreckage of the thing that was my only way home.

Prince Harold is panting lightly, his fingers still tight around Primrose's arm. He casts a heroic glance in her direction, a curl of hair falling artfully across his forehead. "You are safe, princess, do not fear."

Primrose doesn't look frightened. She looks baffled and bleary, distantly annoyed. Harold doesn't seem to notice. He raises his sword once more and points it directly at my chest. "Guards! Seize her!"

I have time for a single airless "*what the shit*" before my arms are wrenched behind me and my wrists are wrapped in cold iron. I writhe against the chains, but I can feel the weakness of my limbs, the stony strength of the men holding me.

Harold shakes his head at me, flicking that perfect curl from his forehead. "Did you think you could evade me twice, fairy?" He gestures imperiously to the tower steps. "To the dungeons."

7

THE DUNGEON ISN'T so much a place as a collection of generic dungeon-ish elements: damp stone walls and iron bars; dangling chains stained with God knows what; brittle bones piled in the corners, cracked and yellow; a decayed sweetness in the air, like a root cellar with something spoiled in it.

In all my twenty-one years of bad luck, I don't think I've ever been this thoroughly, irredeemably fucked. I'm locked in a windowless cell in the wrong reality, wondering how long I can stay on my feet before I'm forced to sit on the stained stone floor. I'm hungry and thirsty and fatally ill. I have no way home. My only friend in this entire backwards-ass pre-Enlightenment world is about to be married off to a sentient cleft chin. Right now, the king is probably debating whether to drown me or burn me or make me dance in hot iron shoes.

I wanted to wrench my story off its tracks, to strike out toward some better ending, but all I've done is change my lines. I made myself the witch, and witches have even worse endings than princesses.

My therapist—who is corny and sincere, but usually right—says when things get overwhelming it can help to make a list of your assets. It's a short list: a small pile of vertebrae in the corner; a tin pail of unsanitary drinking water; several protein-clogged organs; a phone with approximately 12% of its battery life remaining.

I turn it on and scroll through my missed texts, because why not? There's no reason to hoard the charge now.

Charm's sent me a few more wild theories and links to NASA pages that don't load. I figure I have time to kill so I zoom in on the screenshots enough to read—well, skim—okay, *glance at*—the articles. All of them seem to subscribe to the (hypothetical, unprovable) concept of the multiverse, in which there are an infinite number of realities separated by nothing but a few quarks and cosmic dust bunnies. One dude describes them as bubbles in paint, endlessly spawning; somebody else asks me to envision a six-sided die that lands six different ways and spawns six alternate realities. My favorite is the one that describes the universe as "a vast book containing an infinity of pages." I like the idea that I'm just a misplaced punctuation mark or a straying verb who somehow found herself on the wrong page. Beats being a dice roll or a paint bubble.

I wish Charm were here to mock my lack of basic scientific understanding (when you skip half of high school and major in liberal arts, there are certain inevitable holes in your education). I always sort of imagined her beside me at the end, weeping prettily at my bedside, perhaps catching the eye of the extremely hot nurse who works the day shift in the ICU. Maybe they see each other again at my graveside and go out for drinks. Maybe they wind up married with three rescue dogs and a Subaru, who knows?

I type and delete several messages to Charm before going with the painfully effortful: bad news babe. portkey's busted.

that WOULD be bad news except—as I previously mentioned—portkeys are fiction

It takes less than ten seconds for me to send back a cropped version of one her own screenshots with the final line circled in red: "in a universe of infinite realities, there's no such thing as fiction."

She responds with a middle finger emoji, which is fair.

but like, real talk: the magic spinning wheel is broken. I think I might be stuck here forever. or for however long I have left. I've been trying not to feel the clogged-drain sensation in my chest or the shuddering weight of my own limbs, trying not to think of the X-rays that sent Mom straight out to her rose beds, her face cold and hard as a spade.

did you read the stuff I sent you?

of course, I lie.

There's a pause, then: if you had, which you definitely have not, you'd know that alternate dimensional realities are unlikely to be connected by individual physical objects.

charm please. I've had a real long day.

there are no ruby slippers or rabbit holes. if there's a way between universes, which there apparently is, it's something weirder and more quantum-y than a magic fucking spinning wheel. allow me to present my top ten theories thus far. I can see her so clearly: cross-legged in bed in the crappy two-room apartment she rented for the summer, surrounded by a small ocean of printed-out articles and library books and Smarties wrappers. The whole place would smell like burned coffee and laundry and weed, because Charm is essentially a frat boy with brains and breasts.

Her next text is an image of a PowerPoint slide titled, *So You Fucked Up and Got Lost in the Multiverse*. The subtitle reads: *Theory #1: narrative resonance*, followed by a pretty unreasonable number of bullet points.

How many jokey, stupid, helpful slideshows has she made me over the years? In junior year it was, *So You Want to Disappear: Ninety-Nine Reasons to Stick Around, Asshole.* In college she sent me, *So You Want to Murder Your Roommate: Practical Suggestions for Making it Look Like an Accident.*

I stare at the damp gray ceiling for a while before responding. i thought you grew out of trying to save me

jesus zin you're so stupid sometimes. hot, but stupid.

She texts again before I can type anything more than *hey*—

why do you think I majored in biochem? why am I interning at goddamn pfizer??? why was my senior thesis on MAL-09?

I know why. Just like I know why Dad still stays up too late reading message boards and googling unlikely medical experiments, why Mom still attends Roseville's Children meetings every month. Their love has hung above me like the sun, a burning brightness I could survive only if I never looked straight at it, never flew too close.

My phone buzzes again. i never stopped trying to save you. so don't you fucking dare stop trying to save yourself.

I stare, unblinking, the words fractured and blurred through the sheen of tears, and she adds: you promised to come back.

I shove the phone back in my jeans pocket and press the heels of my hands into my eyes hard enough that tiny fireworks pop against my eyelids. At sixteen, I tried to run away from my story and couldn't. So I put away my dreams of adventure and true love and happily ever afters, and settled in to play out the clock. I made my dying girl rules and followed them to the letter. I even wrote Charm a very serious three-page breakup letter and she informed me that (1) I was a dumbass, (2) you can't break up with your best friend, legally, and (3) she preferred blonds anyway.

And she stuck around. Through every doctor's appointment and prescription refill, every *Gargoyles* rewatch and whiny text about my roommate. I pity all those other Auroras and Briar Roses, the sleeping beauties who are alone in their little paint-bubble universes.

I wish I could bleed from my page to theirs, like ink. I wonder if that's more or less what I did. I wonder what happens when you tell the same story again and again in a thousand overlapping realities, like a pen retracing the same words over and over on the page. I wonder precisely what Charm meant by *narrative resonance*.

And then I have my second big, stupid, excellent idea. I retrieve my phone (8%) and write back to Charm: ok.

Then: i'm gonna need your help.

❋ ❋ ❋

THE FIRST GUARD who visits my cell is too scared of me to be any use at all. I badger him with questions and demands while he quivers and slides a bowl of greenish soup through the bars. He retreats back up the steps and I'm left to pace and scheme and consider all the many and varied ways this plan could fail. The soup congeals at my feet, like a pond scumming over.

The second guard is made of sterner stuff, refilling my water pail with hands that shake only slightly. He barely screams when I grab his wrist.

"Unhand me, foul creature!"

"I need to speak to the king."

"And why would our noble king consort with an unnatural—"

"Because I have a final request. Even unnatural creatures are owed some dignity in death, aren't they? Before they die?" I step closer to the bars as I say it, tilting my head upward and putting the slightest tremble in my lower lip. This is the exact fragile-wilting-flower act that got me out of at least 50 percent of my gym classes in high school.

I see the guard's throat bob. He is no longer trying quite so hard to remove his hand from mine. "I—I will pass your request along."

I let go of his wrist and sweep my eyelashes down. "Thank you, kind sir. And may I ask one question more?"

"You may." He's rubbing the place where my fingers held his wrist.

"The wedding. When will it be held?" Three days hence, the king had said, but that was seven days ago.

A suspicious line forms between the guard's brows, as if it's occurred to him that wicked fairies and weddings are an unfortunate combination. He must not be wholly convinced of my wickedness, because he says slowly, "Tomorrow, just after the dawn prayer."

"Thank you." I spread my fingers across my chest and sweep him the best curtsy I can achieve in unwashed jeans. He clunks into the wall on his way out of the dungeon.

I return to my unproductive pacing and scheming, stopping only to cough up weird, mucus-y lumps that I try not to look at very closely. If there were X-rays in this world, I bet my chest would look like a galaxy, the healthy black peppered with white stars of protein.

Hours pass. The king never arrives.

But someone else comes in his place. She descends the steps slowly, velvet skirts dragging across stained stone, rings shining hard and bright on her fingers.

The queen stands on the other side of the bars, entirely alone, watching me down her too-long nose. There's a steely chill in her eyes that makes it clear that my long-lashed, damsel-in-distress persona will get me exactly nowhere. I should have known Primrose's spine didn't come from her father.

I open with a grave "Your Majesty" instead. The queen doesn't so much as blink. I wet my cracked lips. "I would like to make a final request."

"And why should I grant you any requests?" Her tone is so perfectly calm that I see giant flashing warning lights ahead. It's the voice Mom uses on doctors who talk down to me or school administrators who give her shit about all my absences.

"Because," I begin carefully, but the queen cuts me off in the same flat voice.

"Why should I grant anything at all to the creature who cursed my daughter?"

"Because I'm someone's daughter too, whatever else you think I am." God, what if this doesn't work? What if I vanish from my parents' world and leave them with a terrible absence in place of an ending? Running away had seemed so romantic when I was a kid, but I'd planned to leave a note, at least. "And my mother wouldn't want me to spend my last night surrounded by filth and darkness."

Something flashes behind the queen's eyes, red and wounded, before she banishes it. "It is our choices which determine our fates. Each of us gets what we deserve."

"Oh, *bullshit*."

"How *dare* you—"

"I'm sorry. I meant: bullshit, *Your Majesty*. Did your daughter choose to be cursed? Did she choose to marry that dumbass prince?"

The queen seethes at me, that red wound glistening behind her eyes. "There are certain duties—certain responsibilities that come with her rank and birth—"

Watching her choke with rage, a sudden suspicion occurs to me. I lean closer to the bars. "Did you *choose* to marry the king? Or would you have chosen differently for yourself, if you could? If this world permitted you to?"

The queen is silent, her face wracked with rage or despair or maybe both. I can't tell whether she's considering helping me or setting me on fire herself. But why did she come down here without handmaidens or ladies or even guards? Why did she answer my call at all? Perhaps she, too, is hoping for a last-second miracle.

"Listen." I whisper it, one conspirator to another. "Give me what I need, and I might be able to help her. I might be able to give your daughter the first real choice she's had in her life."

The queen stares at me for a very long time. In her face I see the cold weight of the choices she didn't have and the chances she didn't take, the weary years waiting for fate to swallow her daughter the same way it swallowed her. I see her choosing now whether to make her love into a cage or a key.

She smooths her palms down the rich velvet of her gown and asks, quite matter-of-factly, "What do you require?"

❁ ❁ ❁

THE ROSES ARRIVE by the bucket and barrelful, carried by bewildered guards and skeptical gardeners. They must have stripped every climbing vine and rosebush for miles, tying the flowers into hasty bundles and hauling them down to the dungeons to fulfill the fairy's final request. They must think I've gone mad; they might be right.

By the time the last footsteps echo back up the stairs, my cell looks like a poorly tended greenhouse: roses burst from every corner, lining the walls and pressing through the bars. Fallen petals carpet the floor. The air smells green and sweet and bright, like summer. Like home.

I lie on the hard stone, the dampness leaching through my jeans, the petals clinging to the bare backs of my arms. I check my phone to see if Charm wrote back, if she made it to the tower, if the roses are still there—but it makes a final, weary bleat and the screen goes dark.

After that there's nothing to do but fall asleep. I tell myself a fairy tale, the way I did when I was little, imagining a great unseen pen retracing the same letters over and over, the ink bleeding through to the next page.

I begin at the end: *Once upon a time there was a princess who slept surrounded by roses.*

I DON'T KNOW when I start dreaming, or whether it's a dream at all. What do you call the vast nothing between the pages of the universe? The whisper-thin nowhere-at-all that waits in the place where one story ends and another begins?

The world smears sideways around me. A silent wind rushes past.

I see a woman sleeping in a castle bedroom, its windows dark with thorns.

I see a woman sleeping on a mountaintop, broad-shouldered and armored, surrounded by shields and flames. Her nose is crooked and scarred; she scowls even in her sleep.

I see a woman sleeping in a chrome coffin, white frost prickling across the deep brown of her skin. There is nothing but a thin metal hull between her and the star-strewn black of space.

I see a woman sleeping among the wild roses of the deep woods, her hair cropped short and her hand curled around the hilt of a sword.

I see women sleeping in towers and townhouses, attics and lakes, hospital beds and spaceships. Some of them sleep serenely, as if they've accepted their fate; some of them look like they fought fate tooth and nail and are still ready to go another round. All of them are alone.

Except me, because I have Charm. I see her sleeping on top of a grubby comforter in the abandoned guard tower on Route 32. The buckets and vases of roses still surround her, their edges curled black with age, their leaves shriveled. The bleached wing of her hair is fanned like a halo behind her head and there's a misshapen tutu tugged over her jeans. The plastic crown she gave me on my birthday glimmers false gold on her brow. I told her to dress like a princess, and I guess this is as close as she gets.

I'm so relieved to see her I almost wake from this not-quite dream. I wasn't sure it would work—Charm isn't really a sleeping beauty. But she had a mother and father who longed for a daughter, and she shared my curse with me for almost twenty-one years. And she climbed to the top of the tallest tower in the land and slept surrounded by roses. It must have been enough.

Or maybe—I look at her hand, still curled tight around her phone, still waiting for my next text—we're so much a part of one another's stories that the laws of physics bend for us, just a little.

Charm opens her eyes. I see my name on her lips. Her hand reaches up toward me and I reach down to her, and I know, I *know,* that I could step out of this knockoff fairy tale world and go back into my own. I could go home, and to hell with Primrose and Prince Harold and shitty medieval gender roles.

But I promised the queen I would try to change her daughter's fate, and I promised Primrose she wouldn't be alone. And maybe the dying girl rules are garbage, and instead of just trying not to die we should be trying to live.

My hand finds Charm's and I haul her toward me. I feel her body land beside mine on the dungeon floor, smell the slightly chemical citrus of her hair, but I remain in the whirling in-between. I look out at all those hundreds of sleeping beauties, trapped and cursed, bound and buried, all alone. I wonder if they'll even be able to hear me, and if any of them will answer; I wonder how badly they want out of their stories.

The void between worlds is nibbling at my edges, tearing at my borders. I don't know what'll happen if I linger too long, but I imagine it's the same thing that would happen to a chickadee who lingered in a jet engine. I reach my hand out to all the sleeping princesses and whisper the word that brought me into Primrose's world, that sent both our stories careening off their tracks: "*Help*."

I land back on the cold cell of my floor, surrounded by roses and rot. My last bleary thought before I slip into true sleep, or possibly a coma, is that some of the beauties must have heard me.

Because some of them have answered.

❁ ❁ ❁

HANDS ARE SHAKING my shoulders. A voice—a voice I know better than any other voice in the world—is saying my name. "Zinnia Gray. I did not zap myself into another dimension to watch you die. Wake *up*."

I open my eyes to the same face I've woken up to on hundreds of Saturday mornings since second grade: Charmaine Baldwin. She's looming over me with a worried frown and wild hair. I give her a lopsided smile. "Morning, sunshine."

She rests her forehead very briefly against mine. "Oh, thank Jesus."

I sit up slowly, achy and stiff, feeling simultaneously hungover and

still drunk, to find that my list of assets has expanded considerably while I slept: there are now four women crammed into my narrow, rose-filled cell.

Charm, sitting cross-legged with her tutu crumpled in her lap and her head tilted back against the bars, eyes closed in relief. The short-haired girl with the sword and the stubborn jaw who reminds me of every young adult protagonist from the '90s; the Black space princess wearing a silvery suit and a skeptical expression, stepped straight out of science fiction; the armored Viking woman whose name is probably something like Brunhilda and whose shoulders are wider than any three of us shoved together.

All of them came when I called. All of them stepped out of their own narratives to save someone else. All of them are staring at me.

"Uh," I begin auspiciously. "Thank you all for coming." I'm banking on the fairy tale logic of this world to let them understand me. "I think you're all—well, I think we're all versions of the same story, retold in different realities. The universe is like a book, see, and telling a story is like writing on a page. And if a story is told enough times, the ink bleeds through." Charm makes a small, pained sound at the scientific absurdity of my explanation. The other beauties stare at me in unblinking unison.

"So we're . . . the ink? In this metaphor?" It's the space princess, whose expression of skepticism has deepened by several degrees.

"Yes?"

Charm rescues me, as usual. "Don't we have a wedding to stop? A princess to save?"

"Oh, right. So there's another one of us here. She was cursed to prick her finger on a spindle's end and fall into a hundred-year sleep"—a series of grim nods from the other beauties—"except it turns out the curse was supposed to save her from a shitty marriage"—at least two grim nods—"and she's probably standing at the altar right now. I was hoping you could help me bust out of here and save her."

A painful silence follows while they exchange a series of glances. The '90s heroine-type cocks her head at me. "And afterward you'll send us home?"

"Or wherever else you want to go." Assuming I can arrange another moment of sufficient narrative resonance, but I elect not to alarm them with the sketchy details of my sketchy-ass plan.

The Viking woman gives a wordless shrug, tosses her pale braids over one shoulder, and turns to face the barred door. She wraps her scarred fists around the bars and muscle ripples across her back. Ropes of tendon twist down her arms.

I have time to think *no fucking way* before the iron gives a long groan of submission. The bars are warping beneath her fists, bending slowly inward, when a blue bolt of light streaks past my ear. It sizzles through the iron like spit through tissue paper, leaving nothing but a ragged, faintly smoking hole where the latch used to be. The Viking lets go of the bars. The door swings meekly open.

We turn collectively toward the space princess, who is holstering something shiny and chrome that's probably called a blaster or a plasma arc. I hear Charm whisper a reverent *hot damn*.

We ascend the stairs in single file, boots and tennis shoes and bare feet tapping against the stone. A pair of guards wait at the top, hands slack around their spears, entirely unprepared for a legion of renegade princesses to descend upon them like a set of mismatched Valkyries.

In less than ten seconds Brunhilda and the girl with the sword have them kneeling, disarmed, and gibbering, their

own weapons leveled at their throats. I lean down and give a small wave. "Hi, sorry. Where's the chapel? We've got a happily ever after to stop."

There's a queasy second where I think they might pass out before answering, but one of them swallows against his own spearpoint and raises a shaking finger. I thank them both sincerely before Brunhilda clangs their helmets together like brass bells. They slump against the wall and I think a little giddily of the versions of this story where the castle falls asleep with its princess, from kings to cooks to the mice in the walls.

Charm takes off down the corridor and I follow, and then the five of us are flying, running down toward the wedding like last chances or last-second miracles, like twist endings in a story you've heard too many times.

❁ ❁ ❁

LOGICALLY WE COULD show up at the ceremony at the wrong time: ten minutes too early, when guests are still filing into the pews, or half an hour too late, when the chapel is emptying and the princess has already been swept away by her uncharming prince.

But we're in a fairy tale, and fairy tales have a logic all their own.

We skid around a final corner and see a pair of arched doors standing open. Ceremonial-sounding Latin drifts through them, echoing off stone walls. I tiptoe to the doorway and peer around the corner. The room is smaller than I expected, with a dozen rows of pews lined up beneath a vaulted ceiling. Morning light falls through a single circular window, gilding the bride and groom on the dais below.

Princess Primrose looks literally divine, Boticelli's Venus with clothes. Her hair is burnished gold beneath the thinnest whisper of a veil; her gown is a rich rose the precise shade of her lips. Her face is coldest ivory.

Prince Harold looks ridiculous. He's wearing those embarrassing medieval pants that poof out above the knee and he's looking at Primrose the way a man might look at his favorite golf club, fondly possessive.

Charm pokes her head around me and gives a silent whistle. "That's her, huh?"

"Yeah." I pull back from the doorway and chew my lip. "I can't remember if they did the 'speak now or forever hold your peace' thing in medieval times, or if it's one of those Victorian inventions, like brides wearing white, or homophobia. Should we wait and see or—"

But Charm isn't listening, because Charm is already moving. She strolls through the chapel doors and down the aisle like a fashion model with a bad attitude, a deus ex machina in black jeans. "Hey!" Her voice shouts back at the congregation from the arched ceiling, redoubled. The Latin chanting stops abruptly. Charm slides her hands into her pockets and shrugs one shoulder, her chin high. "I object. Or whatever."

The silence is broken only by the slide of satin as the gathered lords and ladies swivel in their seats to look at Charm. The Superman tattoo grins back at them.

Primrose turns slowly on the dais, her face filling with a desperate, painful hope, the kind of hope that has died at least once and is rising now from its own ashes. Her eyes fall on Charm and the hope ignites, blazing hot.

I look past the princess to the throne where her mother sits. The queen looks suitably shocked, her hand held primly before her open mouth, but behind the shock I see an echo of the same hope that burns in her daughter's face, like reflected flames.

The guards stir against the walls, their polished armor clanking awkwardly. I guess guard training doesn't cover bleached blonds interrupting royal weddings, because they all look helplessly up at the dais for direction.

The king recovers his voice. "What are you waiting for? Seize this trespasser!"

I nod to the other beauties still hesitating with me, just outside the door. "That's our cue, ladies." The '90s heroine tosses me a spear she stole from the dungeon guards and braces her sword crosswise. The space princess draws her blaster and does something complicated with the dials and buttons on the side. Brunhilda cracks her neck to one side and gives me a small, ominous smile.

We pour into the chapel after Charm, a horde of misfits bristling with weapons. I swing my spear with all the enthusiasm my scrawny, oxygen-starved muscles can muster, which isn't much, but it doesn't seem to matter—the guards are so thoroughly taken aback by our arrival they appear frozen in place, their jaws hanging loose.

"Primrose, come on!" The princess gathers her vast skirts in two hands and makes it one step down the dais before Prince Harold catches her wrist. The fabric of her sleeve puckers beneath his grip, crushed tight.

Primrose spins back to face him, golden hair arcing behind her, crown askew. The perfect porcelain princess has vanished, replaced by someone angrier and wearier and far less inclined to tolerate bull-shit. "Let go of me," she spits.

If Harold had the sense God gave a dachshund, he would listen to her. He doesn't.

Primrose closes her eyes very briefly, either gathering herself or abandoning herself, before she punches him in the face. I don't know much about hand-to-hand combat, but it's pretty clear that she's never punched anyone in the face before. It's equally clear that Prince Harold has never been punched. He reels back with a profoundly un-manly squeal, releasing her wrist to press both hands to his face and bleat.

Primrose looks sick and giddy as she turns away, even paler than usual. Her feet tangle in the vast drape of her own dress and she topples forward, but Charm is somehow already at her side, arms out-stretched. She catches the princess as she falls, a knight catching a swooning damsel in a cheesy sword-and-sandal movie.

Charm looks down at Primrose, her arm wrapped tight around her waist, and Primrose looks up at her, one hand resting delicately on her breastbone. The two of them remain that way so long I suspect they've forgotten the crowded chapel around us,

the impending guards, everything in all the infinite universes except one another. I don't know if I believe in love at first sight in the real world, but we're not in the real world, are we?

I break away from the other beauties to flick the back of Charm's head. "Let's go, huh?"

"Right." Charm detaches herself with some difficulty and leads Primrose by the hand. I linger long enough to glance up at the queen and give her a final, unmilitary salute. She nods infinitesimally back, a captain remaining with her ship.

I'm turning away when Prince Harold says, his voice thick and fleshy through his swollen nose, "I don't understand." His eyes are on Primrose and Charm, on the place where their hands are joined together so tightly they look like a single creature.

"Well, Harold," I say gently. "They're lesbians." The prince stares back at me with the dull, suspicious squint of a man who has been mocked on previous occasions by words he doesn't know.

"Guards!" The king bellows again, but whatever order he's about to issue is interrupted by a soft gasp from the queen. She appears to have fainted, contriving to drape herself perfectly across her husband's lap.

It would be a shame to waste whatever seconds she's bought us. I join my fellow sleeping beauties and we make our way back down the aisle surrounded by the blue sizzle of blaster fire and the clang of blade against blade. Some brighter-than-average guard has drawn and barred the chapel door, entirely failing to calculate the breadth of Brunhilda's shoulders or the circumference of her biceps. She barely breaks her stride as she crashes through it.

The five of us rush into the hallway and I grab the princess's sleeve. "Primrose! We need to get back to the tower. Can you lead us there?"

"I-I don't know. I'm not asleep, so I don't know if the curse—"

"You were always fighting it before, right? So it could only take hold of you when you were sleeping. Now I need you to *stop* fighting."

Primrose looks like she's considering telling me that's not how it works, that it's impossible, but she pauses. Her eyes flick around to the four interdimensional sleeping beauties gathered around her, armed with swords and spears and space-blasters, and I watch her recalculate her definition of what is and isn't possible.

She closes her eyes. Charm gives her hand a small, encouraging squeeze.

I didn't realize how tense she was, how constantly on guard, until I watch her let it all go. Her shoulders fall. Her arms loosen at her sides. When she opens her eyes, they're the deep, haunted green of undersea caves.

She looks at each of us in turn, dreamy, almost drunk. "Follow me."

WE FOLLOW HER. Up staircases and down corridors, running through deep pools of shadow and beams of dust-specked sunlight, cries of alarm sounding behind us.

I run with the others at first. But something's gone tight and funny in my chest, as if my organs are held in a pair of clumsy fists. My lungs are sacks of wet sand and my pulse is a clock tick-tocking in my ears. *Not now,* I plead with it. *Please, give me a little more time.*

I would laugh at myself if I had the breath to spare. It's what I've always wanted, what I'll never get.

My legs weaken, starved of blood and breath. The other beauties stream past me and I wheeze behind them, too breathless to call for help, even to swear. The gap between us widens. They round a corner ahead and I'm deciding whether to limp faster or rest for a moment against this friendly-looking wall when I hear Charm's voice say, "Everybody hold the fuck up. Where's Zin?"

I lean against the wall, letting the chill of the stones seep through my T-shirt. A vast pair of boots appears in my vision. "Oh, hi Brunhilda. If that's your . . . actual . . ." I have to pause mid-sentence to gulp air. I'm not a medical professional, but that seems like a not-great sign. ". . . name."

"It is Brünhilt." A hand settles on my shoulder, wide and warm. "May I?" It's the first time I've heard her speak. Her voice is surprisingly high, like a hawk calling in the distance.

I'm pretty sure I nod because the next thing I feel is a pair of arms gathering me up and armor grating against my cheek. My body jars with every step but the pain is harmless, almost pleasant, compared to the ache in my chest. Bruises fade, after all.

Charm's worried face swims above me. "Zin?"

"It's fine," I assure her, but my breath whistles weirdly in my throat. She doesn't look comforted.

Clanging sounds echo up the corridor, booted feet and armored legs moving closer. "Let's just go, okay?" I don't hear Charm's answer, but Brünhilt starts moving again. I try to look up once or twice to see how close the guards are and whether we're going fast enough, but everything jounces and rattles and hurts so I give up, lolling against Brünhilt instead. There's a soupy, suffocating lethargy spreading from my extremities, inching up my limbs, tugging me toward sleep.

I tell myself a story to stay awake. *Once upon a time there was a princess cursed to sleep for a hundred years.*

I open my eyes and catch the blurred gleam of Primrose's hair as she leads us up the winding tower steps, her spine stiff and her crown high, a princess refusing to go gently into her own good night.

Once upon a time she asked for help.

And I answered her. All of us did. We followed the lonely threads of our stories across the vast nothing of the universe and found our way here, to this tower, to save at least one princess from her curse. I've always resented people for trying to save me, but maybe this is how it works, maybe we save one another.

I become aware that Brünhilt has stopped climbing just before Charm says, tentatively, "Zin?" I try to respond but succeed only in making a sound like a plunger in a clogged sink. "Was there supposed to be something up here? Like, say, a spinning wheel?" Charm's voice is strung tight.

I struggle out of Brünhilt's arms and stand on fizzing, trembling legs. Her hand hovers at my back, ready to catch me, and I don't trust myself enough to pull away. I blink around the tower room. There's nothing but smooth flagstones and five sleeping beauties, their expressions reflecting five variations of *Now what, bitch?*

There's no spinning wheel. Even the busted remains of the one Harold smashed are gone, neatly swept away by some fastidious guard. Shouldn't it have magically reconstituted itself in our absence? My plan was to prick my finger on something and fall asleep and hope that was enough to send us back into the whirling multiverse—but what the hell am I going to do now?

Distantly, I hear the thudding of boots on the winding tower steps. We don't have long, and if we're captured there won't be any secret pacts or miraculous escapes. I picture the '90s heroine forced into skirts and deprived of her sword; Brünhilt in chains; the space princess peeled out of her chrome and silver armor, stuck forever on a single planet rather than sailing among the stars. Primrose, trapped in her silk sheets; Charm, unable to save her.

I wanted to save us all from our stories, but I should have known better than anybody: there are worse endings than sleeping for a hundred years.

Pain pops in my kneecaps, sharp and sudden. My teeth clack

together. It's only when I hear Charm swearing that I realize I've fallen to the floor. I feel her arm bracing my shoulders, Primrose kneeling at my other side. I want to tell them I'm sorry, that I tried my best, but the tightness in my chest is suffocating me. My pulse has lost its steady tick-tocking rhythm, thundering like hooves in my ears. Darkness nibbles at the edges of my vision.

The floor tilts toward me, or maybe I tilt toward the floor, and then my cheek is plastered against cold stone. I blink once, staring hazily at the boots and slippers and bare feet of the beauties around me. I guess I get a theatrical death after all, sprawled at the top of the tallest tower, pale and fragile as any Rackham princess, but a lot less lonely.

I see it in the half second before my eyes hinge shut: a slender shard lying on the floor. A single splinter of dark wood that might once have belonged to a spindle. *It wasn't a spinning wheel in the original version.*

I feel my lips peeling back over my teeth in a bloodless smile. I've read enough fantasy novels to recognize a last chance when I see one. This is the part where I rally my final strength, calling on reserves of fortitude I didn't know I had to reach my numb fingers for that splinter. With my dying breath I will prick my finger and pull us all into the space between stories, and all the beauties will weep with gratitude and admiration as they escape into whatever new narratives they choose, and I will fall into my final sleep knowing I've done something worthwhile—

Except I don't have any secret reserves of strength. There's no amount of conviction or hope or love that can keep my overstuffed heart from stopping or my oxygen-starved brain from going gray.

My hand barely brushes the splinter when my vision turns the final, empty black of a theater screen just before the credits roll. I feel myself falling down, down into the kind of sleep that has no dreams and never ends.

The last thing I hear is my own name, spoken in a voice that sounds like a heart breaking. The last thing I think is how ironic it is, how fucking hilarious, that Charm should spend her life trying to save me, and I should die trying to save her, and both of us would fail.

10

I FIGURE I'M dead. Again.

True, there's a grayish light glowing through my eyelids and stiff sheets beneath my skin, but I chalk that up to the random sensory misfirings of a dying brain. Ditto for the soft squeaking of orthopedic tennis shoes on waxed floors and the distant beeps of machines. It's the smell I can't seem to ignore: hand sanitizer and human suffering. Surely no version of heaven has hospital rooms.

I open my eyes. There's a paneled ceiling above me. A whiteboard with the name of my nurse and a smiley face written in blue marker. The intrusive chill of oxygen tubing beneath my nose and the prickle of an IV in the crook of my arm. The window is one of those unopenable, industrial affairs, nothing at all like the arrow slit of a castle tower.

I know my regional hospital rooms: I'm in the ICU of Riverside Methodist Hospital on the north side of Columbus.

It occurs to me that one explanation for the

seven days I spent trapped in a fairy tale is that I collapsed on the night of my twenty-first birthday and have spent the past week hooked up to an IV, furiously hallucinating about hot princesses and un-wicked fairies. That maybe I'm actually in one of those bullshit Wizard of Oz stories where the girl wakes up in the final chapter and everyone assures her it was all a dream.

But then—why is there a slender splinter of wood held tight in my fist? I press my thumb against my own fingertips, feeling for blood or bruises; there are none.

"Hey, hon." The words are rough with exhaustion, cracked with relief.

How many times have I woken in a hospital bed to the sound of my father's voice? How many times have I turned my stiff neck to see my parents perched at my bedside with new worry lines carved into their faces, cardboard cups of watery coffee clutched in their hands?

"Hey." My voice sounds like it's coming from inside a rusted pipe organ, a flaky wheeze. "Where's my Prince Charming?" It's the same joke I always make when I wake up from my surgeries and procedures. Usually Dad pulls a wounded, *Am I not charming?* face and Mom rolls her eyes and tousles his hair in a way that tells me she, at least, is thoroughly charmed.

This time they both burst into tears. Dad is the established crier of the family—he was asked to "get a grip or leave the theater" during the last twenty minutes of *Coco*—but this time Mom is crying just as hard, her shoulders heaving, her knuckles pressed to her eyes.

"Hey," I offer rustily. "Hey." And then somehow they're both on the bed next to me and our foreheads are mashed together and I'm crying too. I spent the last week (or maybe the last five years) trying not to let the weight of their love suffocate me. It doesn't feel very suffocating right now.

I clutch them a little closer, tucking my head into the hollow place right beneath Dad's collarbone the way I did when I was little, when my death was far away and neither of us were very afraid of it. We stay like that for a while, shuddering and snuffling at one another, Mom smoothing the hair from my forehead.

Questions intrude, scrolling gently across my brain like the banners behind planes at the beach. How did I get here? How am I not dead? Am I still dying?

I don't really care about most of them. There's only one thing (five things, technically) I care about. I pull back from my parents. "Is Charm around? Or . . ." I don't know how I'm going to finish that sentence—*or any other mythical figures / Disney princesses?*—but I don't have to.

The curtain between my bed and the next is flung back with a dramatic flourish, and there she is: five-and-a-half feet of attitude, a bleeding heart with bleached hair. Charm. She gives me a smile that's aiming for cavalier and landing closer to desperately relieved, then tugs someone else around the curtain. She's tall and slender, with enormous eyes and fragile wrists that extend several inches beyond the sleeves of Charm's leather jacket. It takes me far too long to recognize her.

"*Primrose?* How—"

A helpless, giddy smile slides across the princess's face as Charm swaggers to the foot of the bed and sits casually on my ankles. "Morning, love."

A throat clears on the other side of the curtain and someone says, "There's a three-visitor limit, folks!" in the cheery, steely tone of a nurse on a twelve-hour shift who is not interested in a single ounce of back talk.

Mom and Dad stand. "We'll give you all a minute," Dad stage-whispers, and they edge around my princesses and out into the hall, taking their cardboard cups with them.

I push the button that buzzes my bed upright. "Hi."

"Hi," Primrose answers carefully. "How are you?" She sounds like a tourist who has memorized the local phrases from a guidebook.

I resettle the oxygen tubing beneath my nose. "Alive. So, you know. Pretty excellent." As I say it, I realize it's true: I'm tired and a little stiff, but my heart is thumping steadily in my ears and my lungs are filling and emptying easily, casually, as if they could keep doing it forever. Hope flutters again in my chest, a habit I can't seem to quit. "How did we get back?"

"You fell into an accursed sleep," Primrose answers seriously. I guess that's fairy tale–speak for *a hypoxic coma brought on by advanced amyloidosis*. "And I . . ." Primrose blushes and I find myself mesmerized by the blotchy fuchsia of her cheeks; I hadn't thought it was possible for her to look anything less than perfect.

"And she *kissed* you. You!" Charm shakes her head in mock disgust. "Which was enough to trigger the narrative resonance between universes, I guess. Apparently fairy tales are flexible about gender roles."

A cursed girl sleeping in a tower; an heir to a throne bending to kiss her. And if the heir was a princess instead of a prince, and if it's more like awkward sexual tension between them than true love, well, stories are told all sorts of ways, aren't they?

I run my thumb along the splinter in my hand, the slender last hope which had done exactly nothing to save me. "And the others? What happened to them?"

Charm makes a mystical woo-woo gesture with her fingers. "They took their exits on the cosmic highway between worlds, man." I kick her and she relents. "We all got sucked together into this whirling darkness—the void between universes, I guess—and the other princesses each chose a story to step into. The cryogenic space lady and the Viking lady went home, I think, but the short-haired girl with the sword went elsewhere. She struck me as the adventurous type." I picture her crashing into some other unsuspecting sleeping beauty, a headstrong protagonist out to wreak merry havoc, and feel a weird lurch of something in my stomach. Regret, maybe, or envy.

Primrose finishes the story. "Charmaine took you to this world, and I followed. We landed in the tower of an abandoned castle"—the guard tower of the state penitentiary, I assume—"and Charmaine summoned assistance"—called an ambulance?—"because you wouldn't wake up. I thought for a time that you might be . . ." *Dead.*

"Yeah, me too," I tell her. "I will be soon, statistically." I try to say it with a shrug in my voice, the way I used to, but I can't quite pull it off. There's still a hot spark of hope caught in my chest, scorching my throat.

Charm frowns at me. Tilts her head. "Didn't they tell you?" she asks, and the hope catches fire. I can't speak, can't breathe, can hardly think around the bonfire of my own desire, twenty-one years of suppressed hunger for *more*: more life, more time, more everything. For the first time in my life I let myself believe I might, somehow, be cured.

Right up until Charm says, "I mean, it's not like you're cured or anything, but—" and the fire goes out like an ember beneath a boot. I don't hear the rest of Charm's sentence because I'm busy wishing I could rewind the world and linger in the radiant ignorance of two seconds ago, when I thought my story had finally changed. It's a good thing I already used up my tears for the year.

I stare fixedly, carefully at the wall as Charm stands and shuffles

through a pile of folders and clipboards on the bedside table. She produces an oversized sheet of plastic and waves it in front of me. "It's still pretty rad, don't you think?" Her voice is soft but shaking with some enormous emotion, barely contained. Joy?

I look at the X-ray in her hands. For a long second I can't tell what I'm seeing; it's been years since I've seen my lungs without the white knots and tangles of proteins inside them. Now there's nothing but ghostly lines of ribs hovering above velvety darkness, clean and empty, just like the pictures of healthy lungs in Charm's textbooks.

She holds up a series of smaller photos beside it. Ultrasounds. I see my heart, my liver, my kidneys. A caption in blocky capitals reads *Findings: normal.*

I stare at the images for two seconds, then three. I blink. "I don't understand." My voice is a whisper.

"Zin—the proteins are gone. All the stuff that's been accumulating in your organs is just . . ." Charm snaps her fingers. "The doctors checked your identity like four extra times because they were sure you couldn't be the same girl. They have no idea how it happened."

She gives a smug little toss of her bangs that makes me ask, "But you do?"

Charm smiles at me with the gleeful enthusiasm that usually precedes a science lecture. "Well, I have a theory. I think when you travel to another dimension—which is a *real thing* that happened to *us*, by the way—the laws of physics, of reality itself, bend to match that universe."

"I thought the laws of physics never bent. I thought that's why we call them laws."

Charm sniffs. "Well, maybe they're more what you'd call guidelines, than actual laws. Anyway, the rules of Prim's world are different than ours." My brain, which is still processing the immensity of those clean X-rays, pauses to waggle its eyebrows and say, *Prim, eh?* "In her world there are wicked fairies and magic knives and probably unicorns. In her world, kisses lift curses."

I mull this over for another string of seconds. "But not in this one, huh?"

Some of the fervor leaks out of Charm's face. "No, not in this one. They took about fifty samples and confirmed that your RNA is still fucked. You are still officially diagnosed with Generalized Roseville Malady."

I picture the rules of this world reasserting themselves over my cells, harsh reality swallowing fantasy. I glance sideways at Primrose and understand that it's not just the leather jacket that confused me when I first saw her: her hair is an ordinary blond rather than a shimmering, impossible gold; her eyes are blue rather than cerulean; I think she might even have pores. She isn't a fairy tale princess any longer.

Charm clears her throat and slides the X-rays back into their stack. "But like, this is pretty good. *Very* good. It's like the clock is reset."

I swallow, tasting the plasticky cold of the artificial oxygen in my throat. "So—so how long—?" It's not a question I'm accustomed to asking. I've always known exactly how long I had left.

"They don't know," Charm answers. "It could be a month. It could be another twenty-one years. Welcome to regular-old mortality, friend." Her voice is shaking again and her eyes are shimmering with tears she's too stubborn to shed. Normally this is the point when I would look away from her, when the two of us would retreat to sarcasm and bravado. But God, I'm tired of being too cowardly to let myself love anyone. I catch her wrist and haul her toward me. She falls against my chest and I wrap my arms around her and it turns out I haven't used up my tears after all.

The princess steps around the bed and looks politely out the window while we cry at one another. I rub Charm's back and watch Primrose through the rainbowed distortion of tears. A princess who slept with a poison knife beneath her pillow, who rode into the night to face her own villain, who stands now in the strange light of a new world, unflinching. I don't think the next person Charm falls for will be a coward.

I scrub a hand across my cheeks and tousle Charm's hair. "You're snotting all over my hospital gown, hon."

She slides her gross face across my collarbone and burrows in a little closer. "Fuck off."

"So, *Prim,*" I say loudly, "What do you think?"

The princess looks away from the window, a tendril of yellow hair drifting fetchingly in the air conditioning. "Of what?"

"Of our world." I gesture grandly at the cramped room, with its bland furniture and wipe-able surfaces. "It gets better than the Columbus ICU, I swear to God. There's . . . ice cream? Bet your world didn't have that. And dresses with pockets. Gay rights, at least some places." Charm goes very still against my chest, barely breathing. "You wouldn't be a princess anymore, but you're hot and white and young, so you could be pretty much anything else you wanted. A librarian or a physical therapist or a lion tamer, if those are still a thing." I can see the idea taking hold of Primrose, rising like stars in her eyes. A whole galaxy of possibilities laid out where before there had been a single, narrow story with a single, bitter end. I know precisely how she feels. "Would you like to stay?"

Charm sits up. She looks at Primrose and then away, as if she doesn't care what the answer is. Charm's worst crushes are generally the ones she pretends she doesn't have.

Primrose is looking down at her borrowed clothes, running her thumb along the leather sleeve of her jacket. Her hand is shaking. "Could I?"

I kick Charm again and she clears her throat. "Yeah. I mean, you could stay at my place. I mostly sleep on the couch anyway." This is a stone-cold lie, but I don't call her on it. Some lies are important.

Primrose looks at Charm through her lashes. I see her eyes trace the stubborn line of her chin, the defiant square of her shoulders. "I—yes. I would like that." Charm gives her a watery, puffy-eyed smile, and Primrose smiles back, and I'm torn between rolling my eyes at them and crying some more.

Primrose unglues herself from Charm with an almost audible snapping sound and turns to me, that silly smile still in place. "And what about you? What will you do?"

I open my mouth to answer, but nothing comes out. I just stare back at her, jaw loose, feeling all those galaxies of possibilities spinning around me. I've never thought about the future. I never had one.

Charm's hand finds mine and squeezes. I squeeze back. "I don't know," I answer, and it's the simple, glorious truth.

11

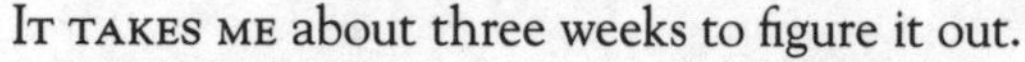

It takes me about three weeks to figure it out.

I spend the time bouncing between home and the hospital and Charm's place. I don't actually need to be in the hospital. The doctors tell me the first few globules of protein have appeared in my organs, but I still feel better than I have in years, and there's still nothing they can do but hand me some steroids and suppressants to slow it down. Mostly I think they just want to continue poking and prodding at me. They keep scheduling me for more samples and tests and biopsies, followed by interviews with panels of doctors whose attitudes have moved from baffled to ambitious, as if they're seeing themselves presenting their findings to packed lecture halls, using laser pointers to circle my miraculously empty lungs. I should be worried about transitioning from dying girl to lab rat, but I can't seem to be worried about anything. And I already know—in a wordless, formless way—that I'm not sticking around.

Between appointments I'm mostly at Charm's place, which is conspicuously less disastrous than it used to be. There are even curtains on the windows now, instead of towels held up with binder clips; I would worry about what this means in terms of how hard she's falling for Prim, except that Prim seems to be falling just as fast. The first time I show up she tells me about the Swiss Army knife Charm gave her with a degree of sappiness generally reserved for bouquets or diamond rings. "It's *mine*! Charm says I don't even need to hide it!" I can't believe how much I missed those exclamation points. "It's a tool *and* a weapon!"

"Yes, but remember there is *no dueling* in Ohio, for *any reason*." Charm says this with the peculiar emphasis that indicates there was another Incident. There's already been problems with a bank teller who didn't use her proper title and the HVAC guy who tried to give Prim his number and wound up with a nosebleed. "What should you do if you get in trouble?"

Prim sobers and recites, "Text you on the phone, like a normal person."

Her education in modernity is going pretty well, all things considered. Charm and I take her on lots of long walks through town, pointing out crosswalks and traffic patterns. We wasted an entire day in Pam's Corner Closet & More, explaining everything from fake fruit to microwaves. There have been some stumbling blocks (toilet paper, the internet, the whole concept of wage labor), but Prim is pretty sharp, it turns out, and I already knew she was brave.

In the evenings we tend to her cultural literacy by getting high and binging classic Disney movies and Austen adaptations (she agrees that the 2005 *Pride and Prejudice* is the superior version, because it is). Charm and Prim let me sit between them on the couch, my head on Charm's shoulder, my feet slung over Prim's legs, all our hands jostling in the popcorn bowl. It feels like all the slumber parties I never had growing up. It feels like a happy ending.

At Mom and Dad's it mostly feels like an endless party. Dad keeps baking cakes for no reason, humming off-key in the kitchen; Mom uses up all her vacation days at work, rather than hoarding them for some looming medical emergency; we reinstitute family game night and I discover, to my deep dismay, that Mom has been going easy on me in *Settlers of Catan* for twenty-one years. She straight-up steals my longest road without even a flicker of remorse.

I have the nagging sense that there are things I should be doing—applying for jobs or joining the Peace Corps or meditating on the profound gift of time—but all I seem to want to do is lounge around Roseville with everyone I love most.

It takes me a while to realize I'm saying goodbye.

I'm putting away groceries with Dad one evening when I pull a fresh set of twin sheets out of the bag, still wrapped in plastic. "Are these for me?"

Dad is halfway inside the fridge, rearranging Tupperware to make room for the milk. "They were half off! I figured you wouldn't want to take your old set with you. You've had them since what, middle school?"

I stare at the fridge door. "Am I . . . going somewhere?"

Dad reemerges with a pot of leftover lentils in one hand and limp celery in the other. He gives me a shrug and a smile that hangs a little crooked on his face, bittersweet. "You certainly don't have to. I guess it just felt like you might, now that you have . . ." He shrugs again. I consider all the ways he might have ended that sentence: a future, a life, a story still untold.

"Huh. Yeah. I guess." I feel it again, that sense of galaxies spinning around me, hanging like fruit ripe for the picking, and I know he's right. I stack diced tomatoes on the counter in silence before clearing my throat. "Would you and Mom be . . . okay, with that?"

He goes very still, a box of Cheerios in one hand.

"I mean, if I left for a while, maybe like a long while, you wouldn't freak out?"

Dad sets the Cheerios down and spreads his hands flat on the counter, his back to me. "When you disappeared, I thought that was it. Charmaine kept saying everything was fine, but I didn't really believe her. I thought maybe you'd run off, and that she was covering for you." His voice is low and thin, like he's forcing it through a tight throat. "It hurt like hell. Of course it did. I kept thinking about all the hours I spent trying to keep you here, trying to save you—or maybe myself—"

"Dad, I'm *sorry*—"

He slaps his palm on the counter. "And what a damn *waste* it was. Of my time, of our time together. I should have let you do whatever

the hell you wanted. I should have spent more time thinking about your life than worrying about your death."

He turns to face me finally, tears not merely gathering in his eyes but already sliding down his cheeks, pooling in the laugh lines around his mouth. He holds his arms out to me. "*I'm* sorry. Go wherever you want, with our blessing." I fall into him, stumbling over half-empty Save-A-Lot bags. "Just text sometimes, okay?"

The next morning I wake up with a slight headache from crying, a curious lightness in my chest, and a calm certainty that it's time to go. This time I pack the essentials: a few weeks' worth of meds, an alternate pair of jeans, my phone charger, my brand-new sheets, still in their plastic. A single splinter stolen from another world.

Mom's in the garden shaking junebugs into a pie pan of soapy water and Dad's sleeping in, so I leave a note beside the coffee maker. *Be back when I can. Expect me when you see me. Love, Zin.*

I'm in my car before I text Charm. Not on the groupchat we've been using for the last three weeks—on which we've finally convinced Prim to stop beginning every message with "To my Esteemed Companions Zinnia and Charmaine,"—but just her.

meet me at the tower, princess.

* * *

IT TAKES CHARM eleven minutes to get there, which is exactly the time it would take to read a text, pull on a pair of jeans, and drive from her place to the old state penitentiary. She must still be sleeping with her ringer on.

I raise a hand in greeting, leaning against the warm stone of the tower. She narrows her eyes at me, hair standing at wild angles, and stalks through the rutted dirt and overgrown grass to lean beside me.

She's close enough that I can feel the heat of her skin, see the rumpled pink lines the bedsheets left across her face. "Morning," I offer.

"Morning," she replies, coolly. "What the fuck?"

"Charm, please don't get upset—"

"If you ever speak to me in that tone of voice again, I will do crimes to you."

I should've known this would be way harder than leaving a note for my folks. I shut my mouth and fiddle with the wooden splinter in my hands. It's spent the last three weeks in my pocket, and the edges are already beginning to smooth with use. The end is still plenty sharp.

I feel Charm's eyes on my hands, hear the soft rush of her breath. "You're running, aren't you."

It isn't a question, so I don't answer it. I nod once to the ground.

"May I ask why?" Her voice is so carefully, ferociously calm, but I hear the bite beneath the calm, and the pain beneath the bite. "Why, now that you are magically healed, would you—"

I interrupt her in a soft, level voice. "I'm not healed. Not really." She already knows that. I showed her the little grayish blooms on the X-rays, my curse as-yet un-lifted. "All I have is more time."

She makes a surly, stubborn noise. "Which you could spend with *us*." I wonder if she realizes how quickly and tellingly her *me* has transformed into an *us*.

I don't look at her, speaking instead to the hazy green of the horizon. "I've spent every day since second grade with you, Charm, and I'm grateful for every second of it." I scuff my shoe against a dandelion, staining the earth yellow. "But even at the very best of times, there was a part of me that was just . . . playing out the clock. Waiting. Wishing I could save myself somehow, but never thinking I could aim higher."

"Higher?"

I clear my throat, wishing the truth was just a little less cheesy. "Saving others. I should have gone to all those stupid protests with Roseville's Children, I should have at least *tried*, and now it's too late." Last week a reporter from CNN asked to do a profile of me as "the oldest surviving victim of GRM." I never wrote back, but the word *victim* burrowed under my skin and itched at me, a brand-new allergy.

Charm doesn't say anything, so I keep talking to that green horizon. "I can't stop thinking about the others. Not just the other kids with Roseville's Malady, but the other sleeping beauties. The girls in other worlds who are dying or trapped or cursed, who deserve better stories than the ones they were given. Who are all alone." I run my fingertips across the point of the splinter and I know by the sharp sound of Charm's breath that she understands. That she sees the infinite pages of the universe turning before me, a vast book filled with a thousand wrongs that need righting, a thousand princesses that need rescuing, or at least a hand reached toward theirs in the darkness. "I don't know how much time I have, but I know what I want to do with it."

Charm exhales very slowly beside me. "And they said a folklore degree was impractical."

"Not if you're a cursed fairy tale princess, it turns out."

It's a weak joke, but Charm smiles for the first time since she stumbled out of her Corolla. "Maybe we got it wrong. Maybe you weren't the princess, after all. Maybe you're the prince." She rubs her Superman tattoo as she says it.

I shrug at her. "Or maybe we got the wrong story altogether. Maybe GRM is more like a poison apple than a curse, and there's seven dudes waiting to put me in a glass coffin when I die. Maybe my true love's kiss will revive me." I kick at the dandelion again. "Maybe there's a cure out there in one of those other worlds."

Charm gives me a sharp, sideways glance before squinting at the rising sun. "Nice to know you're trying to save yourself. Finally."

"Yeah, so maybe you can stop trying to save me. Finally."

I don't even have to look at her to feel the mulish set of her jaw. God, she's stubborn. I feel like I should warn Prim before I go. Then I remember the exclamation points and wonder if I should warn Charm instead. "Look, just—don't work for fucking Pfizer. Don't stick around Roseville. Go do something, anything else. Whatever you want. And take Prim with you."

"You are not the boss of me," Charm answers reflexively, but I can see the dangerous softening of her jaw at the mention of Prim's name. She swallows and adds, casually, "Hey, by the way: I love you." Her hands are jammed in her jeans pockets now, her eyes are still on the sky. "You don't have to say anything back—I know about your rules—I just thought you should know before you—"

I tip my head against her shoulder, right where Superman's hair curls against his forehead. "I love you, too." It's surprisingly easy to say, like the final tug that unties a knot. "It was a stupid rule."

"Hot, but stupid, like I've always said." Charm's voice is rough and gluey, full of tears again. "Will you come home? When you're ready?"

"Cross my heart."

"Okay." Charm turns and kisses me once, hard, on the top of my head. "I hope you find your happily ever after, or whatever."

"Already did," I say, and it's possible that my voice is a little gluey, too. "I'm just looking for a better once upon a time."

We don't say goodbye. We just stand for a while, my cheek still on her shoulder, watching the sun rise over Muskingum County. Eventually Charm sighs and walks back to her car. She turns and blows me a final, brassy kiss before she gets inside.

The tower still smells faintly of roses. I find them curling and drying in their buckets, their petals gathering in drifts against the walls. I watch Charm's car through the scummed windows, feeling the gathering heat of summer, thinking about stories that are told too often and the ink that bleeds from one cosmic page to the next and the stubborn arc of the universe. Charm's car vanishes around a bend in the road, sunlight flashing gold against the windshield, and then I'm a girl in a tower again.

But this time it's not midnight. This time I'm not drunk on despair and cheap beer, hoping desperately for a way out of my own story. This time, when I press my finger to the end of a splintered spindle, I'm smiling.

A MIRROR
MENDED

to everyone who is doing their very best just to live, happily

1

I LIKE A good happily ever after as much as the next girl, but after sitting through forty-eight different iterations of the same one—forty-nine, if you count my (former) best friends' wedding—I have to say the shine is wearing off a little.

I mean, don't get me wrong, I worked hard for all forty-nine of those happy endings. I've spent the last five years of my life diving through every iteration of Sleeping Beauty, chasing the echoes of my own shitty narrative through time and space and making it a little less shitty, like a cross between Doctor Who and a good editor. I've rescued princesses from space colonies and castles and caves; I've burned spindles and blessed babies; I've gotten drunk with at least twenty good fairies and made out with every member of the royal family. I've seen my story in the past and the future and the never-was-or-will-be; I've seen it gender-flipped, modern, comedic, childish, whimsical, tragic, terrifying, as allegory and fable; I've seen it played out with talking woodland

creatures, in rhyming meter, and more than once, God help me, with choreography.

Sure, sometimes I get a little tired of it. Sometimes I wake up and don't know where or when I am, and feel all the stories blurring into a single, endless cycle of pricked fingers and doomed girls. Sometimes I hesitate on the precipice of the next story, exhausted on some fundamental, molecular level, as if my very atoms are worn thin from fighting the laws of physics so hard. Sometimes I would do anything—anything at all—not to know what happens next.

But I spent the first twenty-one years of my life being Zinnia Gray the Dying Girl, killing time until my story ended. I'm still technically dying (hey, aren't we all), and my home-world life isn't making headlines (I pick up substitute teaching shifts between adventures, and have spent the last couple of summers working the Bristol Ren Faire, where I sell the world's most convincing medieval fashion and ephemera). But I'm also Zinnia Gray the Dimension-Hopping, Damsel-Saving Badass, and I can't quit now. I may not have much of a happily ever after, but I'm going to give away as many as I can before I go.

I just skip the after-parties, that's all. You know—the weddings, the receptions, the balls, the final celebratory scenes before the credits roll. I used to love them, but lately they just feel saccharine, tedious. Like an act of collective denial, because everybody knows that happily is never really *ever after*. The truth is buried in the phrase itself, if you look it up. The original version was "happy in the ever after," which meant something like "hey, everybody dies and goes to heaven in the end, so does it really matter what miseries and disasters befall us on this mortal plane?" Cut out two little words, cover the gap with an *-ly*, and voilà: The inevitability of death is replaced by the promise of endless, rosy life.

If Charmaine Baldwin (former best friend) heard me talking like that, she'd punch me slightly too hard for it to be a joke and cordially invite me to chill the fuck out. Primrose (former Sleeping Beauty, now part-time ballroom dancing instructor) would fret and wring her pale hands. She might remind me, bracingly, that I'd been granted a miraculous reprieve and ought to count myself lucky! With an audible exclamation point!

Then Charm might casually mention my five years of missed appointments with radiology, the too-many prescriptions I'd left unfilled. At some point the two of them might exchange one of their *looks*, ten thousand megawatts of love so true its passage would leave my eyelashes singed, as if I'd stood too close to a comet.

And I would remember sitting at their wedding reception while they slow danced to that spacey, ironic Lana Del Rey cover of "Once Upon a Dream," looking at each other as if they were the only thing in the only universe that mattered, as if they had forever to look. I would remember getting up and going to the bathroom, meeting my own eyes in the mirror before I pricked my finger on a shard of spindle and vanished.

And hey, before you get the wrong idea, this isn't a love triangle thing. If it were, I could simply say "throuple" three times in the mirror and summon Charm to my bedroom like lesbian Beetlejuice. I'm not jealous of their romance—they love me and I love them, and when they moved to Madison for Charm's internship, they rented a two-bedroom apartment without any discussion at all, even though the rent is ridiculous.

It's just that they're so damn *happy*. I doubt they've ever lain awake at night, feeling the bounds of their narratives like hot wires pressing into their skin, counting each breath and wondering how many are left, wishing—uselessly, stupidly—they'd been born into a better once upon a time.

But that's not how it works. You have to make the best of whatever story you were born into, and if your story happens to suck ass, well, maybe you can do some good before you go.

And if that's not enough, if you still want more in your greedy, selfish heart: I recommend you run, and keep running.

❁ ❁ ❁

ALL THAT SAID, this particular happily ever after is a real banger. It's another wedding reception, but this one has tequila shots and a churro cart, and every single person, including the bride's great-grandmother, is dancing me under the table.

I showed up two weeks ago, following the distant, familiar echo of a young woman cursing her cruel fate. I landed in a palatial bedroom that looked like it was stolen straight from the set of a telenovela and met Rosa, whose one true love had choked on a poison apple and fallen into a coma. The apple threw me, I'll admit, and it took me a while to get the hang of this place—there are more sudden betrayals and identical twins than I'm used to—but eventually I smuggled Rosa past her wicked aunt and into her beloved's hospital room, whereupon she kissed him with such passion that he snapped straight out of his vegetative state and proposed. Rosa stopped kissing him just long enough to say yes.

I tried to bail before the wedding, but Rosa's great-grandmother slapped the spindle out of my hands and reminded me that her wicked aunt was still out there seeking revenge, so I stayed. And, sure enough, the aunt showed up with a last-second plot twist in her back pocket that might have ruined everything. I locked her in the women's room and Rosa's great-grandmother put a *¡CUIDADO!* sign out front.

It's after midnight now, but neither the DJ nor the dancers are showing any signs of quitting. Normally I'd have slipped out the back hours ago, but it's hard to feel existential dread when you're full of churros and beer. Plus, the groom's second or third cousin has been shooting me slantwise looks all evening, and everyone in this dimension is so dramatically, excessively hot I've spent half my time blinking and whispering, "Sweet Christ."

So I don't run away. Instead, I look deliberately back at the groom's second or third cousin and take a slow sip of beer. He jerks his chin at the dance floor and I shake my head, not breaking eye contact. His smile belongs on daytime TV.

Ten minutes later, the two of us are fumbling with the key card to his hotel room, laughing, and twenty minutes later I have forgotten about every single dimension except this one.

It's still dark when I wake up. I doubt I've slept for more than two or three hours, but I feel sober and tense, the way I get when I linger too long.

I make myself lie there for a while, admiring the amber slant of the streetlight across Diego's skin, the gym-sculpted planes of his back. I wonder, briefly, what it would feel like to stay. To wake up every morning in the same world, with the same person. It would be good, I bet. Even great.

But there's a slight tremble in my limbs already, a weight in my lungs like silt settling at the bottom of a river. I don't have time to waste wanting or wishing; it's time to run.

I pick my clothes off the floor and tiptoe to the bathroom, feeling for the handkerchief in my jeans pocket. Wrapped safely inside it is a long, sharp splinter of wood, which I set beside the sink while I dress. I can and have traveled between dimensions with nothing but a bent bobby pin and force of will, but it's easier with a piece of an actual spindle. I'm sure Charm would explain about the psychic weight of repeated motifs and the narrative resonance between worlds if I asked, but I don't ask her anything anymore.

I don't travel as light as I once did, either. These days I carry a shapeless backpack full of basic survival supplies (Clif Bars, bottled water, matches, meds, clean underwear, a cell phone I rarely turn on) and the useful detritus of forty-eight fairy tale worlds (a small sack of gold coins, a compass that points toward wherever I'm trying to go, a tiny mechanical mockingbird that sings shrilly and off-key if I'm in mortal peril).

I sling the pack over my shoulder and glance at the mirror, knowing what I'll see and not really wanting to: a gaunt girl with greasy hair and a too-sharp chin who should definitely text her mom to say she's okay, but who probably won't.

Except, the thing is, it's not me in the mirror.

It's a woman with high, hard cheekbones and hair coiled like a black silk snake on her head. Her lips are a startling false red, painted like a wound across her face, and there are deep pink indents on either side of her brow. She's older than most sleeping beauties—there are cold lines carved at the corners of those red, red lips—and far less pretty. But there's something compelling about her, a gravitational pull I can't explain. Maybe it's the eyes, burning back at me with desperate hunger.

The lips move, silent. *Please.* One hand lifts to the other side of the glass, as if the mirror is a window between us. Her fingertips are a bloodless white.

I've been in the princess-rescuing game long enough that I don't hesitate. I raise my fingers to the glass, too, but there doesn't seem to be anything there. I can feel the heat of her hand, the slight give of her skin.

Then her fingers close like claws around my wrist and pull me through.

❁ ❁ ❁

YOU MIGHT THINK interdimensional travel is difficult or frightening, but it's usually not that bad. Picture the multiverse as an endless book with endless pages, where each page is a different reality. If you were to retrace the letters on one of those pages enough times, the paper might grow thin, the ink might bleed through. In this metaphor, I'm the ink, and the ink is totally fine. There's a brief moment when I'm falling from one page to the next, my hair tangling in a wind that smells like old paperbacks and roses, and then someone says *help* and I tumble into another version of my own story.

This time, though, the moment between pages is not brief. It's *vast*. It's a timeless, lightless infinity, like the voids between galaxies. There are no voices calling for help, no glimpses of half-familiar realities. There's nothing at all except the viselike grip of fingers around my wrist and a not-insignificant amount of pain.

I mean, I don't know if I technically "have" a "body," so maybe it's not real pain. Maybe my conviction that my organs are turning themselves inside out is just a really shitty hallucination. Maybe all my neurons are just merely screaming in existential dread. Maybe I'm dying again.

Then there are more pieces of story rushing past me, but I don't recognize any of them: a drop of blood on fresh snow; a heart in a box, wet and raw; a dead girl lying in the woods, pale as bone.

The fingers release my wrist. My knees crash against cold stone. I'm lying flat on my face, feeling like I was recently peeled and salted, regretting every single beer and most of the churros (although nothing I did with Diego).

I attempt to leap to my feet and achieve something closer to a woozy stagger. "It's alright, it's okay." I hold up empty hands to show I mean no harm. The room is spinning unhelpfully. "I'll explain everything, but if there's a spindle in here, please don't touch it."

Someone laughs. It's not a nice laugh.

The room settles to a slow lurch, and I see that it's not a lonely tower room at all. It looks more like the apothecary in a video game—a small room stuffed full of stoppered bottles and glass jars, the shelves loaded with books bound in cracked leather, the counters strewn with silver knives and pestles. If it belongs to a wizard, there are certain indications (a yellowing human skull, chains dangling from the walls) that they are not the friendly kind.

The woman from the mirror is sitting in a high-backed chair beside a fireplace, her chin lifted, gown pooled around her ankles like blood. She's watching me with an expression that doesn't make any sense. I've met forty-nine varieties of Sleeping Beauty by now, and every single one of them—the princesses, the warriors, the witches, the ballet dancers—has looked surprised when a sickly girl in a hoodie and jeans zaps herself into the middle of their story.

This woman does not look surprised. Nor does she look even slightly desperate anymore. She looks *triumphant*, and the sheer intensity of it almost sends me to my knees again.

She studies me, her brows lifted in two disdainful black arches, and her lips curve. It's the kind of smile that doesn't belong on Sleeping Beauty's face: sneering, languorous, strangely seductive. Somewhere deep in my brain, a voice that sounds like Rosa's great-grandmother says, *¡CUIDADO!*

She asks sweetly, "Why, what spindle would that be?" which is when I notice three things more or less simultaneously. The first is a small silver mirror in the woman's left hand, which does not seem to be reflecting the room around us. The second is an apple sitting on the counter just behind her. It's the sort of apple a child would draw, glossy and round, poisonously red.

The third is that there is no spinning wheel, or spindle, or shard of flax, or even a sewing needle, anywhere in the room.

Somewhere deep in the bottom of my backpack, muffled by spare clothes and water bottles, comes a tinny, warbling whistle, like a mockingbird singing out of key.

2

Sure, okay. I should have figured it out a little faster. But in my defense, my brain was recently soaked in Sol Cerveza, dragged through the liminal space between worlds, and tossed at the feet of a tall woman with silken hair and a dangerous smile.

Also, in five years of adventuring through the multiverse, I've never once made it out of Sleeping Beauty. And let me tell you, I tried. I hung my hair out of high windows and bought apples from old ladies at the farmer's market; I went dancing until the stroke of midnight and asked my father to bring me a single rose from the grocery store. None of it worked. Charm theorized about clusters of related realities and drew graphics that looked like the branches of some great interstellar tree. I pretended like I understood when really all I understood is that there are some rules you can't break.

But now, somehow—my eyes flick to the silver mirror in the woman's hand—the rules have changed. It occurs to me that I have no idea what's going to happen next. A thrill shoots up my spine and buzzes at the back of my skull.

"You," I say, and my voice is shaking now, but not with fear, "are not a princess."

Her perfect brows arch half an inch higher, and I wonder dizzily if this world has eyebrow threading. "Not anymore, no." She touches the pink indent at her left temple, which I'm suddenly sure was left by the weight of a crown.

"So where am I?" But it's a simple equation (apple + mirror + royalty) with only one answer. There are no spindles here, and no fairies, but I'd bet my left lung there are seven dwarves living deep in the woods. "Who are you?"

Her triumph flickers very briefly, as if she doesn't like that question much. "You may call me Your Majesty, or My Queen, should you find yourself begging for mercy."

I've heard more than a few villainous threats, but none delivered with such bored sincerity. My excitement dims somewhat. "Right. Cool. Well, it's an honor." My eyes slide to the only door. I'm several feet closer than she is. "I'm sure you're wondering how I got here—"

Her eyes flash, the triumph swallowed by a bottomless, fascinating hunger that makes me forget, for a moment, that I'm in the middle of an escape attempt. The mockingbird in my bag sings an octave higher. "And I would just love to tell you about it. But, uh, is there a bathroom I could use, first?"

The queen tucks the hunger away with practiced ease, like someone leashing a dog; some very unwise part of me is sorry to see it go. She says with polite amusement, "No, I don't think so."

"Oh." I take a sidling step toward the exit. "Could I at least have something to drink? I have this condition, see, this mysterious illness." Generalized Roseville Malady (GRM) isn't actually that mysterious, but premodern monarchs aren't generally familiar with terms like "amyloidosis" or "in utero genetic damage." "It causes me great suffering, and will one day surely kill me." My only symptoms at the moment are a high heart rate and a headache, which could be explained by being hungover, freaked out, and—sue me—a tiny bit horny, but I drag my hand dramatically across my brow anyway.

The queen looks profoundly unmoved. "How tragic," she says passionlessly. The part of me that isn't busy calculating the distance between me and the exit and the likelihood of dying in a fairy tale I don't even like goes: *huh.* Twenty-six years of terminal illness has taught me to anticipate and weaponize pity, however tedious and gross it feels—but the queen's face is the definition of *pitiless.* It would be gratifying if it weren't so inconvenient.

I take another step, edging behind a chair. "It is, truly it is." The queen is watching me in a way that reminds me uncomfortably of a lean-boned stray watching a very stupid robin. "It's a sad tale, which I will relate to you, at length and with footnotes, should you desire it, Your Majesty." On the final syllable I shove the chair hard, sending it tumbling between us, and rush for the door.

I make it, hands slapping hard against the wood, fingers fumbling for the latch—

Which is, as it turns out, locked.

I stand facing the door for a long moment, breathing hard into the silence.

"Oh *dear,*" says the queen. "Let me get that for you." I turn to see her carefully righting my tossed chair, setting the mirror on her workbench, and taking a long green ribbon down from a hook. She saunters toward me with a swaying, careless step that makes me think again of a hungry cat, if cats wore crowns and gowns the color of fresh kidneys.

She stops far too close to me, and there might be the teensiest, tiniest delay before I move my eyes from the clean line of her collarbone up to her face. There's a curl in her lip that tells me she noticed.

Her eyes fall to my throat and my brain leaps unhelpfully to that fucked-up Gaiman short story where Snow White is a vampire, and then, even more unhelpfully, to an undergraduate lecture about the inherent homoeroticism of Western vampire literature.

The queen lifts the green ribbon between us. I have time for two very brief and stupid thoughts (*Where's the key?* and *God, that mockingbird is loud*) before her other hand snakes past me and the ribbon is wrapped around my neck.

❁ ❁ ❁

IT DOESN'T SEEM that bad, as garrotings go. The queen barely knots the ribbon before stepping away. But in the startled second it takes my hands to reach my throat, the ribbon has wound itself so tightly that I can't fit my fingers beneath it. It pinches harder, crushing veins, clenching around my windpipe. I try to scream, but nothing emerges except a wet wheeze.

Dark spots bloom across my vision. The back of my head cracks against the door. One of my fingernails snags and rips as I try and fail to tear the ribbon away, and then I'm falling and thinking, with extreme irritation: *I've been here before.* I have been on my knees in some distant Disney-knockoff castle, fighting for air and not finding it. That time there was a princess to kiss me back to life; this time there is a queen to watch me die.

Which is bullshit, because I'm not supposed to die yet. I'm supposed to have years, maybe even decades, and I'll be damned if somebody else's evil stepmother is going to steal them. On this bracing thought, I lunge for the queen's legs. Except it turns out your muscles need oxygen to function, so what I actually do is flop face-first at her feet.

I hear a distant sigh. Hands under my arms, dragging me across the floor. The cold click of metal around my wrists. Just when my vision has contracted to a single point of light and my limbs have gone so numb they feel like bags of wet sand, the ribbon disappears.

There's an ugly little stretch of time here that mostly consists of drooling and choking and the sickly sound of vomit hitting the floor. Let's skip over it.

When I can see again, I find my arms manacled awkwardly above my head, with just enough loose chain to rattle but not enough to either stand or lie down. The queen is carefully emptying my backpack onto the counter, examining each item with mild interest and sorting it according to some ineffable system of her own devising. The socks and underwear are piled together; my phone is held briefly at arm's length, as if she is considering her own reflection in the dark glass of the screen, before being placed carefully beside the knife.

"What," I begin, but I have to stop to wheeze hoarsely between each word. "The *fuck*. Is wrong. With you."

The queen doesn't answer immediately. She's holding my little mechanical mockingbird up to the light; the bird is now producing a pitch only dolphins can hear. "Oh, you're perfectly fine," she assures me without a single atom of remorse. "It would only have sent you into an enchanted slumber."

"*Only?* Jesus Christ, lady, don't they have human rights here? I didn't do anything to you and you just—you—" This time it's a sudden, helpless rage that chokes me. I still dream of my own death sometimes, except now it's a memory instead of a prophecy. I feel my lungs massing with misbegotten proteins, my pulse weakening, my mouth full of air I can no longer breathe. I don't even like holding my breath in the pool anymore or putting my face under the blankets; it turns out I really, really dislike being strangled.

I breathe in through my nose and out through my mouth, just like my stupid therapist taught me, until I can snarl, "Just whack me in the head next time, you fucking psychopath."

"Noted," she replies coolly, still studying the mockingbird. Eventually she sweeps it to the floor and crushes it quite casually beneath her heel. There's a small, pathetic crunch, like several finger bones snapping at once, and the mockingbird is quiet. The silence leaves me chilled, dry-mouthed, unable to believe I permitted myself even a single homosexual impulse about this woman.

She turns a level, businesslike gaze on me. "Now, let us talk. I require your assistance."

It's hard to pull off a mocking laugh when you're shackled to someone's wall and they're looking at you like you're a lock they will either pick or break, but I give it a good effort. "Really? Because I could swear you just choked me with a magic murder ribbon."

"It's a bodice lace, actually."

"I figured." I may not know this story as well as Sleeping Beauty, but I'm still a folklore major with a significant Grimm obsession. In their version, called either Schneewittchen or Schneeweißchen depending on the edition, the wicked stepmother tries to kill Snow White with a poison comb and a bodice lace before she goes for the apple, which are sufficiently weird murder weapons that my favorite professor even wrote an article about them ("Mirror, Mirror: Vanity as Villainy in the Western Imagination"). If Dr. Bastille were here, she'd probably be asking the queen whether her choice of tools represented a sublimated reclamation of the male monopoly on violence, whereas all I can think about is how badly I want to punch her in the throat. And how I'm going to escape, and whether I have a chance in hell of taking that mirror with me.

The queen watches my sour, snarling mouth for a moment before sighing and dragging her chair to face me. She sits, her kidney-colored gown falling in another perfect sweep around her feet, her face tired beneath the makeup. "Please understand that I will do whatever I must to get what I need." Her eyes are concerningly sincere. "No one will interrupt me. No one will save you." Her accent is lightly burred, her words blunt, nothing like Prim's vaguely British, grammatically suspect speech. I wonder if Charm has finally removed the word *whence* from her vocabulary, and then quickly stop wondering, because thinking about Charm is like thinking about an amputated limb.

"And really," the queen continues. "It is no great favor I ask of you. I only need to know how you do it."

I curl my lip and ask scornfully, "How I do what?" But there's only one thing she could possibly want from me, however unlikely it seems. The hunger has returned to her eyes, and it strikes me, with a sudden, plunging chill, that I've seen it before: staring back at me out of every mirror since I was old enough to understand my own story.

"I want to know how you get out," she grates, and for the first time her voice is something less than perfectly calm. "I want to know how you leave your world and find another."

A heartbeat of silence. Another, while her eyes bore into mine and my brain produces nothing but strings of panicked question marks (*?????????*). I try very hard not to look at her mirror.

"Tell me," she says, imperious, barely leashed, and I feel my chances of getting out of this with all my fingernails and teeth declining precipitously.

I swallow hard and say, "I'm sorry, I don't know what you mean," because I've seen enough Marvel movies to know that it's generally frowned upon to hand the obvious villain the keys to the multiverse. I don't have a clear idea what she'd do with the ability to zap herself into other versions of Snow White, but I doubt it's anything good, and more importantly, fuck her.

The queen's mouth flattens. She holds my very twenty-first century backpack by one fraying strap, her eyebrows raised very slightly.

"Oh, that? I got it from a wizard in a kingdom far from here. I'm happy to draw you a map, if you'd like to talk to him." All I need is about two minutes un-shackled so I can prick my finger and peace the hell out of here, preferably with that magic mirror in tow. I would like to know where it came from, and how the queen found out about multiple worlds in the first place, and why her eyes are so ravenous, so familiar, but it doesn't seem worth lingering to find out.

"I am not," she says gently, "a fool."

"Okay, fine, you got me! I'm from another world. But frankly"—I rattle my chains at her—"I don't see why I should tell you shit."

She rises from her chair, face twisting. The air seems to gather and darken around her like a personal thunderstorm. "Because if you don't, you writhing *maggot,* you miserable *louse,* I will feed your beating heart to the carrion birds. I will knap knives from your bones and use them to flense the fat from your breathing body." She pauses, perhaps to appreciate her own alliteration. "I am the *queen.*" There are no sibilants in that sentence, but she manages to hiss it anyway.

My lips peel back from my teeth as I look up at her, not fearless but pissed enough to do a good impression. "Oh, please, you're just the bad guy. The villain, the evil stepmother. You're the Wicked Witch of the East, bro."

She opens her mouth, but I interrupt, entirely unable to resist. "You're going to look at me and you're going to tell me that I'm wrong?

Am I wrong?" At least Charm will be proud of me if these turn out to be my last words.

I watch the queen teetering on some internal precipice, perhaps deciding between the thumbscrews or the pliers. Instead, she tucks her fury carefully away. It's like watching a woman shove a mattress into a pillowcase. She strides to a crowded bookshelf and asks abruptly, "What's your name?"

"Zinnia Gray. Of Ohio."

She takes down a slender volume with a bright red spine, incongruous in the gloom of her workroom. "Aren't you going to ask me my name, Zinnia Gray? Or do they not have manners in Ohio?"

"Whereas here it's customary to chain your visitors to the wall." She studies my face with finite patience, one fingernail tapping the book, until I sigh. "Fine. What's your name?"

Obnoxiously, she doesn't answer. She slinks back over to me and stands, paging through her book. I crane my neck upward, expecting to see a book of hexes or poisons, something with embossed silver and dyed leather, but the cover is simple red canvas, lightly scuffed. It has a tatty ribbon glued to the binding as a bookmark and a purplish stain on the back, and there's something very, very familiar about it. Like, *distressingly* familiar. The kind of familiar that your brain refuses to process because it just doesn't make sense, like seeing your first grade teacher in the grocery store.

I can't read the title upside down and backwards, but I don't have to, because I already know what it says. This book—this *exact copy* of this book, with the tatty ribbon and the grape juice stain on the back cover—has been on my bedside shelf since my sixth birthday. It's the 1995 reprint of *Grimms' Fairy Tales*, with Arthur Rackham's original 1909 illustrations.

This is, I find, my limit. I've been sucked into a story that doesn't belong to me, garroted, chained up, and questioned by a queen, but seeing a fairy-tale villain with my favorite childhood book is apparently the place where my disbelief draws a hard fucking line in the sand and says: *No way*.

But the book persists in existing, solid red against the white of the queen's fingers, whether or not I believe in it. She finds the page she's looking for and turns the book around, kneeling before me. One page is a full-color plate of a sleeping girl with skin the color of chewed gum and seven small men gathered around her. The other page is dense text with a title in curlicued faux-Victorian font: *Little Snow-White*.

"You were right, of course," the queen says, conversationally. "I *am* the villain, the stepmother, the wicked witch, the evil queen." Her face is racked with furious grief, lips twisting with something far too dark to be humor. She leans past me, so close I can feel the heat of her cheekbone against mine, the slight stirring of my hair as she whispers, "*I don't have a name*."

3

THE QUEEN DRAWS slowly back from me. She meets my gaze for a long, taut moment, her expression fierce but her eyes full of the impotent ache of someone who knows how their story ends and can't change it. I see, or think I see, the faint sheen of bitter tears before she whirls away. The door slams as she leaves and I remember, for the first time in several minutes, to exhale. I suspect I'd feel that way even if the queen hadn't been threatening to rip out my beating heart; she has that kind of presence, an intensity that thickens the air around her.

I knock my head ungently against the wall and order myself to get it together. Luckily, or unluckily, I've been in enough perilous situations by now that I don't waste too much time panicking or regretting my life choices or shouting *SHITSHITSHIT* in all caps. I've developed a simple system.

Step one, which turns out to be equally useful in staving off panic attacks and escaping dungeons, is to make a list of your physical assets. I have a book of fairy tales that shouldn't exist on this narrative plane, a piece of spindle in my back pocket, two bobby pins tucked in my shoe, and a finite number of minutes before the queen returns.

Step two is to make a plan. The obvious choice is to wrangle the splinter out of my jeans, jab my finger, and whisk myself back to the Sleeping Beauty–verse. But I could also go for the bobby pins and try to pick the lock on my shackles (don't laugh—once I realized how often various kings and fairies were going to be tossing me into dungeons and throwing me in the stocks, etc., I spent a serious number of hours watching lock picking YouTube videos. I only have about a 50 percent success rate in the real world, but I've found that fairy tale locks are inclined to pop open at the first sign of narrative agency).

Step three is to get moving. I hesitate for a fraction of a second before going for the pins instead of the splinter. Partly because it would require some pretty uncomfortable contortions to reach my back pocket, whereas all it takes is a half split to grab my ankle, but also because I'm curious. Not about the queen—despite her hungry eyes and her silken hair and the way she looks at me, like I'm something vital, desperately necessary to her survival—but about everything else.

I waggle the bobby pin in the lock while I assemble a list of questions, including but not limited to: How did I pop into Snow White? How did my childhood book wind up in an alternate universe? Did the queen steal it, or did it spontaneously manifest? Is that mirror some kind of palantír/all-knowing orb situation that lets her peek into other worlds? If I steal it, will I be able to escape my story forever? And, PS, has my casual world-hopping had some unfortunate and unforeseen effects on the narrative integrity of the multiverse?

I can't stop myself from picturing the slideshow Charm would assemble for the occasion: *So There's Something Fucky Happening to the Multiverse: Ten Implausible Theories.* Or maybe, *So You're a Little Bit Hot for the Villain: We've All Been There but This Isn't the Time, Babe.*

But Charm stopped answering my texts six months ago, over basically nothing. The last message I have from her is two paragraphs long and calls me "a pretty shitty friend" and "an irresponsible lackwit," among other things. Prim must be rubbing off on her.

Just about the time my wrists are chafed bloody and my tendons are cramping, the manacles pop open. I rub the numbness out of my fingers, shove my stuff back into my pack, and tuck the mirror carefully on top. Its surface is a perfectly mundane reflection, but it feels heavier than mere silver and glass should.

The door isn't locked, which means the queen underestimated me after all. I feel a fleeting, embarrassing twist of disappointment.

I'm three steps into the hall when a heavy hand falls on my shoulder and a cheery voice says, "Pardon, miss."

There's a man standing just outside the workroom door. He has a generic, uncomplicated handsomeness, like one of the lesser Hemsworths, and I'd guess from his callouses and clothes that he's a woodcutter, or—aha!—a huntsman.

I raise my chin to an aristocratic angle. "Unhand me, sir! I am the Lady Zinnia of Ohio, and the queen herself invited me to—"

But he's shaking his head earnestly. "Sorry, miss. Back in you go." He tugs politely at my shoulder as if I'm a pet trying to escape her crate.

"You are mistaken." I keep my voice shrill and disdainful, but my hand is already in my back pocket.

"Her Majesty said if I saw a skinny wastrel in men's trousers I was not to let her escape—"

The huntsman stops because I've driven my fist toward his throat with the long splinter sharp between my knuckles. He catches my wrist in a hand roughly the size and shape of a baseball mitt. He gives my arm a shake that makes my bones creak, and the splinter falls from my nerveless fingers.

He shakes his head again, tsking as he picks up the splinter. "None of that, now. Her Majesty also said I was to whip the flesh from your ribs and leave you hog-tied, awaiting her pleasure, if you gave me any difficulty."

I try to wrench my hand away, but I have the upper body strength of a wet paper doll. I'm not even sure the huntsman notices. "That—okay, that is definitely not necessary." I soften, letting my lashes fall and my lip tremble. "Please, sir, don't hurt me." This seems like a fairly traditional retelling of Snow White, which means the huntsman is a giant softy with a track record of disobeying his queen.

He looks visibly torn, like a good kid thinking about breaking curfew. "Well, let's just get you locked back up, eh? Then she'll be none the wiser." He lays a conspiratorial finger along his nose, which isn't something I thought anyone ever did in real life.

"No, that's not—"

But it's too late. He hauls me back into the queen's work room and snaps the manacles back over my wrists. He must not be quite as stupid as he looks (which is, to be clear, a very low bar), because he searches me, confiscating the bobby pins, and tosses my backpack out of reach. He pats me clumsily on the head as he leaves, pausing only to flick something into the fireplace. A matchstick, maybe, or a long wooden splinter.

And then I'm all alone, except for the ashes of my spindle and the questions I can't answer, and the coldly comforting thought that the queen didn't underestimate me after all.

❊ ❊ ❊

You wouldn't think a person could fall asleep with their arms cuffed above their head and their neck dangling at a sickening angle, but I'm here to tell you they can.

I wake some hours later to find the light slanting long and heavy through the window and the queen sitting once more in her chair. She's fiddling with something in her lap, and her face looks different in the absence of hunger or hatred: younger, softer.

I try to move my fingers and make a tiny wheeze of pain.

She doesn't look up. "Good morning. Or rather, good evening." I guess she's switched to good cop mode. She holds a little golden object up to the light before setting it gently on the floor beside me. It's my mockingbird, dented and battered but whole once more. "It's a clever little device. Took me the whole afternoon to put it right."

I got that mockingbird from a twelfth-level artificer in a steampunk version of Sleeping Beauty; I doubt very much that a short-tempered medieval witch could repair it. I attempt a sneer, but my lip cracks and bleeds. "If you fixed it, how come it isn't singing?"

"Because I mean you no harm."

I make a noise of pure disbelief and the queen's eyes flash beneath those lowered lashes. She moves. There's a silver gleam, a rush of air, and then there's a wicked point pressing into the bare skin above my collarbone. The little bird breaks into a shrill song, somehow even less melodic than before. Apparently she really did fix it. Under the circumstances—with her knife at my throat—I find my capacity for admiration is somewhat limited.

The queen drags the knife up my neck, scraping along my jugular, pushing uncomfortably into the soft meat beneath my jaw. My chin lifts reluctantly. Her eyes burn into mine, scornful, scorching. "When I threaten your life, I promise you will know it."

I glare back, unflinching, deliberately unimpressed, until the queen's jaw tightens. She sits back with a faint *hnnh* and tucks the knife back into the red drape of her dress. The mockingbird warbles into silence once more.

"I was hoping," she says, with a sweetness entirely at odds with the clenched muscle of her jaw, "that you and I could start again. Here."

She sweeps to her feet and turns a key in my manacles. My arms flop gracelessly to the floor, the fingers swollen and useless as minnows gone belly-up in the bucket.

The queen leaves me clumsily rubbing at my own limbs while she settles beside the fire. There's a second chair across from her and a small table heaped high with food between them. "Come. Help yourself."

I'd like to be prideful and heroic about it, but I haven't eaten in a full day and it's not like I'm going anywhere with dead fish for arms. I stumble into the chair and make a clumsy grab for a pewter cup. You never realize how good water tastes until you've spent a day hungover and chained to a wall.

She waits until I've made it through a full pitcher and three rolls before she speaks. "Let me state my position more clearly." Her voice is earnest, her face carefully contrite. She definitely noticed me noticing her—again, sue me—because her makeup has been carefully reapplied and the laces of her dress tightened so that her breasts are squashed higher. I wonder if this is how she seduced poor Snow White's dad out of his kingdom, and if she even knows who she is when she's not playing the bloodthirsty villain or the helpless femme.

"I am a foreigner and a widow, with nothing but a throne to protect me. But I know now that I will lose that throne, along with my life. And I . . ." She places one hand on what, I am mortified to report, can only be described as her *heaving bosom*. "I need your help, Zinnia Gray."

I skip the apples on the tray and reach for a fourth roll instead. "Again, if you wanted my help, the manacles were not an amazing start."

Another little flash of annoyance, but her voice remains penitent. "A mistake, born out of great need. I'm sorry."

I pick bread from between my molars. "So that mirror of yours. What's it do?"

I can almost hear her teeth grinding. "It shows the truth."

"Where'd you get it?" My voice is casual, my eyes on her face.

"I didn't *get* it. I made it. A woman in my position needs to know the truth at all times." There's the faintest blush of pride in her voice. I count magical objects in my head—comb, bodice lace, poison apple, mirror, my own mockingbird—and decide to believe her. It's a pity she mostly uses her considerable skills for homicide.

"Neat," I say. "Now, can I have my pack?" Suspicion is obvious on her face. I turn both hands palm up. "No, for real, I have to take my meds—magic potions, whatever—twice a day. You'll recall the terminal illness I mentioned."

"That was not a ruse?"

"I mean, yes, it was"—and so is this—"but it's also true. Now give me my shit unless you want me to drop dead in the next twenty minutes." That's horseshit, of course. These days I forget my meds for weeks at a time, approaching them with the sporadic guilt that inspires people to buy multivitamins. It's weird, actually, after living for so long under a strict regimen of pharmaceuticals and appointments, injections and X-rays. I used to be visibly, obviously sick in a way that made parents look away from me in grocery stores, as if my very existence was a bad omen. But now I mostly pass as a healthy person, carrying the GRM like an ugly secret, a bad seed in my belly. It's almost a relief to announce it like this, even if it's mostly a lie.

I snap my fingers and the queen's mouth thins—God, I love bossing around royalty—but she fetches my backpack and tosses it into my lap. I make a show of fishing out ziplock baggies and plastic boxes labeled with days of the week, surreptitiously shoving the mirror deeper into my bag.

The queen watches me count pills into my palm. "What is the nature of this . . . illness?"

I swallow a lump of steroids and blood thinners. "Did you read that whole book of fairy tales?"

A regal nod.

I make a ta-da gesture at my own chest. "You're looking at the protagonist of a bleak contemporary version of Aarne-Thompson tale type 410." My smile tastes bitter. "Little Brier-Rose."

"The . . . pro-tagonist?"

"The main character. In 'Little Brier-Rose,' the protagonist is Brier-Rose."

The queen breathes an *ah* of understanding. She steeples her fingers and says delicately, "In that case, I would imagine you would have a certain sympathy with my situation—"

I cut her off. "And the book. Where'd you get that?"

She's visibly annoyed now, the edges of her innocent act fraying badly, but her voice is still measured. "It appeared three days ago on my shelf."

"No shit?"

Her brows lower several centimeters, in offense or worry. "It is not the only strange appearance in recent months. The cook found a golden egg in the belly of a goose she cut open for dinner, and a fortnight ago, the huntsman said he met a wolf in the woods."

"I mean, isn't that where wolves should be?"

"It . . ." The queen looks pained. "Spoke to him."

"Huh." Am I in some kind of fairy tale mash-up? Is Chris Pine about to pop out and sing Sondheim lyrics in a confused accent?

The queen gathers herself with the expression of a woman who is determined to regain the reins of the conversation. "People do not like strange things. Golden eggs, talking wolves . . . They are seen as ill omens, portents. Acts of witchcraft." Her eyes flicker. "They will soon want a witch to burn."

I make a show of looking around her workroom, with its skulls and pestles and unpleasant things floating in jars. "They won't have to look very hard, will they?"

A flat look. "Quite. And if that book is to be believed, the people will get exactly what they want. You understand why I want out."

And honestly, I do. I've spent most of my life trying to dodge the third act of my story, and the rest of it trying to save other sleeping beauties from theirs; I know exactly how it feels to find yourself hurtling toward a horrible ending.

The difference is what Dr. Bastille would call an issue of *agency.* I steeple my fingers. "Or—and I know this is a big leap for you—you could just stop trying to murder your stepdaughter. It would save everyone a lot of grief."

The queen's face flattens further, her mouth a grim red slash.

"Ah, I see. The chickens are already on their way back home to roost, then. How long has Snow White been in her glass coffin?"

The lips peel reluctantly apart. "A long time."

"Bummer." I throw the word at her with the same pitiless stare she gave me.

She doesn't seem to find it as flattering as I did, because she says in a harsh monotone, "And do you know how my story ends?"

I elect not to explain about institutions of higher education and the department of folklore. "Snow White marries the prince who fell in love with a dead child in the woods—I mean, my story is yikes, but that's double, maybe triple yikes—and they live happily ever after."

"My story, I said." Her lips twist in an expression that's only distantly related to a smile and her voice acquires the stilted rhythm of recitation. "*Then they put a pair of iron shoes into burning coals—*"

"You don't have to—"

"They were brought forth with tongs and placed before her. She was forced to step into the red-hot shoes and dance until she fell down dead." She stares hard at me when she finishes, the lines on either side of her mouth like a pair of bleak parentheses.

I stare back, trying not to look grossed out. "Sure, yeah, the German peasantry liked a good comeuppance." Or at least, the Grimms did. There were plenty of other stories floating around the European countryside at the time—weirder, darker, stranger, sexier stories—but the Grimms weren't anthropologists. They were nationalists trying to build an orderly, modern house out of the wild bones of folklore.

"And you think that's *justice*? That I should die dancing in red-hot shoes?" The queen's voice is trembling very slightly, her fingers curling into the wooden arms of her chair.

"No, I mean, I'm not a capital punishment person—my mom's into the prison abolition movement"—she's into all kinds of activism these days, as if all the energy she'd been reserving to hate Big

Energy on my behalf had been redistributed to every other modern supervillain—"but this feels like a 'live by the sword, die by the sword' situation, you know?"

The queen stares at me for a murderous moment, then closes her eyes. "Help me." I didn't think a whisper could sound so imperious.

"If I were begging for my life, I might add a question mark and a 'please.'"

Her eyes remain tightly shut, as if she fears she will throttle me if she sees my face. "Help me, please." She doesn't quite manage the question mark.

I lean forward across the table, drawing out a long, vicious pause before I say, "Nah."

The queen's eyes fly open. Her face is so bloodless her lips look oversaturated, a little unreal. "*Why?*"

"Because I'm not setting an evil queen loose in the multiverse! Because somewhere in the woods right now there's a little girl stuck in an enchanted sleep for no reason except your malice, your *vanity*." I'm aware that I'm no longer playing it cool, that my voice is shaking with honest vitriol, but I can't seem to stop. "She didn't deserve it, she deserved to grow up, to meet a normal dude and live a normal life, to just *live*—"

I bite the inside of my cheek hard, but it's too late. The queen's eyes are alight, her smile small and red. "Oh, Little Brier-Rose, you feel *sorry* for her. Poor Snow White, so pretty, so pure." She shakes her head, mock-pity on her face. "You think this is *her* story."

The queen leans closer over the table, her lips peeling away from her teeth. "You know nothing, Zinnia Gray of Ohio."

The first wobbly notes of mockingbird-song are rising and I'm getting ready to flip the food tray in her lap and make a run for it when there's a hard knock at the door.

The huntsman's voice comes clear and cheerful. "My Queen, a messenger has come from across our borders. You are invited to a royal wedding this very evening!"

❋ ❋ ❋

THE ROOM GOES very still, except for the shallow sound of the queen's breathing, the tick of her pulse in her throat. The two of us sit like awkward statuary until the huntsman prompts doubtfully, "My Queen?"

Her throat makes a small, dry rasp as she swallows. "A wedding," she repeats.

"Yes, Majesty. This very evening!" The huntsman is afflicted with exclamation points too. "Shall I give the messenger your answer to his invitation?"

"Not . . . yet." The queen is paling, wilting before my eyes. She looks suddenly much younger, and it occurs to me for the first time that every queen was once a princess.

"Oh." A scuffing sound on the other side of the door, like a large man shuffling his feet. "It's just, he's waiting in the great hall now, and he brought so many guards with him to escort you, and—"

The queen summons enough regality to say, firmly, "Offer them food and drink while I make myself ready."

"Yes, Majesty."

When there are no subsequent boot steps, she adds, "That will be *all*, Berthold."

"Yes, Majesty." He clomps dutifully down the hall.

The queen still hasn't moved. Her skin is the grayish-white of last week's snow, or cheap dentures. She could almost be mistaken for the protagonist of this story if it weren't for the faint pink marks of the crown on her brow. I could almost feel sorry for her if she hadn't poisoned a child and shackled me to a wall.

"*Berthold*, huh?" I slouch back in my chair, ankles crossed, eyebrows up. "He seems bright."

She answers absently, one shoulder twitching in a shrug. "He has his uses."

"*Oh*, it's like that?"

I'm being a dick on purpose, maybe trying to provoke her into anything other than this congealed panic, but her expression barely flickers. "Do you have any idea how difficult it is to find a lover who isn't angling for the throne? He was . . ." Her lip curls, and I can't tell if it's the huntsman or herself she disdains more. "Kind."

It doesn't seem very helpful to remind her that he betrayed her and let Snow White live, so I don't say anything.

Eventually the queen gathers herself, blinking twice and exhaling sharply. If she were a knight, I imagine she would lower her visor, but since she's an evil queen, she stands and stalks to her workbench.

It takes less than a second for her to whirl back to face me. "Where is it? What have you done with it?"

A brief, hissed exchange follows, wherein I try and fail to deflect her accusations ("Where's what?" "You know what, you thieving pustule!" "Okay, calm your tits, it's in my backpack." "Calm my *what*?"), and then she's clutching the tarnished frame of her mirror, whispering to it. I can't hear the words, but I don't have to. Maybe it's in the original German, or maybe it's the Grimms' translation: *Mirror, mirror in my hand, who is the fairest in the land?*

In Sleeping Beauty stories, I've come to recognize certain moments—tropes, you might call them, repeated plot points—that have an echo to them. Pieces of the story that have been told so many times they've worn the page thin: the christening curse, the pricked finger, the endless sleep, the kiss. You can almost feel reality softening around you, at those times.

I feel it now, as the wicked stepmother whispers to her mirror.

I don't know what she sees in the glass, but the queen's throat moves as she swallows. "It's too late."

"Yeah." I make a face, hissing through my teeth. "I recommend you decline this invitation." It never made much sense why the wicked queen showed up at Snow White's wedding, anyway.

A scathing glance in my direction. "Do you really think I have a choice? Do you think she sent all those men as an honor guard?"

I shift in my seat, stomping the tiny worm of pity in my stomach. "So pull some witchy shit. Disguise yourself. Knot your sheets together and climb out the window. Run."

"That would buy me days, maybe weeks. And even if I somehow escaped her reach, what would I do? Hide in a little house in the woods, rotting away?"

The pity vanishes. "Oh, you mean like Snow White did? To escape *you?*"

Her eyes narrow to vicious slits. She says, "I. Have. To. Get. Out," with extra periods between each word.

"That's what I just said." But I know that's not what she means. I reach, not very casually, for the straps of my backpack.

The queen stalks toward me, the mirror still clenched in one hand, the air thickening around her. Stray hairs lift in an invisible breeze, tangling like dark branches across the cold moon of her face. "You will tell me how it's done." This time it's not a question or an order; it's a promise.

So, okay, it was exciting to find myself in a different fairy tale, to feel for the first time the possibility of diverging from my own dreary road, but it's time to go. I stumble out of my chair, backing away, running my free hand against the shelves in search of something, anything sharp. A knife, a splinter, a tooth, a shard of bone. There's nothing.

The queen is close now. She reaches for my collar and twists it in one clawed fist, drawing us together. I can see the plain bones of her face beneath the creams and cosmetics, the hard line of her lips.

And I have no spindle and no tower, no roses or fairies or handsome princes, but I have a monarch close enough to kiss. It'll have to be enough.

I straighten my spine and tilt my face recklessly upward—and, oh God, I have to stand on tiptoe to close the last inch between us, which is both embarrassing and embarrassingly hot—and kiss her.

It's an undeniably weak kiss: a nonconsensual crush of lips and teeth that I would feel pretty bad about if she hadn't been on the verge of nonconsensually torturing me. She breaks away, of course—but not instantly. There's a tiny but critical delay, a moment that makes me wonder how long it's been since the queen met someone outside of her control, and if she might harbor a low taste for sickly, sarcastic peasants.

Then she's glaring and panting, reaching for her knife while her cheeks turn patchy pink. I shouldn't care, because I should be disappearing right now.

Except I'm not.

Nothing is happening. The world is not thinning around me, the infinite pages of the universe are not rustling past. It didn't work, and both of us are extremely screwed.

Something draws the queen's eyes away from me. She looks more closely at the mirror in her hand, and her eyes go wide.

She drops my collar and catches my hand instead. Before I can pull away—before I can even begin to form the word *hey!*—she presses our hands to the glass surface of her mirror.

Except there is no glass. Just our hands, falling into nothing at all.

4

It's cold, between worlds. There's no air, but it whips past me, smelling of frost and first snows. The only warm thing is the queen's hand locked tight around mine, dragging us into a story that doesn't belong to either of us.

My knees hit earth, moss-pillowed and green, and the queen falls beside me with a squashy thud. She makes a sound like air leaking out of a tire, and I'd make fun of her if I didn't feel the same way. My cells are frazzled, as if my entire body was recently microwaved, and it takes me longer than it should to stand and look around.

Trees. Soft, springtime air. Extremely melodic birdsong. The whole scene has a strange haziness to it, like a pre-Raphaelite painting or an old VHS tape.

The queen staggers to her feet in front of me and spreads her hands wide in triumph. "I didn't need you after all, Zinnia Gray. I saved *myself*, as I always have and always will."

I roll my eyes so hard it hurts a little. "Oh yeah? Then who's *that?*"

The queen's victorious smile sags a little at the edges. She follows my gaze over her left shoulder, where a glass coffin lies between the trees. A girl with a cute black bob is lying beneath the glass, her face lit by a single, perfect sunbeam, her hands folded limply around a bouquet of flowers.

The queen stares. She opens her mouth, closes it, and opens it again. "I don't know," she answers.

"Are you serious? Did you hit your head?"

"No, I know who it is, but—" The queen swallows, her eyes fixed on the unsettling white of the girl's face. "That's not *my* Snow White."

"Yeah, I didn't think so." I tuck both hands in my pockets, squinting around at the scenery. "Your world was a little more Gothic, but this place has a 'now-in-Technicolor' vibe." I can tell she doesn't understand, so I say meanly, "Congratulations, you made it to a different world! But you're still in the same story."

The queen looks dazed, staring down at Snow White with the beginnings of revulsion creeping into her eyes. "Why is the light like this?" She reaches her hand tentatively into the sunbeam. Something violet drifts into her palm. "Are there *flower petals* falling over her?"

I don't answer because I'm busy sidling behind her. I snatch the mirror out of the queen's hand and fling it sideways at the trunk of a tree. I'm hoping for a dramatic shatter of glass, but the frame just *thwumps* disappointingly against the bark and falls to the ground, perfectly whole. There's a half second's held breath before both of us dive for the mirror.

The queen shoves past me and I tackle her around the waist. It devolves quickly into a wrestling match, our clothes streaked with moss and dirt, our breath coming fast.

The queen is stronger and meaner than me. "*No,*" she pants. "I am—not"—she pins me between her knees and lunges for the mirror—"staying here!"

I try to slap the mirror out of her grip but she turns the glass to meet my hand, and it flies through it, passing back into that cold nowhere.

The last thing I hear is the queen laughing.

* * *

THIS TIME WE land somewhere dim and damp, like one of those basements that never quite dries out. Opening my eyes takes more effort than it should, and I can't tell whether it's the GRM or the unwilling trips through nowheresville.

The first thing I see is a stranger's face smiling down at me. It's a cute face: freckled and gap-toothed, framed by tangled hair the color of coal. Her lips aren't red as blood and her skin has seen too much sun to be compared to snow, but I know a protagonist when I see one. "Hi," I rasp.

"Good morning!" God save me from princesses and their exclamation points.

"Morning. Where's—" I sit up abruptly, blinking the room into focus. But it's not a room. It's a cave, with a sandy floor and tidy fire pit.

The girl—woman, really, she's got at least a decade on the cherubic kid in the coffin—settles cross-legged beside me. "Your angry woman?" She has a burbling, throaty sort of accent.

"She's not my—yeah, her."

She gestures with her chin toward the entrance of the cave, where more than a dozen men are struggling against a tall, dark-haired figure. There seems to be a lot of swearing from all parties.

"Who are those guys?"

The stranger smiles fondly at them. "Mine. They took me in when my mother tried to murder me, and I've been here ever since." She confides this without much concern, as if attempted filicide is one of life's little misfortunes.

"Ah." My brains feel like hot Cheez Whiz, but I distantly remember versions of Snow White where she's adopted by robbers or brigands rather than dwarves. Spanish, maybe? Or Flemish? Either way, I'm pretty sure her mom takes another shot at her, and she deserves a heads up. "Listen, Snow White," I begin.

"Sneeuwwitje."

"Listen, Sneeuwwitje—"

The queen shrieks from the cave entrance. "Zinnia! Tell these ruffians to unhand me!"

I shout back without turning, "Tie her up tight, boys, she's super dangerous." There are muffled sounds of fury in response, a definite uptick in swear words.

I try again. "You might already know this, Sneeuwwitje, but your mom is definitely going to try to kill you again. So if anybody shows up with an apple, or a comb, or whatever, just say no."

Sneeuwwitje nods solemnly. "She gave me a demon's ring, which sent me into a deep sleep. How did you know?"

I squint at the stained leather of her clothing, the calluses across her palms. "If she already put you to sleep . . . how come you aren't married to a prince right now?"

"Oh, I told him no. I have seventeen husbands already." An extremely compelling dimple appears, presenting a convincing argument that a man might share one-seventeenth of this woman and count himself lucky. "Eighteen just seemed greedy."

"Sure, yeah," I say faintly, making a distant mental note that not all princesses need saving.

Someone shouts a warning. Footsteps pound across the sand. The queen's fingers close around my ankle and she grins fiercely up at me, a doubled trail of blood leaking from her nose and a mirror in her hand.

I have time to say, "Oh, for fuck's sa—" before the world dissolves again.

❋ ❋ ❋

THE NEXT WORLD has the sleek, blue-lit aesthetic of far-future science fiction. The walls are stacked with cold metal coffins. Waxen faces stare from their small, frosted windows, dead or sleeping, their lips a sickening, poisonous red.

The queen hisses between her teeth and flings us back into the void.

We land on a steep and lonely mountainside. For a moment I think we're alone, but then a branch cracks. A long-legged dog trots past us, its coat silken silver, its eyes fixed on some invisible purpose. Six more follow at its heels, a soft river of paws and skulls and sterling fur.

"*What*—" the queen begins, but a woman comes loping into the view after the dogs. She has hair the color of the moon and a dress the color of snow, and her eyes widen when they land on the queen. For a moment I think she might bare her teeth or set her hounds on us, but then her eyes slide to me. She bows her head, as one would to a fellow soldier in a long war, and runs on after her dogs.

The two of us are left standing together in the pine-scented silence, unsure whether we've been blessed or cursed. The queen takes my hand almost gently this time before she lifts the mirror again.

A college campus full of ivy-eaten buildings and signs in Korean, where one extremely beautiful boy is offering an apple to another equally beautiful boy.

A sumptuous wedding feast that seems to involve seven ogres and a princess in a gown of richest red.

A hunched woman offering a comb to a little girl, her lips curving in a cold smile.

I can feel myself coming undone, unspooling into the endless whirl of dead girls and coffin lids, wicked mothers and poison apples. The same story repeated again and again, like a woman standing between two mirrors, reflected into infinity.

And then another forest, curled and black beneath a starless sky. I wrench my arm away from the queen and pluck the mirror from her other hand. She's too weak to stop me, her skin clammy and chilled, her limbs shuddering.

She rolls onto her stomach beside me, panting into the dark muck of leaves and earth. "This is where you draw the line?" she spits. "*This* is where you choose to stay?"

She has an extremely good point. The woods around us bear no resemblance at all to the first forest we landed in, with its flower petals and birdsong. The trees here are knotted and bent, like snapped bones that have healed poorly, and the darkness is the kind that makes your eyes ache if you look at it too long. I've hit a couple of versions of Sleeping Beauty that edged into horror, and returned with new scars and probably some undiagnosed PTSD. Charm threw a fit about it, and the next time I left home I found a new pocketknife and a first aid kit in my pack, along with a note reading *Don't die, bonehead* in Prim's fancy calligraphy.

So, no, I don't love the Grimm-dark vibe of these woods, but I'm tired on a subatomic level, my muscles shaking and my teeth chattering, and I'm done channel surfing at someone else's whim. "Why not?" I make an effort to crawl away and manage several consecutive feet before collapsing against my own backpack, mirror still in my hand. "Look, you've got to give it a rest. You're going to kill yourself at this pace."

"As if you care about my fate." Her voice darkens, silky and low. "Beyond your base desires, of course."

"My what?"

The queen raises herself to her hands and knees just so she can do a haughty glare at me. "It's a little late to feign indifference. You *kissed* me."

I'm torn between explaining that my kiss was actually a failed escape attempt and clarifying that there's nothing especially base about desiring a tall, dangerous woman with terrible vibes (whomst among us, etc.). Instead, I say, "Whatever. I just need a break from that mirror, okay?"

"Then tell me how to get out of this damned story." The queen's voice is ragged, pushed far beyond exhaustion but still unwilling to bend. It would be admirable if it weren't extremely annoying. "Tell me, and I swear I'll stop."

"Bite me."

"Now is not the time for your crude fantasies!" She climbs unsteadily to her feet, takes two wavering steps in my direction. "You have no idea what it's like to fight for your own right to exist. To know yourself doomed, yet to keep striving—"

I throw a wad of leaves at her. "Cry me a fucking river, woman. You just found out how your story ends *last week*. I've spent my whole life under a death sentence."

The queen is clawing wet leaves out of her hair, teeth flashing white in the gloom. "You think I haven't?" Her voice is a strangled hiss. "I may not have known about the iron shoes, but I was always headed for a bad ending. I was an ugly second daughter with uncanny power, and then I was a foreign bride who bore no heirs. Now I am a queen who is feared only slightly more than she is hated, and my time is up. But I have fought tooth and nail to survive, and no pretty little princess is going to stop me."

This little monologue leaves me with two not entirely comfortable sensations. The first is the sudden, lurching shame of my worldview being wrenched out of shape as it occurs to me that Snow White might not be the only victim here. The second comes from the word *pretty*, which the queen tried to hurl at me like a slap, but which faltered mid-flight and landed quite differently. I find myself struggling to form a sufficiently scathing response, or any response at all.

But she's not even looking at me anymore. She's staring into the abyssal black between the trees with a long-suffering expression. "Oh, not another one."

There's a fragile amber light flickering closer, like a candle held in a shaking fist. Scurrying footsteps. The terrified panting of someone running for reasons that are not recreational.

The queen looks inclined to melt into the shadows and let this character pass us by, their narrative uninterrupted, but I stand woozily and say, "Hello?"

I catch a glimpse of a young girl with brown skin and terror-struck eyes before I realize the lantern has left her night-blind. She slams into my diaphragm and we go down in a pile of limbs and elbows while the queen gives a small, pained sigh.

The girl scrambles to her knees, already trying to launch herself back into the tangled dark of the woods, but I catch her shoulder. "Hey, it's okay. We're not going to hurt you."

She shrugs my hand away. "I have to hide—they're coming—"

"Who? The huntsman?"

She nods, wheeling to look behind her as if she expects to find a henchman lumbering out from behind a tree. The woods are perfectly still.

I know she'll be all right on her own—she's due to find a friendly bunch of dwarves or fairies soon, and the huntsman probably isn't even chasing her—but she's a lot younger than the other Snow Whites we've seen, and much more frightened. I find myself saying, "Don't worry, we'll help you find a safe place."

The queen makes a strangled noise of protest and I shoot her a repressive look. "*Won't* we?"

"I don't see why I should," she huffs.

"God, you're the *worst*."

"You think you're such a hero, but you won't help me—"

"Maybe if you acted just a *smidge* less evil I'd consider it."

The queen lunges, fangs bared, but I raise her mirror and waggle it warningly. "Ah-ah. You wouldn't want to break this, now would you?"

It's at this point, when the queen's face is a twisted rictus of fury, her eyes fixed on her precious mirror, that the young girl shoves between us.

She raises her lantern high and says, "I'll find it myself," over one shoulder as she passes us.

I pause long enough to give the queen a "now look what you did" face before hurrying after Snow White. I rummage in my pack one-handed and produce a battered wooden box. "Here, this'll tell us where to go." I open the compass and wait for the needle to wobble to a stop, directing us northeast.

The girl leads the way, striding past humped roots and clawing branches, and I follow her without consulting the queen, because it's not like she'll let either me or the mirror out of her sight. We haven't made it ten paces before I hear her stomping and muttering after us.

The woods darken and thicken around us. Briars tug at our clothes and small, slinking creatures rustle just past the bright ring of lantern light. A few reluctant stars blink like filmy eyes through the branches, but the moon refuses to rise.

The young Snow White never slows down or hesitates. I wonder briefly what could scare a kid like this, who walks so fearlessly through the dark, and decide I'd rather not know.

Eventually another light shines through the trees: a pair of lit windows, warm and inviting, wildly out of place in the thorned and twisted wood.

I point Snow White toward the windows. "Okay, there's probably somebody in there who can help you out. Just do whatever they say and stay away from strangers, and you'll . . . be . . ." I trail away, because there's a small bird silhouetted in one of the windows, the first we've heard or seen all night. Something about the shape of it rings a very distant and unlikely bell in my head.

It flutters toward us and perches directly above me, lit from below by the shuddering yellow of Snow White's lantern. It fixes me with a single bright and clever eye and I know, suddenly, where I've seen this bird before.

I whisper, softly and a little desperately, because this is more than six impossible things and breakfast is still a long way off, "No way."

But the multiverse in all its infinite weirdness, answers: *Yes way.*

The door of the hut opens and an old woman stands in the spill of light looking exactly as she did five years ago, when I sat at her table drinking tea with a different folkloric princess.

I feel dizzy, suddenly uncertain, as if I might have fallen into the gap between stories and gotten stuck. "Z-Zellandine?"

Zellandine, for her part, does not look even slightly surprised to see me. She points her chin inside the hut and says tiredly, "Well, come on, then."

5

It's the young Snow White who moves first. She strides into the fairy's house with a stiff spine and an expression suggesting that nothing in front of her could possibly be worse than whatever's behind her. Zellandine welcomes her with a grandmotherly nod, gesturing to a seat around the table. There's a rightness to the shape they make against the light, two silhouettes repeated in a thousand variations of a thousand stories: the old woman welcoming the weary traveler, the witch inviting the child inside, the fairy godmother sheltering the maiden.

Then Zellandine turns back to us and the rightness vanishes. We eye one another—three straying characters who have run off the rails of their own stories and collided in someone else's—before Zellandine grimaces as if to say, *What a mess,* and chucks her head toward the other three chairs around the table.

Her hut is exactly as I remember it, cottagecore with a witchy edge, blue-glass bottles on the shelves and herbs strung before a crackling fireplace. The only difference is that the kitchen table has four chairs now, and four cups of tea on mismatched saucers.

We sip our tea in uncertain silence, not looking at one another. Zellandine butters bread and sets it in front of our Snow White, who eats with the determined efficiency of someone who doesn't turn down free calories. In the fuller light of the hut she looks even younger than I thought, her cheeks still gently rounded, but she lacks a little kid's wide-eyed trust. Her expression is closed and watchful, precocious in the bleak, uncanny way of a child who has spent too much time thinking about how and when she'll die. It's the expression I'm wearing in every one of my school photos.

"You'll find a bed made, upstairs," Zellandine tells her gently.

Snow White's eyes cut to the bright-lit windows, shining like beacons into the black sea of trees, and Zellandine adds, even more gently, "I'll keep watch tonight."

Snow White nods in grave thanks, one hand on her chest, then repeats the motion to me and—after a moment's hesitation—the queen. The queen's eyes widen very slightly. I suppose wicked stepmothers aren't often thanked.

Zellandine clears the cups as Snow White climbs the steps to the loft, which I'm 98 percent sure didn't exist the last time I had tea in this hut. "There are three beds up there," Zellandine observes.

The queen makes a visible effort to un-slump herself from the table. "I thank you, but I'm afraid Zinnia and I must be on our way." Her tone aspires toward chilly rebuke, but lands closer to *very tired*.

"Oh my God, give it a *rest*." I tap the silver frame of her mirror on the tabletop. "You can get back to your jailbreak first thing in the morning. I promise."

Even her venomous glare is exhausted. After a long and weighty pause, she grates, "Your word that you will neither flee nor damage the mirror while I rest."

I'm tempted to roll my eyes, but I restrain myself to a flat stare. "Sure, yeah. Scout's honor." I slide the mirror across the table and she stops it with two long fingers against the frame, her lips slightly parted in shock. "See what you get when you ask nicely?"

The queen cuts me a look, dark and inscrutable, before following Snow White upstairs.

"Sorry about her," I say to Zellandine. "She's the villain, obviously."

Zellandine unties her apron, fingers slower and older than I remember them, and settles across from me. "Oh, we villains aren't all bad." A flash of humor in the pale blue of her eyes.

"No, she's like, a *legit* villain, not a misunderstood protofeminist fairy."

Zellandine makes a very neutral sound, her eyes glinting with that subterranean humor. "We don't all get to choose the parts we're given to play. You should know that better than most."

I think unwillingly of all the other roles the queen was given: the ugly princess, the barren queen, the foreign monarch. A string of women with just enough power to be hated and not quite enough to protect themselves. I swallow a lump of inconvenient sympathy. "Sure, okay, but we all get to choose what we do *next*. A sad backstory is no excuse for being a dick. I should know."

This feels to me like a solid rhetorical win, but Zellandine undermines it by murmuring, "You should, yes," under her breath.

"And what's that supposed to—"

"How's the princess?" Zellandine asks it blandly, even pleasantly; there's no reason the question should feel like a sucker punch.

I try to make my face equally bland and pleasant. "She's good. Fine.

She's married now, actually." My smile feels weird but I can't seem to make it un-weird. "Doing the happily-ever-after thing, I guess."

Zellandine gives me a nod containing more sympathy than is strictly warranted. "So how long has it been since you last saw her?"

"A while. A few months." Six months and twelve days, but whatever. "Anyway, I don't know why it matters. What matters is *what the hell is going on*? What are you *doing* here?"

Zellandine doesn't look even slightly thrown by the topic change; it's annoyingly hard to surprise a prophetic fairy. "I could ask you the same thing," she replies evenly. When I squint, she lifts one shoulder. "This isn't your story either."

"Yeah, well, that's not my fault. I'm headed back to the Sleeping Beauty–verse as soon as I can." I don't mention the secret, wild hope that I don't have to return to my own story at all. That I've found a way to break free of this endless cycle of cursed girls and pricked fingers, to punch through the walls of my own plot and bust into other narrative dimensions like a fairy-tale Kool-Aid Man. And if I can make a new beginning for myself in some other story—what's to stop me making a new ending too?

There's a pause before I can speak through the hope now crawling up my throat. "I was kidnapped by an evil queen. How did *you* get here?"

Zellandine sits back in her chair, watching me as if she knows exactly what I didn't say. "It's happened a few times now. I step outside and find myself in deep woods I've never seen before, on a mountaintop that isn't mine. Once, I woke to find my house all covered in sweets, with gingerbread for shingles and boiled sugar for window panes."

I think: *Oh shit*. I say: "Oh shit." I remember the talking wolf in the queen's world, my juice-stained copy of Grimms' fairy tales, things shaken loose from their moorings and set adrift. "You're slipping between stories."

Zellandine tilts her head. "There do seem to be a lot of tales that require someone old and magical living alone in the woods. I don't mind it, mostly—cursing the occasional haughty prince, letting a handsome knight or two warm themselves by my fire." I check her face for innuendo and find it suspiciously absent. "But it's been happening more and more often. And I'm starting to feel like . . ." She trails away, her hand stroking the inside of her wrist. The flesh there has milky translucence I don't remember from five years before.

"Like butter spread over too much bread?"

"Yes, like that," she breathes. "And I confess, I was fond of my home on the mountainside. We miss it." Her blackbird trills to her, but I hardly notice because the word *home* is rattling between my ribs like a stray bullet, carelessly fired. I think of my phone, fully charged but turned off, zipped in one of those inner backpack pockets no one ever opens. I think of three hands buried in the same popcorn bowl. I think of Charm's face the last time I saw her, asking me for something I couldn't give.

"Well." I clear my throat, searching for levity and finding nothing but sickly sarcasm. "You have to admit, your story kind of sucked."

"But it was mine." Zellandine's tone is sharper than I've heard before, grief-edged. She bites the inside of her cheek before adding, "I might not have chosen it, but I always chose what to do next."

"Often on other people's behalf, if I remember right."

I meant it as a stinging rebuke, but Zellandine is nodding thoughtfully. "To their detriment, I think now. I was trying to save others from a fate like mine, but perhaps I was taking away their own right to choose, to make of their stories what they would."

She gives me such a mild look that I bristle defensively. "Hey, I'm not—it's not like that. I'm helping people fix their stories. And if they can't be fixed, I help them escape."

Zellandine is still looking at me with that weaponized mildness. "Oh, I don't think any of us escape our stories entirely."

"Prim did."

"Did she?" I want to sneer that I don't think Perrault or Disney ever pictured Sleeping Beauty marrying a hot butch with an undercut and a Superman tattoo, except I have this horrible sinking feeling that she might be right. I mean, I said it myself: *She's doing the happily-ever-after thing, I guess*.

I raise my hands in mock-surrender, abruptly exhausted. "Well. I'm sorry about the narrative slippage. But I'm glad you were here tonight." My chair scrapes against wood as I stand and make my way toward the steps.

Zellandine speaks just as my hand lands on the railing. "I don't understand what's happening to me, or how." She turns, her eyes catching the dying red of the hearth, and in that moment I see her as she must be in other stories: the fairy who curses kingdoms, the crone who punishes ungrateful travelers, the witch who waits in the woods.

Her mouth twists, wry and tired, and she is only Zellandine again. "But I think both of us know why."

❁ ❁ ❁

ZELLANDINE'S BEDS ARE squashy and warm, piled deep with flannel and down, but I sleep in fitful bursts. Each time I drift toward unconsciousness I'm woken by some small noise—the scritching of skeletal black branches at the window, the distant shrieks of night birds—and left wide-eyed and panting in a pool of adrenaline. Snow White is apparently accustomed to sleeping through horror movie sound effects, but every time I look toward the queen's bed, I catch the lambent white of open eyes before both of us turn away.

Breakfast the next morning is gray and quiet. I chase my oats in miserable circles, muffling phlegmy coughs in the crook of my elbow and refusing to wonder if they sound wetter than they did yesterday, if tiny protein buds are already sprouting along my bronchial tree like deadly Christmas lights.

The queen doesn't look great either. There are spongy bruises beneath both eyes and her makeup is mostly smeared away, leaving her looking like a painting that sat too long in direct sunlight. Several determined freckles are poking through the remains of her face powder, forming an unexpected constellation.

Zellandine settles at the head of the table and folds her hands in a businesslike manner. "We didn't introduce ourselves properly last night. I'm Zellandine, an old friend of Zinnia's."

She looks expectantly at the queen, who looks, for no reason, at me. For the briefest moment I see something raw and bleeding behind her eyes, like an unstitched wound, before she gathers the edges of herself and presses them back together. "You may call me Your Maj—"

"Eva." I interrupt. The queen gives me a glare that's more searching than scorching. I don't like the vulnerable set of her eyes, another glimpse of that red wound in the middle of her, so I lean over and stage-whisper, "Short for Evil Queen."

While she's still sputtering, I gesture to the poor kid sitting next to me. "And this, of course, is Snow White."

Snow White has been eating her oats in determined silence, looking at the windows as if she's waiting for something to emerge from the trees. At the sound of my voice, she flinches so badly she sends her bowl shattering to the floor. She doesn't seem to notice, crouching in her chair with her eyes pinned on me.

"Oh, my bad," I say mildly. "Is that not your name?"

She answers slowly, as if she half expects me to sprout fangs and pounce. "No. You don't—" Her eyes narrow, moving from my face to my jeans to the backpack propped against my chair. "You're not . . . from here, are you?"

"Nope. I'm an interdimensional tourist, just passing through."

She stares for another long, hard second before saying tersely, "My name is Red."

"Huh." There are several Red-variants running through Western folklore—Rose Red and Little Red, for a start—but I'm not sure what any of them would be doing in a Snow White story. (Yes, there is technically a Grimm story titled "Snow-White and Rose-Red," but it has nothing whatsoever to do with the other Snow White; yes, it is very confusing. Take it up with Jacob and Wilhelm.)

Well. The name Snow White always had uncomfortable implications about racialized standards of beauty; maybe in this world, her mother named her for the drop of blood, rather than the snow it fell on.

"Hi, Red." I say it as comfortingly as I can, which isn't very. "You should be safe now. Zellandine is a powerful fairy, and she'll keep you hidden from your wicked stepmother."

Red's eyebrows scrunch together. "My what?"

"Or mother, or sister, or whoever—"

"Perhaps," Zellandine suggests, with a touch of asperity, "the girl could tell her own story."

After a beat, during which I stick my tongue out at Zellandine and the queen sighs as if she regrets every decision that led her to be sitting at this table, Red does. It takes approximately two sentences to confirm that we are very, very far from the singing woodland creatures and flower-strewn forests of Disney. We're not even in one of the

Grimms' bloody fantasies, with their violent morality; we're someplace darker and wilder and much older, where the villain has a terrible hunger, and the hero is the one who survives it.

Red, it turns out, is not a princess. She's a shepherd's daughter from a poor village at the edge of the woods. Every winter, the queen sends her hunters to snatch the strongest and healthiest children and drag them back to her lair.

"Nobody knows what she does with them. Ivy says she gives them candies and jewels, but Ivy's stupid." Red's voice is flat and even. "I think she plucks out their hearts and eats them. Either way, nobody ever sees them again."

A small, appalled silence follows this. It's the queen—Eva, I suppose, since she's not the queen of anything around here, and the name seems to annoy her so deeply—who speaks first. "But why would she do that?"

Red gives her a look suggesting the cannibal queen's personal motivations are fairly low on her list of concerns. Zellandine speculates about the latent magical properties of innocent hearts and the power that could theoretically be gained through ingestion, but I miss most of it because I'm busy hissing back and forth with Eva. ("Hold up, Miss Moral High Ground, didn't you ask for Snow White's lungs and liver?" "Yes, but I wasn't going to *eat* them! I'm not *depraved*!")

I shush Eva, which she visibly hates, and turn back to Red. "And your family, your parents—they just let her take you?" I consider Red's hair, pulled away from her face in pretty twists, and remember my dad braiding my hair every day before school, his fingers gentle. Someone must love her. "They didn't fight for you?"

Eva makes a scathing noise that tells me more than I wanted to know about her own parents, but Red answers with a soft and terrible brevity. "They did."

Eva seems to be struggling with something, her lips working until she says, almost angrily, "Why don't you all leave? Or hide?"

"She always finds you," Red says, her voice still soft. "She talks to the moon, people say, or maybe a magic mirror. And then . . ." Her eyes flick to the window again, and this time the warm brown of her skin goes ashen. "And then her huntsman come to fetch you."

There's something funny about the grammar of that sentence, but it's only when I hear the crunch of many pairs of boots through the woods, then the thud of many fists on the door, that I understand I misheard her. She didn't say *huntsman*, with a singular A; she said *huntsmen*.

❁ ❁ ❁

My first, profoundly unhelpful thought is: *This isn't how it goes*. There's supposed to be a witch disguised as an old woman, an apple the color of blood, a pretty coffin in the woods. There's supposed to be three chances and a happy ending. But instead there are fists pounding on the door.

A shrill voice shouts, "We know you're in there, girlie! Come out, queen's orders!"

Red is out of her chair, backing against the counter, fingers curling around a bread knife. Zellandine is rising, tightening her apron with trembling fingers. Only Eva and I remain frozen, like a pair of mannequins in a bustling department store.

By the time Zellandine opens the door, her hands are not shaking at all. "You must be mistaken, good sirs. There's no one here but me." It's a brave effort, and a doomed one. She barely says the words before a thin-faced man shoulders his way past her, eyes roving hungrily around the cottage. More men pour in behind him. They all have the same stringy, unhealthy look, and they all wear the same yellowish necklaces. The necklaces rattle oddly when they move, like chattering teeth. It takes me too long to realize that's what they actually are: human teeth, strung on leather cords. Acid boils in my throat, sick and hot.

The leader points to Red. "Come with us."

She shakes her head once, knuckles pale around her bread knife, chin still high, and God, this kid deserves better than this bloody, brutal story. One of the huntsmen draws a knife of his own, one never intended to slice bread, but it turns abruptly to ash in his hand. Greasy flakes drift silently to the floor.

"I did not invite you across my threshold, boy," Zellandine growls behind him. But she's panting as she says it, the flesh of her face gone white and thin as onionskin. Back in Primrose's world she'd seemed ageless, invincible, a woman who could turn knives into feathers with the slightest flick of her eyelash. But maybe that was only true in her own world, and the rules are different in this one. Maybe power has a price here, and she's paying it.

The knifeless huntsman seems to sense her weakness, because he turns and shoves Zellandine hard, as if she's not a witch but merely an old woman. Someone yells, and it's only once I'm on my feet that I realize it was me. The huntsmen are all staring at me and the strap of my pack is tight in my hand, and it's not like I have a stellar life expectancy anyway. I sling it into the leader's face.

The fight that follows is brief and embarrassing. In less than a minute I'm facedown on the floor with someone's knee ungently separating my vertebrae. A hand snarls in my hair and smacks my face almost perfunctorily against the floor. Everything goes staticky and muffled after that, my vision stippled with black starbursts.

There are boot steps. A fleshy thud and a strangled cry. The head huntsman asking, from far away, "What about you? Going to give us trouble?"

A pause, taut with the promise of violence, followed by Eva's voice speaking a single, thin syllable. "No."

The huntsmen leave then, pausing only to offer a few casual kicks to my rib cage as they pass.

In their absence, the only sound is the steady *splish* of my blood against the floorboards and the whine of the door as it swings in the wind, and—in the distance, fading fast—the cries of a brave little girl who has come, at last, to the end of her bravery.

6

"So, OBVIOUSLY"—MY PACK whumps onto the tabletop—"we have to go after her."

I'm hoping if I say it with enough calm authority, we can skip the part of the conversation where Eva gets whiny and morally gray about it, but apparently not, because she says, "I assure you we do not," without even opening her eyes. Her hands are propped on the kitchen counter, her head hanging low. Her fancy braids are hanging loose down the back of her neck now, nothing at all like the sleek black crown she wore when I first saw her in the mirror.

"I mean, I agree, ideally there would be more of us, and Zellandine would be conscious." After my ears had stopped ringing and my nosebleed had slowed to a jellied ooze, I bullied Eva into helping me scoop the fairy off the floor. I have no idea how we would have gotten her up the stairs, but luckily we didn't have to. The steps had vanished, replaced by a single bed in the corner, the sheets already turned down. We tucked Zellandine under the covers and received a wan smile in return. Her cold fingers covered mine. "You'll go after her, won't you?" she asked resignedly. I nodded. The fingers tightened. "But afterward—go *home*. Things are tangling, the lines are blurring. You can't keep running forever." My second nod was more of a noncommittal jerk of my chin. Zellandine's eyes narrowed. "Every story ends, Zinnia."

She appears to be sleeping now, her blackbird perched on the bedpost, considering her with one worried eye and then the other.

"But you know what they say." I give the queen a hearty shrug. "If wishes were fishes."

Eva opens her eyes then, but only to squint at me as if she has a sudden headache. "Then what?"

I consider. "Never mind. The point is, we have to go."

Her mouth hardens. Her eyes close again. "No, we don't."

I'm unpacking and repacking my backpack, dispensing with unnecessary weight. I unzip an inner pocket and lay my phone carefully on the table. "You know," I say, trying very hard—medium hard—well, a little—to keep my tone polite, "maybe we wouldn't have to go save a kid from a cannibal queen if you'd put up literally any fight at all, but you chose to *sit* there while the rest of us—"

Now Eva spins to face me, lips curling away from her teeth. "And what did that get you, exactly?" She closes the distance between us and reaches abruptly for my face. I stare her down, refusing to flinch or look away, but her thumb brushes with surprising softness across my chin. It comes away smeared with glutinous red. "I have tried before to explain my position, but perhaps you did not understand." Her voice vibrates, thick with emotion. "Everything I have done, everything I will do, serves one purpose: to *survive*."

And there is an un-small part of me that understands that, and more than understands it. Sympathizes with it, admires it, even—

okay, yes—desires it. (The way she looks right now, her eyes blazing with that bottomless life-hunger, her face lit with an intensity that burns straight past prettiness and toward something far more dangerous . . . No jury would convict me.)

But I've tried just surviving. I spent twenty-one years pouring all my want and will toward it, adhering to a set of rules—*move fast, go hard, don't fall in love, try not to die*—that left me with exactly one friend and zero plans. And in the end, none of it mattered anyway. In the end, it was just me and my nonnegotiable illness, and the only reason I survived was because someone else (a couple of someones, technically) saved me.

So I just look at Eva for a while, in all her selfish, ferocious, sexy will to survive, and shake my head. "Fine." I hold down the power button on my phone and wait for the screen to light up, steadfastly refusing to think why I'm turning it on or who I might call. "But I'm going."

Eva's eyes flicker. "*Why?*"

"Because . . ."

There are noble ways to finish that sentence (because Red is brave and clever and she deserves better; because the hot nerd on *The Good Place* was right, and the meaning of life basically boils down to what we owe to each other) and less noble, potentially more honest ways (because as long as I'm saving other people I can forget, briefly, that I can't save myself; because storming an evil fortress is easier than showing Charm my X-rays and watching her understand, all over again, that I'm not in it for the long haul, that there's still a trolley barreling toward both of us).

I finish boringly. "Just like, because. Someone should."

Eva's expression remains hard and fixed, like a marble statue titled *Monarch Who Is Unmoved by the Pleas of the Peasantry*, but there's an odd wistfulness in her eyes, almost as if she envies me. As if she wishes she, too, were a stupid twenty-six-year-old with the reckless bravery of the terminally ill rather than the predictable villain doing the predictably villainous thing. I think of Zellandine telling me that we don't get to choose our stories, but we get to choose what we do next.

A very bad idea occurs to me then. I slide my arms into my backpack straps and meet her eyes very squarely. "If you come with me and help save Red, I'll tell you how to get out of this story." I lean forward and tap the back of her magic mirror, which is never far from her hand. "For real."

Eva's eyes move from the mirror to my face, widening as she realizes I don't just mean *out of this particular version of this story* but *out of this kind of story more broadly*. Out of her own horrible ending, away from the cruel logic of her character arc.

Her face finally moves, and it takes me a moment to recognize the expression for what it is. I've seen her sneer, and smirk, and bare her teeth in a dozen cruel grins, but this is the first time she's genuinely smiled at me.

I'm obliged to blink several times. "So." There's an answering smile spreading helplessly across my face. "It's a deal?"

❁ ❁ ❁

In retrospect, it's possible that Eva and I could have spent more time in the planning stage of our rescue attempt.

All we really did was consult the magic mirror, which confirmed that Red was still alive (Eva had stared at Red's face, terrified and tear-streaked, with something very close to guilt), and shove supplies in my bag. Bottled water and snacks, my cool magic compass, her cool magic mirror, a functioning, fully charged phone, and two of Zellandine's sharpest knives, which we—well, I—fully intended to return.

But after we stepped across the threshold there was a slight, inaudible *pop*, and a rush of wind that smelled very faintly of roses. When we turned around, Zellandine and her hut were gone.

There didn't seem to be anywhere to go after that except onward. I pulled out my compass and thought of Red, with her watchful eyes and her grim mouth, her hair twisted by someone who fought for her and lost. The needle spun southwest, and the two of us followed it.

It was an uneventful journey. Most things—and boy, did this forest have more than its fair share of Things—didn't bother us, either because of the knives or because they were looking for even bigger, juicier Things to eat. Around lunch (half a carrot cake Clif Bar apiece, which Eva considered with scientific curiosity, palpating it gently before realizing she was expected to consume it), something horrible landed on my open pack. It tore at the contents, shredding and shrieking, long talons flashing.

Eva had it pinned to a tree with her knife through its heart before I could properly scream. I would tell you what kind of animal it was, but I have no idea, and looking at it made my brain cramp. So I'll just say it was bad. Like, if a snake fucked a tarantula and their baby died in a tar pit and was later reanimated by a necromancer who graduated at the absolute bottom of his class.

"Thanks," I said in a voice that was a mere two octaves higher than usual.

I received nothing in response but a contemptuous curl of Eva's upper lip. But both of us moved more carefully after that, and startled at small noises. By the time dusk settled over the woods—although I'm not convinced it's ever fully not-dusk here; it seems to exist on a limited palette ranging from gloaming to gloomy—we were shivery and tense, and I'd spent the last several miles trying and failing to think of a funny name for the twitch in my left eye.

Eva held up her hand and I flinched backward. "What, where—"

She was pointing silently through the trees. I followed the line of her finger and saw it: a high stone wall stained a viscous, tarry black. I looked upward through the dark lace of the leaves, and that was the moment it occurred to me that Eva and I could have prepared better for what struck me now as a laughable attempt at a rescue mission. We could, for example, have brought siege weaponry, or a smallish army, or one of those big mech suits from *Pacific Rim*. Instead, we brought two kitchen knives and an assortment of underpowered magical objects, like video game characters rushing to the boss battle without leveling up.

I say, "Oh, *yikes*," which really undersells the enormity of the yikes we're facing.

I mean, sure, when one is looking for the lair of a cannibal queen, one expects to encounter a certain degree of spookiness. One might anticipate something resembling the Beast's castle pre-makeover, with gargoyles and buttresses and more lightning storms than is statistically likely. One does not anticipate what I'm seeing now, which is a jagged ruin of black glass and bones that makes the Black Gate of Mordor look like the Barbie Malibu Dreamhouse. Trees press against the walls, reaching over the battlements with fawning fingers. Dark, winged things circle the towers, screeching in too-human voices.

"Well." Eva makes a sardonic gesture at the walls. "What are we waiting for?"

After another brief round of hissing ("This was your idea." "I know! There's just like, more skulls than I was expecting! Give me a second."), I gather myself and say calmly, "Okay, there has to be a back way in."

"I very much doubt it. If I built an impregnable fortress to hold my desperate victims, I certainly wouldn't—"

"Yeah, I know, but there's *always* a back way in. Trust me." Eva's face makes a funny flinch, which I can only assume is her natural response to the concept of trust, but she trails huffily behind me as we circle the wall. A few guards go clomping past us along the battlements, but none of them seem to see us creeping below them. I guess this isn't the kind of place that people often try to get into.

After less than fifty feet of sneaking, a damp, foul breeze emerges from somewhere nearby and wafts across us. It smells like old meat and human suffering, and it leads us without much trouble to a rusted, weed-choked grate set in the earth.

I wave my hand and whisper, "Voilà. A back way in."

Eva squints sourly at the sewer grate. She sniffs. "It must be nice. Being the protagonist."

I give her my cheekiest smile and say, "It suits you." It comes out more sincerely than I intended, and Eva's eyes flick to mine, then away.

I haul the grate aside and shimmy down the hole, landing with a fairly repellent plop. The water (it is not water) is sludgy and cold, running halfway up my thighs. It feels like an obvious moment for Eva to cut and run, but she lands beside me without fuss and strides onward, looking—just for a moment, in the dark—a little like a hero.

❁ ❁ ❁

WE WADE THROUGH the muck for just long enough that I'm starting to worry that these sewers function as actual sewers rather than plot devices and don't lead anywhere useful, but then we hear things echoing off the wet stone walls: cries and pleas, the miserable *clink-clink* of chains dragging across stone floors. The unmistakable sounds of a castle dungeon.

There's a grate directly above us, casting a sickly shard of light across Eva's face. I nod upward. "This is our stop."

We slither out into a space that looks like a slightly larger version of the sewer we just left, except that there are greasy torches spitting along the walls and cells with iron bars for doors. Most of them are empty, and some of them contain . . . pieces . . . that I refuse to look at long enough to identify. We pass a cell with actual, live occupants, but my heart sinks when I see that they aren't children.

But one of them is a tall woman with a proud arch to her nose and warm brown skin. The others are slumped listlessly against the walls, but this woman is on her feet, reaching through the bars to wiggle a shard of bone in the lock. Her hair is twisted neatly away from her face.

She gives us a wary once-over as we approach the bars, but apparently we don't look like a threat or salvation. She returns her attention to the lock, manacles clanking softly against the bars.

"You're Red's mom, aren't you." I don't say it like a question, because it isn't one.

At the sound of the word *Red* her eyes snap to my face. "Where is she? Who are you? Did they catch her?"

I hiss the word "*chill*" between clenched teeth, just as a broad-shouldered man stands and sets a hand on the woman's shoulder. She chills, reluctantly, but her eyes are a pair of knives pressed to my jugular.

I decide to be blunt and quick. "The huntsmen took her a few hours ago."

The woman closes her eyes. The big man grunts as if he's taken a physical blow.

"It's okay, we'll save her." I look up and down the dungeon, wishing for my bobby pins. "We'll, uh, we'll find a guard and steal the keys—"

I'm trying to comfort her, but Red's mother isn't listening to me. She's speaking in a calm voice to the big man behind her. "Looks like we're out of time, love."

He sucks air through his teeth. "It'll be loud. Bring them down on us."

"Let them come." Something in her voice makes me think of snapping bones, blood on the walls.

The man tears a seam at the hem of his shirt and withdraws a waxy twist of paper. He unwinds it to reveal a mound of grainy black sand, which he pours neatly into the keyhole. I have the somewhat humbling suspicion that I'm not necessary in this story, that I'm lucky I even got a speaking part.

The woman raises her hands and seems to recall, at the last moment, that Eva and I exist. "Stand back," she says. We do.

She strikes her manacles against the bars, sending showers of angry white sparks over the lock. Once, twice. All the prisoners are standing now, watching her, murmuring to one another. I can feel the weight of their hope like a physical thing, urging her on. I wonder how many of their children were stolen.

On the third strike, a tendril of smoke leaks from the keyhole. Shortly afterward I find myself lying flat on my back with a shrill ringing in my ears. The air smells hot. I think one of my incisors is loose.

I sit up to see Red's mother stepping through the mangled remains of her cell door, black smoke trailing her limbs. She's followed closely by the big dude (Red's dad? I don't want to make assumptions about heteronormative family structures in alternate universes, but the way he shadows Red's mom suggests he belongs to her) and the rest of the villagers. They flock silently around her as if they're waiting for a command, which I guess they are. Red's mother sends the oldest and youngest villagers down into the sewers and assembles the rest into rough formation. She nods once to me, like a commander acknowledging a new recruit, and sets off, heading upward out of the dungeons and into the castle itself.

I feel like I should ask questions, like *where are we going?* or *what happens when the guards turn up?* But Red's mother still has that sharpened bone in her fist, and her father's expression suggests an entire armed battalion would present only a fleeting obstacle.

We don't meet anyone. We climb stairs, and then more stairs, the air warming as we rise. The old-meat stink of the cells is replaced by something worse: a boiling, greasy smell, like bubbling fat. By the time we're aboveground I have a decent guess where we're headed. Red's mother opens a final door and I'm sickened to find out I'm right.

The kitchens are empty. The hearths are banked, the counters bare, the knives hanging clean and wicked from hooks on the wall. And in the corner of the room, huddled in a wire cage like chickens or goats ready for the slaughter, are the children.

They look up when we enter the room, the whites of their eyes gleaming in the dark. Most of them have the glazed, numb expressions of people whose adrenal glands and tear ducts ran dry a long time ago. The last time I saw that look on a kid's face was on my floor of the children's ward, and for a moment I want to split and run, not stopping until I find a world worth lingering in.

One of the kids lifts her chin, body braced against the wire as if she's hoping to get in one last punch before they carve her for the table. I spend half a second admiring the sheer guts of her, and then Red sees her mom.

All the fight runs out of her like cheap dye, leaving her looking like what she is: a frightened girl who wants her mother. Her lips shape a word I don't know and then her mother is on her knees beside the cage, hands jammed through the wire, and her father is smashing his boot against the lock again and again, and if the guards weren't already on their way, they are now.

"Be *quiet*." Eva's strangled whisper arrives long after the ship has sailed. The lock shatters. The children crawl out, some of them still dazed, some of them beginning to cry in sudden, shocking bursts. Red vanishes between her parents, their arms interwoven, their heads bent together. The shape of them—this family trapped in this god-awful horror movie of a world, surrounded on all sides by bad endings, still clinging stubbornly to one another—makes my heart twinge, so I look away.

When I'm done blinking back a weird wave of tears, Red is standing in front of us. She looks from me to Eva and back. "You came after me."

I consider explaining that actually her mom and dad had the whole thing pretty much in hand, but I figure we should get points for effort. "Yep."

Her eyebrows are crimped in the middle. "But you don't even know me."

"Nope."

"Why?" This time, for whatever reason, she addresses the question to Eva.

"Because . . ." Eva flounders, looking around the kitchens as if hoping to find another zombie snake-tarantula to fight rather than finish this sentence. Her eyes skate across mine. She ends quietly, with a wry twist of her lips that isn't half as disdainful as she'd like it to be. "Someone had to."

Red hugs her then, which makes Eva's face do several complicated contortions. It lands on a fixed expression that reminds me of a school calculator that's been asked to perform too many impossible functions and is reduced to flashing *ERROR* on the screen. She makes eye contact with me over Red's head, a clear plea for help that I pretend not to see.

I always like this part. The happily ever afters that come after are too sweet for me, like grocery store frosting, but this moment right here, when you feel the relief of a bad ending averted, a wrong righted—this is the good shit.

(I give a mental middle finger to Zellandine, because I'm not *running*, I'm being *helpful*, even if Red's parents didn't really need my help.)

Eventually, Red's mother comes to collect her, pausing to give us a dignified nod.

The room empties as the villagers disappear back down the stone steps, led by Red and her family. I watch them go, still full of that heady, giddy pride.

I can tell from Eva's expression—eyes dark, lips slightly parted, head tilted back—that she feels it too. "It's nice, isn't it?" I murmur.

"What is?"

"Being the good guy."

She snorts at me, but her eyes catch mine. I'm smiling brazenly up at her, wondering a little dizzily what it would be like to kiss her for real, on purpose rather than out of necessity, when a voice behind us says cliché-ly, "Well, well, well."

And I know that I have a very few seconds to act. I could run. I could turn and fight. I could prick my finger on the tip of my own knife and hope I fall out of this B-horror movie of a universe. Instead, I do what I've always done when I'm cornered, what I always will do. I text Charm.

In the moment before hands close around my arms and my phone is dashed to the floor, crashing into a dozen useless plastic pieces, and this shitty story takes me in its jaws again, I manage to type nine characters and press send: atu 709 sos

7

A CONFESSION: I was totally expecting her to be ugly. Which is pretty fucked up of me, but in my defense, Western folklore persistently and falsely equates a character's physical appearance with their inner morality, so like, it was a pretty safe bet that the evil cannibal queen would look like Anjelica Huston after she peels off her mask in *The Witches*.

But when her goons wrench my arms behind my back and spin me to face her, it turns out she's not ugly at all. She is, in fact, one of the least ugly things I've ever seen (yes, including Prim, who is so beautiful that people squint and blink when they talk to her, like they're trying to have a conversation with the sun). The queen is young and doe-eyed, with long, soft lashes and gently rounded cheeks. Her skin is the phosphorescent white of a Renaissance angel, and her lips are a bright, arterial red, as if she's just eaten a bowl of fresh cherries or, perhaps, the raw hearts of stolen children.

I think, intelligently: *Huh.* And then I think,

slightly more intelligently, my stomach sinking fast: *I know who you are*. "You're—Snow White!" I'm aiming for a nice *j'accuse!* moment, but it's clear from the expressions around me that I'm literally the only person who didn't know.

Snow White smiles at me. It's a very good smile, sweet as springtime, but her voice is pure ice. "You may address me as Your Majesty."

My eyes move of their own accord to Eva. She's putting up a much better fight than me, struggling against three huntsmen as they wrestle her wrists behind her back. One of them knocks the backs of her legs and sends her crashing to her knees. Another buries his fist in her hair and wrenches her face upward, baring the fragile column of her throat. She doesn't look much like a queen compared to Snow White—her face is hard and plain and a little too old, her teeth bared in bitter fury—but looking at her, I feel a big, weird rush of loyalty.

"Sorry," I tell Snow White. "I've already got one of those."

Snow White's sweet smile doesn't falter when she orders her men to strip us of our belongings and lock us up, awaiting punishment for our crimes against queen and country.

So here I am, in the dungeons again. Naturally.

I've seen a decent number of dungeons in the last five years, but these are among the least pleasant. It's the meaty smell of human remains, probably, or maybe the gelatinous burble of the sewers beneath us, or maybe the extreme unlikelihood of our escape. Both our arms are shackled above us and the huntsmen took everything up to, and partially including, our clothes. I'm barefoot and hoodie-less, shivering sporadically in my T-shirt, and Eva's kidney-colored gown is gone. All she's wearing now is one of those shapeless, colorless underdresses that I'm pretty sure is called a shift, or maybe a chemise, laced up the front with a limp green ribbon. It ought to be at least a little bit sexy, but it just makes her look small and vulnerable, like something recently shelled.

"Okay, so." I cough wetly. "That could have gone better."

Eva's head is tilted back against the wall, her eyes closed. She doesn't respond, so I add a small, insufficient, "Sorry."

She exhales in the manner of someone who is counting slowly to ten before replying. "You're sorry." Her eyes are still closed. "You forced me to accompany you on a mad, doomed mission to rescue a girl I barely know who didn't even need rescuing. You promised me a way out and I risked everything to get it, as I always do—" She pauses, perhaps to count to ten again. "And now I'll die, just like I was always going to. But you—you're *sorry*."

"I mean, I'm also going to die, by the way." Well, probably, depending on how pissed Charm is, and whether she remembers the Aarne-Thompson-Uther index, and whether I can get my hands on the damn mirror again. "So yeah, I'm sorry. But honestly, it feels like you're failing to take responsibility for your own actions here? Like, maybe if you hadn't decided to murder a kid for the crime of being hotter than you, everything would've turned out great. You could've lived to a ripe old age in your own world." I try and fail to keep a green thread of envy out of my voice. I can't imagine the privilege of a long life, but I know I wouldn't waste it with petty, vaguely un-feminist villainy. I'd—

I snap the sentence in half, but the images come anyway, unbidden: Mom's roses blushing in spring, family game night, Charm forcing us all to get matching tattoos on her thirtieth birthday. And—maybe, someday—a place of my own: a houseplant, or even a pet, a daily commute, a savings account because I would have something to save for. A whole life that I'd never have to leave.

I'm breathing in through my nose and out through my mouth,

trying not to cry, when Eva says dismissively, "You don't know what happened."

I lose the pattern of my calm breathing. "You know that red book of fairy tales you found? It belongs to me—belonged, I guess, since you left it behind in your stupid world. My dad gave it to me when I was a kid and I read it at least fifty times and then got a folklore degree and read it fifty more times. I promise, I know how the story goes."

"Of course you do," Eva says to the ceiling. Her voice is mocking, almost smug, as if no one could possibly understand her.

"Hey, I've got nothing but time." I try to spread my arms invitingly and succeed only in rattling my chains. "If you want to give me a long, sympathetic speech about your motivations, be my fucking guest."

Eva answers whip-fast and vicious. "Or maybe you could just *think* for two consecutive seconds. My Snow White was a pretty little girl who sang to songbirds and trusted old women selling apples. I am a witch and a queen who has devoted her life to the accumulation of power. If I'd wanted to kill her, don't you think she would be *dead*?"

I open my mouth, and then close it slowly. Fairy tales are riddled with illogical coincidences and obvious plot holes, but most of us learn to skip over them, like you skip the squeaky step on the staircase. "Okay, I'll play," I say. "Why didn't you kill her?"

Eva is looking at me now, her mouth framed by those bitter lines, her freckles like pinpricks of blood in the dim light. "Because I didn't want to. She was only a child, and I'm not a monster." A defiant lift of her chin. "But I couldn't allow her to stay, either. She was the king's only legitimate heir, and I'd failed to give him any others. After he died, but before she came of age . . . I had power. *Real* power—not whispers behind the throne or politicking in the shadows, like my mother had before me. I alone sat on the throne, I alone wore the crown. I was the *queen*."

It's the kind of line the scheming, power-mad queen might deliver in a fantasy novel, but Eva doesn't look mad. She looks wistful and sad, like a woman recalling the golden days of her youth. "And I knew all of it would vanish the second my stepdaughter married. Or maybe sooner—there were already nasty rumors that I was a witch rather than a woman, that I'd murdered Snow White's father."

"But, like . . ." I run my tongue over my bottom lip, trying to decide if there's a tactful way to ask and resolving that there isn't. "Did you?"

Her shoulders move in what I interpret as a shrug, although it's hard to tell at this angle. "Yes."

"Why?"

Eva's eyes harden. "I already told you. Everything I did, I did to survive." Her lashes shutter. "My husband married me because I was young and he needed heirs. When I failed to give him any, he was . . ." A hideous, weighty pause here. ". . . Displeased."

Oh, Jesus. I'm suddenly sick of these faux-medieval worlds and their shitty gender politics, all the pretty stories we tell about ugly worlds. A terrible sympathy crawls up my throat and lodges there, just behind my tongue. "You've used that word twice now. Failed." I fumble in my grab bag of therapist terminology and emerge with a pathetic "You didn't fail."

Eva has met my insults and jabs with bared teeth, but now, when my voice is low and sincere, she flinches. "What would you know about it?"

I meet her eyes. "Well, for starters, I can't. Get pregnant, I mean." She stares at me for a long time, her eyes wide and suspiciously glassy. I give her my best manacled shrug, because she strikes me as the kind of person who would be forced to kill me if I saw her cry. "Bodies are a real roll of the fucking dice, dude."

She swallows. "They—yes." She swallows again, visibly compartmentalizing, wrenching her story back on the rails. "Anyway. The princes began to arrive before she was fifteen. They lounged around my castle, eating from my table while they wooed my stepchild and plotted to take my throne. She was so young . . . but they came anyway. Every hungry second son who wanted a kingdom of his own."

Eva's eyes are narrowed now, her jaw firm. "So I did what I had to. I chased Snow White away, sent her running into the forest pursued by the only man I was certain would never harm her. Berthold came back with that pig's liver, thinking himself so clever, and I thanked him so prettily."

I recall Berthold's handsome, affable, slightly stupid face. I suppose if I genuinely wanted someone assassinated, he would not be my first choice. It occurs to me that the queen must have known he wouldn't hurt me, either, if I tried to escape.

Eva continues on a long sigh. "I'd hoped never to hear from Snow White again. But she didn't run far enough, and soon there were whispers about a pretty girl hidden in the woods, and the princes were circling like damned vultures, and I thought—if she were dead, or seemed to be dead, they would desist." Another sigh, even longer. "It seems I underestimated their appetites."

Now feels like the moment to apologize or sympathize, or, ideally, to stroke her straggling hair away from her face and press my lips tenderly to her forehead. But we're six feet apart and she probably hates my guts. "Look, Eva—Your Majesty, I—"

"All I wanted was power." Her lips make a bitter shape. "I know how I must sound, what you must think of me, but I only mean power over *myself*. Power to make my own choices, and arrive at my own ends."

"It's called agency." And they said my humanities degree would never come in handy. "It's like, the power you exert over your own narrative."

"It's what protagonists have, then."

"Sometimes even protagonists don't get much of it. I mean, did you read Little Brier-Rose in that book? My story sucks ass."

"Yes, I read it. It does indeed 'suck ass.'" She pronounces the phrase with aristocratic precision, and I make a mental note to teach her more modern swears, provided the two of us survive our forthcoming execution. "But at least it belongs to you. Your name is right there in the title. The only name I have is"—her voice hitches, like a thread catching a stray nail—"the one you gave me."

And, God help me, she sounds genuinely grateful. For a mean little nickname I invented just to annoy her. This strikes me as so backwards and awful that I find myself talking, the words falling out in a guilty, desperate tumble. "Charm—she's my best friend—well, she was, until I screwed it all up—she says the key is narrative resonance."

A flare of hope in Eva's eyes, quickly snuffed. "The key to what?"

I take a short breath. "Moving between worlds."

Eva says nothing, her eyes burning with the same desperate hunger that sent me tumbling into Prim's world in the first place, that keeps me skipping from world to world like a stone across the cold surface of the universe. I find myself looking away, unable to stand the sight of so much hope, even secondhand. "So, the universe is like a book, right? And each world is like a page. And if you tell the same story enough times, you can bleed through to another page."

"You mean—I must write down my own story?" Eva looks like she would open a vein and use her own blood as ink if I told her to.

"No, not literally." Although the thought loosens something in the back of my skull, a question I'd been ignoring. I keep ignoring it. "You have to *enact* a familiar part of your plot. And then you can sort of slip between worlds and go somewhere else." Charm is way better at explaining this stuff than me. I miss her, suddenly and fiercely, the way I haven't let myself in six months and thirteen days. Or, if I'm being honest, five years.

I swallow a knot of snot. "But like, it only works in your *own* story, usually. I'd only ever zapped into other versions of Sleeping Beauty until you and your magic mirror landed me here."

"So . . ." Eva closes her eyes. "We need the mirror."

"I think so, yeah."

"*Why?* It's just a mirror I enchanted to show me the truth."

My chains give an uncomfortable rattle. "I think—well, Zellandine thinks that the universes are getting squooshed together?" I applaud my own use of the passive voice. "So your mirror maybe slipped a little into other stories, and showed you other truths."

I can feel Eva studying me. "It's your fault, isn't it? That's what that fairy meant. The worlds are merging because you won't finish your story."

"Excuse me for not wanting to stand around and wait to die."

"Oh, I quite understand." Her tone turns acidic, blackly triumphant. "But then, I'm the villain."

I don't say anything in my defense, because there's not much to say. Maybe I'm the villain too.

Eventually, I feel Eva's bitterness drain away. "The mirror showed me you, out of all the possible people in all the universes." It sounds almost like an apology. "Why?"

"Well, what were you doing at the time?"

"I was looking into the mirror, obviously." She adds, far less sharply, "Wishing for a way out."

"Well." I remember standing in that hotel bathroom, on the run from another happily ever after that wasn't mine. "So was I. As it happens."

She meets my eyes then, and something passes soft and silent between us. A wordless understanding, a sympathy so profound it approaches symmetry. It makes me think I was wrong, and the mirror in the hotel bathroom showed me my own reflection, after all.

"When you kissed me—" Eva begins, and my heart does a maneuver that feels like jumping off a high dive. "It wasn't desire. You were just trying to trigger this narrative resonance, weren't you?"

My heart belly flops. "Yeah. It didn't work."

"So, without the mirror . . . we're stuck here." Her voice is ashen.

"Looks like it."

Silence unfurls between us. I should be formulating unlikely escape plans, but all I can think about is the sight of Red with her parents, the love strung like a cat's cradle between the three of them. They must have known since the day she was born what fate awaited her, and it didn't stop them caring. It didn't stop my stupid, stubborn parents, either, or my stupid, stubborn best friend. The last time I spoke to her she said we had to talk, and I could tell from her voice that it wasn't about my share of the rent or the laundry I left in the washer until it got moldy. *Sure*, I said, and then I went to my room, pricked my finger, and peaced out without even leaving a note.

And if I die in this sick version of Snow White, I'll never get to tell her how fucking sorry I am.

If Eva hears me crying, she has the decency not to say anything. "I really am sorry," I say thickly. "I'm sorry you didn't get out of your story, but if it helps—at least you're not the villain anymore. If you ever were."

She's quiet so long I don't think she'll answer. And then, when I'm sunk deep in a stupor of regrets and should-haves and aching joints, she whispers, "Thank you."

A few hours after that, they come for us.

I find, if I tilt my shoulders and wrench my arms to the side, that I can just reach Eva's hand as they march us through the castle. Her fingers wrap tight around mine, and we're dragged together toward the climax of our stories.

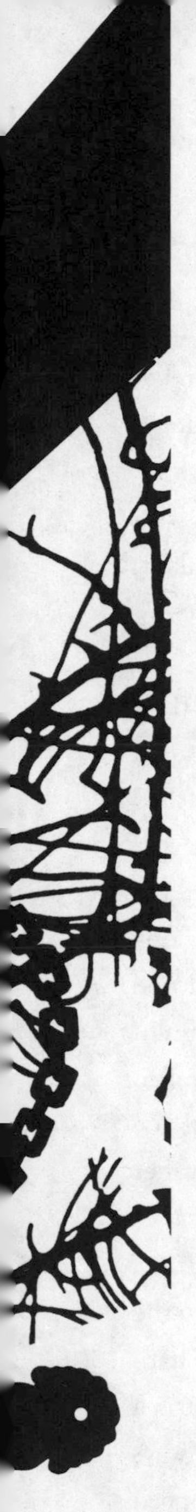

8

I ALWAYS IMAGINED dying in a hospital room, which is sort of funny because it means some treacherous part of my subconscious always wanted to go back home before the end. I pictured my mom and dad on one side of my bed, Prim and Charm on the other, and lots of really high-caliber drugs singing me to sleep.

I did not picture my bare feet on black stone. I didn't picture an airless courtyard or a low, greasy bonfire. I sure as hell didn't picture anyone walking beside me, her fingers biting into mine as if I am her last hope in the world, or she's mine. My hands are numb and bloodless from hours hanging above my head, but I don't let go.

The huntsmen unshackle our wrists and toss us to the ground before the fire. We crawl toward one another without speaking, our spines bumping as we turn to face the ringed huntsmen. The queen—or Snow White, or whatever twisted amalgamation she is in this world—comes sweeping through their ranks with a supervillain's sense of timing. Her hair is still silky black and her skin is still that unsettling alabaster, but her cheeks seem a little less round this morning, her lips a shade less red.

It feels like a good moment to say something quippy and brave, demonstrating my cocky resilience in the face of certain death, but nothing comes to mind. If I had my phone, I would text Charm in all caps: NOW'S THE TIME BITCH

Snow White stops a few feet away from us. "I'm quite cross with you, you know. Children aren't easy to catch." She looks petulant, disturbingly babyish. "They were bound for such a glorious purpose."

"What, dinner?"

Snow White's petulance darkens. "They were meant to keep their queen in the eternal youth that suits her best." Eva makes a small noise of understanding beside me, and Snow White's long-lashed gaze transfers to her. "It was my mother—well, stepmother—who first learned the trick of it." She says it like a secret, although there are huntsmen all around, their ivory necklaces chattering with every tiny movement. "I don't know how old she really was when she married my father, but she looked only a year or two older than me. I think." A doubtful look, as if it's been so long that she can't quite remember. "She might have carried on forever if she hadn't tried to steal the wrong heart." Snow White's fingers tap the white hyphen of her clavicle.

"Look." I wet cracked lips. "That's super awful and traumatizing, and I'm sure you need therapy, but like . . . Why did you turn into the exact same kind of monster? Why couldn't you just chill and live happily ever after?" I'm mostly talking at random, trying to give Charm a few extra seconds to pull off a miracle and rescue me, like she always has before. I wonder if, sometime over the last six months, she stopped sleeping with her ringer on.

Snow White's head tilts, nose scrunching. "It's not really a happily ever after if it *ends*, is it?"

I think I say something here—*it's not like that* or *you don't understand*—but I can't hear it over the rising noise in my head, the sudden bile in my mouth. Is that what I've been doing, these last five years? Trying to outrun my own ending? Throwing away every chance at happiness just because it was fleeting?

I swallow acid. "Every story ends," I whisper. I don't even know which of us I'm trying to convince. Eva shifts beside me so that her shoulder is pressing hard against mine.

Snow White is looking at us like we're very young children; maybe we are, to her. "Well, *yours* will. But I have a few questions before it does." She withdraws something slim and silver from her skirts and turns it to face us. For a confused second I think she's showing us a picture on a phone screen—I see two faces, two sets of desperate eyes—before I understand that I'm looking at a mirror.

My mouth goes dry and sandy. My mind goes perfectly blank. Eva goes very, very still.

Snow White strokes the mirror's surface with one pale fingernail. "This mirror of yours. It has shown me things. Other lands. Other worlds, perhaps." I see the future with helpless, ugly clarity: an immortal cannibal wandering from world to world, plucking princesses from their tales like ripe fruit from the trees. She's warped her own story into a gory horror flick; what could she do to the multiverse?

She asks sweetly, "How do I get there?"

"W-why would you ever want to leave your own world?" Other than the perpetual twilight and freakshow fauna. "You've got a great setup here. A lovely, um, lair, and loyal henchpeople."

Snow White makes a moue. "The villagers are getting restless. They're a tiresome bunch, always *fomenting* and *resisting*. It's harder and harder to get what I need." She pinches the flesh of her throat, where the skin has sagged almost imperceptibly. (I have the unhelpful thought that Dr. Bastille would have an absolute field day with this version of Snow White. "The Fear of Age in the Age of Fear: Representations of the Crone in Modern Folk Horror.")

Snow White smiles her sweet, springtime smile. "They're nothing at all like the little *lambs* I see in other worlds. So I will ask you again: How do I get there?"

I don't answer and neither, somewhat to my surprise, does Eva. Her silence fills me with a weird, reckless pride. "Sorry, I'm just getting the most intense déjà vu, you know? I feel like I was just questioned under torture by an evil queen like, yesterday."

This provokes a brief, whispered argument with Eva ("Torture is a strong word." "Well, if the shoe fits." "If the shoe fits what?" "God, never mind."), at the end of which she clears her throat and says audibly, "I'm sorry I hurt you. I shouldn't have."

It feels like the sort of apology you make because you're pretty sure it's your last chance. I move my hand so that my fingers cover hers, because I'm pretty sure she's right. "It's cool," I say inadequately.

Snow White is watching us closely, looking from our faces to the place where our hands touch. She makes a resigned *tsk*. "I can see you're both terribly stubborn. I'll find my own way. I certainly have the time." She makes an imperious gesture and one of her huntsmen steps forward, drawing his sword with a sound like scraping bone as he comes for us. It's all happening way too fast. I thought I could burn more time bullshitting—I thought Charm would still find her way across the universe for me, even without the mirror, because the rules don't apply to us—

But the huntsman doesn't impale either of us. He steps around us to the edge of the fire and reaches into the coals with the tip of his sword. He extracts an ugly tangle of iron. It looks like the kind of thing you'd see in a museum, a mass of old metal with an obscure, chilling label reading *Scold's bridle, 17th c.* or *Pear of anguish, 18th c.*

Then Eva sobs, harsh and sudden, and I realize that I'm looking at two pairs of iron shoes, the metal straps glowing a dull, hellish red.

I curl my fingers tight around Eva's, but her hand is limp and damp in mine. I turn to face her, kneeling, speaking in a desperate rush. "It's okay, I'm sorry, we're going to be alright." But Eva isn't looking at me, or even at the shoes. Her eyes are on Snow White, who has already forgotten us and is now staring into the mirror's surface with a chilling, predatory patience.

Eva's expression as she looks at the queen is not one of panic, or loathing, or even despair. Her face has an eerie coolness to it, a carved-marble quality that makes my chest hurt for no reason. "Hey, listen, Charm knows we're here. She could still save us, okay?"

Eva's eyes move to mine slowly, squinting as if the two of us are standing on opposite sides of a very wide river.

"I hope she does," she says softly. Then, just as softly, she kisses me.

It's dry and gentle. It feels like an apology, or a farewell. "Thank you." She whispers the words against my lips.

The very small part of my brain that isn't occupied by the imminent approach of my own painful death or the salt-sweetness of her mouth manages to say, "For what?"

"For showing me I do not have to be the villain, the evil stepmother, the Wicked Witch of the East Bro. For giving me . . ." Her eyes move back to Snow White, and her lip curls, revealing a slim white line of bared teeth. "Agency."

It's at this point that Eva begins unlacing the front of her dress. My brain splits into two competing factions, one of which is cheering and sounds a lot like Charm on girls' night at the gay bar, and the other of which is thinking how sad it is that Eva has endured so much, only to lose her mind now. "Eva, babe, what are you doing?"

She doesn't answer, drawing the ribbon slowly out of her shift. Except it's not a ribbon, is it? It's a bodice lace.

A syrupy weight settles over my limbs. I notice small things: the minute tilt of Eva's body away from mine. The taut cord of muscle in her neck, the divot in her cheek as she clenches her jaw, bracing herself to do something terrible and brave and stupid. I reach for her. Too late. Eva has already launched herself across the courtyard, knifing through the air like a falcon with dirty white feathers. She collides with Snow White, and then there's a splintering, shattering sound, like a dropped wineglass. Something sharp slices across my cheek.

The courtyard falls into a numbed silence as every eye looks at the ground, at the place where the magic mirror lies in broken shards. I see our faces reflected in the shards, split and doubled, frozen in shock.

There's a large sliver of glass right beside me, close enough to touch. The face reflected in this piece does not belong to the huntsmen, or either of the queens, or even myself. It's a face framed by a long wing of bleached blond hair, with a septum piercing and an expression suggesting homicidal intent, or at least serious bodily harm. The lips of the face are moving, repeating the same name over and over, interspersed with swears: *Zinnia, Zinnia, goddammit Zinnia.*

"Charm, holy shit—" I reach for the shard and my fingers fall through the glass, into the cold rush of the great nothing between worlds. I feel myself tilting into it, falling forward, but I dig my toes into the stones. "Eva, it's Charm! Come on!"

Eva is crouching before the queen with blood oozing from one nostril. She looks back at me and understanding flashes across her face. But she doesn't run to me. She could have. I want that on the record. She could have taken my hand and run, and left this world under the thumb of its wicked queen for another century or two. She could have chosen to survive, like she always had.

Instead, she draws the bodice lace tight between her hands. It gleams sickly green in the firelight.

Eva nods once to me, with a fey, rueful smile, as if to say, *Well, someone has to*, before she surges to her feet and wraps the ribbon around Snow White's throat.

Warm fingers grab my wrist, pulling hard. The last thing I see before I go is Eva—my not-so-wicked queen, my heroic villain—falling beneath the weight of her enemies.

9

I LAND HARD, flat on my back, feeling like a lump of Play-Doh forced through a cheese grater. The sky above me is no longer low and purple, but a bright, suburban blue crisscrossed by jet trails. A few oak leaves slap peacefully against one another. Damp earth soaks through the back of my T-shirt.

I'm in Charm and Prim's backyard in Madison, a place I wasn't totally sure I'd ever see again and from which I now desperately and ironically want to leave.

"Well, if it isn't Little Miss SOS."

I sit up—a considerable, even noble effort, which Charm does not appear to appreciate in the least. She's kneeling beside me, her nose running badly, her cheeks blotched with ash. Prim is on my other side, her enormous eyes crimped with worry. She brushes dirt from my shoulder, plucks something from the greasy nest of my hair.

Behind them is the tiny metal fire ring they bought for their microscopic yard. There's a pair of flip-flops inside the ring, still smoldering gently, sending up chemical curls of bluish smoke.

I give Charm a quick, woozy smile. "Knew you'd figure it out eventually."

A look of relief crosses her face, there and gone again. She throws a sullen glance at the fire ring. "I liked those shoes."

"Uh." The flip-flops are hot-pink plastic. I can see the dollar store sticker still stuck to the underside of the left shoe. "I owe you a pair?"

Charm shrugs. "It's fine." It's clearly not.

"Okay, whatever. I actually need to go back to where I was, like right now, so if you have another pair to burn that would be great. And maybe a mirror?"

Charm doesn't move. "Aren't you forgetting something?" Her tone is cordial, but her eyes are thin and hard.

"Thank you?"

"Maybe try, 'I'm sorry, Charm.'"

"Okay, I'm *sorry*." It comes out bratty, audibly insincere. "But I really have to—"

"Shut the fuck up and listen for a second?" Charm's civility vanishes; she was never a good bullshitter. Prim winces as Charm leans in. "Let's recap our situation, shall we? So, first, I tell you I've got something important to talk about, and you say, 'Sure thing, babe!' But then you Spider-Verse into another dimension and leave me hanging." I have the sinking suspicion that this speech has been rehearsed, more than once, with and without slides. Prim is creeping for the back door now, leaving me to my fate. "Second, you don't talk to me for six months. Which is very mature and chill. Then, third, you send me a damn Aarne-Thompson-Uther index number—even though you specifically told me that system was, quote, 'a Eurocentric mess' that 'should be retired from anthropology syllabi'—and failed to respond to any of my requests for clarification. Leaving me to spend the last seven hours frantically acting out the goddamn plot of goddamn Snow White, ever more certain that you'd already bitten into a poison apple or been assaulted by a wandering prince or some—"

There's a lot more to the speech, judging by the rising volume and level of aggression, but all I can think about is Eva's small, sad smile right before she wrapped the bodice lace around Snow White's neck. Like she knew the choice would damn her and didn't care, because at least she was choosing her own damnation.

I interrupt Charm by throwing my arms around her. She stiffens, then hugs me back so hard it feels vindictive. "You're such a little shit, you know that?"

I pull away. "Yeah. And I'm really, really sorry. I *am*. But I have to find a way back into Snow White right now. I have to save—"

Charm tosses both hands in the air. "Some stranger? What about us, Zin? What about *me*, you absolute *turdbucket*."

"I know! I'm sorry, but people need me, okay?"

Charm chews the inside of her cheek before saying, in a voice that could only be accurately measured by the Kelvin scale, "That. Is what I'm trying to tell you. Bonehead."

A small, extremely uncomfortable silence follows this statement, during which Charm watches me with red, tear-sheened eyes and I call myself every bad name I can think of. It strikes me that neither heroes nor dying girls are very good at sticking around, at the ordinary work of living: calling your friends back and remembering their birthdays, going to the doctor for regular checkups, taking care of the people you love.

Charm sits back, cross-legged, ripping disgustedly at the grass.

"You're so busy mucking around in other worlds you don't even care about the freaky shit happening in your own."

"Like what kind of freaky shit?" I ask, very mildly. But I think I know.

"Like fairy tale shit. I bought one of those frozen apple pies—shut up, they're good—and when we cut into it we found a bunch of blackbirds. Prim's shoes turned to glass one night while she was dancing. Your mom's roses went nuts in December, blooming while there was still snow on the ground."

I unglue my tongue from the roof of my mouth and say carefully, "That's not so bad, is it?"

"Well, it's not great." Charm is tearing the grass up in great handfuls now, her nail beds stained neon. "The birds were all dead and putrefied. Prim's shoes shattered under her—*nine* stitches, she missed weeks of class. And your mom's roses died down to the roots. She tore them all up."

"Oh."

Charm fixes me with a blunt blue eye. "Is it your fault?"

"Maybe."

"Will it get worse?"

"Uh, maybe. Yeah." I look away from her. "If I don't stop."

"Then . . ." Charm presses the heels of her hands into her eyes. "Jesus, why don't you?"

"I should. I will! But . . ." But somewhere along the line, Eva became one of the people I'm supposed to take care of, and she needs me, and the physical laws of the multiverse can go straight to hell. "But first I need to borrow your phone."

Charm stands. She stares down at me with an expression somehow worse than anger, or even disappointment. It's a sort of bitter, self-directed chagrin, as if she's annoyed that she allowed herself to be disappointed by me again. She slams her phone down on the plastic card table as she leaves.

It takes me a minute to guess her passcode (8008, because Charm still has a seventh grader's sense of humor), and another minute to find the faculty contact information on Ohio University's site.

The phone slips against the clammy sweat of my face. "Hi, this is Zinnia Gray. Is Dr. Bastille available?"

❁ ❁ ❁

"So—AGAIN, HYPOTHETICALLY—HOW COULD the protagonist get back into that Snow White story without the magic mirror?"

Dr. Bastille sighs on the other end of the line. It seems to go on a very long time, as if she's holding her phone in front of a box fan. "Well, *hypothetically*, if you were my student and you came into my office and told me . . . everything you just told me"—over the last six to eight minutes, I've given her the SparkNotes version of my life, framing it all somewhat unconvincingly as the plot of a very meta novella I'm working on—"I would be legally and morally obligated to refer you to campus counseling services."

"Good thing I'm not your student anymore, huh."

"Zinnia, that's not better. You see how that's not better, right? If a random person came into my office to talk about the fairy tale multiverse, I would probably swallow my personal convictions about law enforcement's role in the violent maintenance of race and class hierarchies"—this is ivory tower speak for *fuck the cops*—"and call security."

"Sure, I get that, but what if I was very convincing and desperate-seeming, and you were sort of compelled to advise me despite your better judgment?" I'm trying to bully her into a specific narrative role—the expert consultant/holder of arcane knowledge who offers wise counsel to the protagonist in their hour of need and saves their bacon—but I can feel Dr. Bastille resisting it. She's never much liked playing prescribed roles.

I hear her pulling the phone away from her face, saying *I'll just be a minute, love* to someone else. A woman's voice says something about dinner reservations in a tone suggesting they have been made and broken before.

Dr. Bastille sighs into the receiver again. "Alright. Given the parameters of the story you just told me, it is my professional opinion that you've written yourself into a corner."

"What does that mean?"

"It means you're screwed."

"I—okay." The grass feels very cold on my bare feet, the sky very high above me.

"You said the only way to cross into other tale types was by way of a particular enchanted object. A useful MacGuffin which is now, according to you, broken. So your protagonist doesn't have a magic mirror, and neither does the villain-slash-love-interest—a trend in popular fiction which I find beneath you, by the way"—Dr. Bastille elects to ignore my sighed *I wish*—"and I don't think the physical laws of this universe allow for the creation of enchanted objects. Do they?"

I'm circling the fire pit now, letting the plastic-smelling smoke sear my eyes. "I guess not."

"Which seems like it might be a good thing, because your protagonist's hypothetical wanderings were doing substantial damage to the fabric of the space-time continuum, were they not?"

"But like, why?" My voice goes high on the last word, wobbling perilously. "Why is it such a big deal if I—I mean, my character—doesn't just lie down and wait for the trolley to hit her? Why can't she run away?"

I can hear a familiar creaking through the line, as if Dr. Bastille is leaning back in her office chair and pinching the bridge of her nose. She did this often in our advisee meetings. "In this novella, you've posited narratives as literal worlds. So stories are the organizing principle of the multiverse—which raises some serious world-building questions, by the way, like where these story-verses come from in the first place, since the existence of any story implies the existence of a storyteller." She pauses to address her date: *No, you go ahead, I'll meet you there.* "Anyway, you've created a universe that runs on plot, and a main character who smashes plots like a human wrecking ball. In refusing to complete her narrative arc, she is compromising the integrity of the universe."

"Oh." The smoke scorches my eyes, burns the inside of my nose. "Then this is it. It's over."

"It does seem a dissatisfying climax."

"Yeah. Well." My nose is running badly now. "Thanks for your time."

"Sure." The creak of her chair, the shush of arms sliding into coat sleeves. Dr. Bastille's voice softens very slightly when she says, "I'd be happy to read it, when it's done."

"Read what?"

"The . . . never mind. Good luck, Zinnia." She hangs up.

I set Charm's phone back on the card table and sink slowly to my knees. My eyes are too full of tears to see much beyond fractal green, but I search the grass with my hands, crawling in circles. All I find are beer caps, a few waterlogged roaches, the sharp tops of acorns.

There are no shards of magic mirror in Charm's backyard. Which means Dr. Bastille was right. I'm screwed, and so is Eva.

❁ ❁ ❁

I PACE THE yard for a while, inventing and dismissing a dozen unlikely schemes. It occurs to me eventually that I'm doing what my therapist would call *bargaining*, and that bargaining is a stage of grief.

Charm and Prim are in the kitchen, speaking in tense, low voices. They stop when the screen door shuts behind me. Charm gives me a searching stare, which I return blankly until she turns back to the dishes. Prim looks fretfully between the two of us for a moment, but there's no real question which side she'll pick. She unfolds a dish towel and dries a mixing bowl at Charm's side.

I walk down the hall to the bedroom that is supposedly mine but which actually functions as a walk-in closet. I pick my way through yoga mats and wrapping paper, trash bags of winter clothes, a laundry basket filled with velvet gowns, pewter goblets, all the crap I hadn't sold at the Ren faire before I disappeared. The futon is buried, so I sit on a box of unassembled furniture with THREE IN ONE! written across the side in bubbly, childish letters.

I stare at the wall and test the words on my tongue: *The end.* It's not such a bad ending, I guess. It's a sort of cosmic compromise with the universe. I don't get to magically cure my disease and con my way out of my own plot, but at least I didn't drop dead at twenty-one; Eva doesn't get to live as a hero, but at least she didn't die a villain.

It's not exactly happily ever after, but that's a pretty bullshit concept anyway. Honestly, I don't even know why I'm crying.

Later, long after the clink of dishes has faded and the tears have left my cheeks stiff and dry, the door inches open. I assume it's Charm coming back for round two, but it's Prim. She steps easily through the detritus and clears a space on the futon. Neither of us say anything for a while. She just sits there with her perfect posture and her perfect hair, and I notice the fine lines at the corners of her mouth, the slight pucker of skin beneath her eyes.

She doesn't look old or anything, just ordinary. Like any other girl who wakes up every morning and makes coffee a little stronger than she prefers because that's how her wife likes it, who shops at the farmer's market every Saturday, who will look in the mirror in ten years and start googling eye creams even though her wife insists she's always had a thing for crow's feet. Maybe happily ever after isn't a totally bullshit concept, after all; maybe, if I can't have my own, I can at least find the decency not to ruin this one.

I inhale. "I know I've been a shitty friend. And a lackwit, and all those other things Charm called me."

"Well, actually." Prim gives a small, embarrassed cough. "I sent that text."

I don't say anything, relishing the rare feeling of having the moral high ground. Prim squirms for a minute before adding, in a rush, "I was upset because Charm was hurt—*again*—and she was just going to keep giving you chances to hurt her, and I didn't want to watch."

Okay, maybe I'm not on the high ground after all. "I know. It's just . . . I guess I wasn't ready to talk about appointments and treatment plans and all that stuff. I didn't want to be *worried* over, you know? I wanted to make my own choices, choose my own consequences, live my own—"

"Zinnia," Prim interrupts, softly and gravely. Her gaze is very sober. "We want to adopt."

"Um, that's good? Does this place allow pets?"

She blinks at me, and an expression of great pity crosses her face.

"No. It doesn't." Her eyes move to the box of furniture I'm sitting on. I look down and notice for the first time that there is a picture of a blissful-looking baby on the front. The small print explains that the contents of the box can be used as a bassinet, crib, and toddler bed as your "little one" grows.

I feel suddenly very, very young and very, very stupid. "Oh," I say weakly.

"That start-up offered Charm a full-time position last year, and she took it. So the timing feels right, and it turns out I want children very much, once I realized they could be obtained outside of heteronormative and patriarchal conceptions of marriage." I remember Charm telling me last year that Prim signed up to audit some classes at UW; apparently she liked them.

"Wow, I'm so . . ." Happy? Terrified? Abruptly conscious of the passage of time and fearful of my changing position in what was, until recently, a trio of friends? My voice shrinks. "I didn't know."

"Well, you wouldn't." Prim doesn't sound especially sympathetic. "You left when Charm tried to tell you. She wanted to ask about using this bedroom, once the paperwork was filed."

"Oh," I say again, even more weakly. I dampen my lips. "So . . . how's it going? I heard it can take a while."

Prim's cool composure slips. She looks away and swallows twice. "We never filed the paperwork, actually. Charm hasn't signed it."

A chill settles in the pit of my stomach, a premonition of guilt. "Why not?"

Prim's posture is imperfect now, her shoulders bent. "She says it's because she's not ready to give up beer, but I think she's scared."

"Of what?"

Prim rarely snaps—you can take the princess out of the royal court, but you can't take the royal court out of the princess, or something—but now she snaps, "Of doing it without her best friend, maybe."

The guilt arrives, cold and heavy as a swallowed stone. "Look, I'm really, *really*—"

She interrupts. "Or maybe she's just scared of messing it up, the way her parents did. Adoption . . . wasn't easy for her." This is a massive understatement; I once overheard her mom lamenting Charm's (unremarkable, classically teenaged) behavior to my mom. *You'd just think she'd be more grateful, wouldn't you?* Mom had looked at her like she was a new kind of fungus on one of her rose bushes. I'd never told Charm, but it's not like she didn't know the score.

"Yeah, I can see that."

Prim picks at invisible lint on the futon. "I'm scared, too, to tell the truth. My childhood was not particularly easy either, but . . ." She shrugs, as if the next thing she says isn't that important. "I wish I could talk to my mother."

I move over to the futon, sitting so close our shoulders touch. "Hey, at least there's no wicked fairies in this world." It's an effortful joke.

Prim laughs, equally effortfully. "Well, not yet. But I saw those glass slippers, and the dead birds. This world is not so safe as I had hoped."

The guilt doubles, or maybe quadruples. It's a wonder I have any room left for ordinary human organs. I fumble for something comforting to say and emerge with "No world is very safe, in my experience."

It seems, inexplicably, to help. Prim straightens again and nods at no one in particular. "No. Which means all that matters really is who you have standing at your side. Charm and I have each other, and if that has to be enough, it will." She pauses, perhaps having run out of grand proclamations. "But where I come from, fairy godmothers are traditional. Twelve seems excessive, but if I had a daughter I should hope for at least one."

She meets my eyes as she says the word *one*, her expression simultaneously arch and a little anxious. Like she's just asked me to carry something large but fragile, infinitely precious, and isn't sure I'm up to the task. Like she wants to trust me, but isn't sure she should.

I have the absurd urge to kneel. Fresh tears prickle in the corners of my eyes. "That would be—*I* would be—" I swallow. "Like, I know I haven't been that reliable lately, and I can't promise that my GRM will stay in remission or whatever—but it would be my honor."

Prim nods without breaking eye contact. Her gaze feels like a sword touching each of my shoulders, not especially gently. "Good." She inhales sharply and draws something from her pocket. "We'll talk more when you come back, then."

I know I'm not at my sharpest—having been zapped into a dozen different universes, lightly tortured, imprisoned, kissed, nearly executed, rescued, and chastised by pretty much everyone I've ever met—but this feels like a real left turn in the conversation. "Come back from where?"

Prim hands me the thing she took out of her pocket. It's long and silver, and in its surface I catch the blue flash of her eyes, the glare of the cheap light fixture above us.

It's a long, broken shard of mirror. "I pulled it from your hair when you first arrived."

I could kiss her. I could ask her what the hell took her so long. I could weep, because hope is so much more terrifying than despair.

I draw a breath that shakes only slightly. "Tell Charm I'm coming back, okay? For good, this time. Cross my heart." I don't wait for Prim to agree, or tell me to be careful. I hold the shard so that it reflects a jagged piece of my own face, and whisper to it: *Mirror, mirror.*

In an objective and literal sense, there's no way Eva is the fairest of them all—her face is too square and her mouth is too wide, and she's maybe a smidge too old—but that's the face the mirror shows me when I ask, and the mirror never lies. Maybe beauty really is in the eye of the beholder, and if the beholder is willing to ditch her friends and damage the fabric of space and time for someone, the mirror logically assumes they're past the point of objective beauty standards.

Which I guess I am, because Eva's face makes it suddenly difficult to breathe. I fall toward her, diving through nowhere, feeling like a smear of toothpaste being squeezed out of some cosmic tube. I'm braced to land in hellish chaos—a burning castle filled with murderous huntsmen, perhaps, or a public execution—but I find myself standing in a small, whitewashed room with lots of windows and no blood at all.

It doesn't look like the sort of room that could

conceivably exist anywhere in Evil Snow White's castle, or even in the same world. The light slanting through the windows is an ordinary dusky gold rather than the malevolent violet of endless twilight; the fire in the hearth is cheery and warm and probably was not made to heat iron shoes or boil human soup. The whole place reminds me strongly of Zellandine's hut, except a little emptier and newer.

I would assume I'd made a wrong turn in nowheresville if it weren't for Eva. The queen—*my* queen—is sitting at a small table, fiddling with something shiny.

I make a small, embarrassing sound in the back of my throat, nearly a whimper; she looks up.

And she's—fine. A little tired, maybe, but not tormented or terrified. There's a crust of red around one nostril, but no mortal wounds. She's still wearing her sheer white shift, grimed with prison filth, but there's a plain cloak draped over her shoulders now. Her feet are bare on the floor, the skin smooth and unhurt.

One side of her mouth tilts. There's a light in her eyes that doesn't quite manage to be a wicked gleam. "Why, Lady Zinnia," she drawls. "Have you come to rescue me?"

"I . . ." I glance around the room, which persists in being almost aggressively nonthreatening. "This was a whole lot cooler in my head. How come you don't need rescuing?" I remember, very distantly, wishing more of the princesses would rescue themselves. "The last thing I saw was the huntsmen coming for you, on account of how you assassinated their immortal monarch."

"Yes, well, you left before it got interesting."

She says it with a sly bat of her eyelashes, but another pound of guilt settles in my stomach. I'm surprised there's room, at this point. "I didn't mean to." I make myself meet her eyes. "Leave, I mean."

Eva shrugs, performatively careless. "Why not? I would have."

"But like, you didn't. You could have, but you chose to stay." Which means an actual storybook villain has more moral fiber than I do, apparently. "Anyway, Charm pulled me through the mirror. I wouldn't have left you there, I swear."

Eva looks away and says quietly, "I know." She looks back. "Maybe that's why I stayed." The intensity of the eye contact following this statement makes me think she doesn't hate my guts at all, actually, and if the multiverse stopped breaking and people stopped attacking us for a minute we could do a lot better than a couple of hurried, clumsy kisses.

"Here, sit down." Eva gestures to a second chair. She isn't blushing, but her throat is pinker than I remember it being. "If you'd stayed another thirty seconds or so, you would have seen Red and her people storm the courtyard, cast Snow White's crown into the fire, and declare the glorious revolution."

I blink a few times. I'm not sure any version of Snow White ends with an anti-royalist uprising. "No shit?"

"None whatsoever. Apparently, her parents were highly placed in the revolutionary movement, and Red convinced them to accelerate their plans on our behalf." Eva's smile is small and wry. "It never occurred to me that the person you save might save you in turn. Perhaps survival is less solitary than I'd thought."

I think of Charm and Prim, who saved me, who are still hoping I'll stick around and hold up my half of the bargain. "That's been my experience, yeah." My voice sounds thick in my ears.

"I believe they'll crown Red as their new queen soon. I mean, I overheard some very dense discussion of the monarchy as a symbolic rather than political position, and something about a body of elected representatives, which all sounds rather messy, but"—Eva shrugs—"I suppose it's close enough. The innocent girl sits upon her throne, the wicked witch is dead."

"Is she? Dead, I mean."

Eva looks at my face and then quickly away. "No," she says softly. "I don't know how her story will end, or whether redemption is possible for a creature like that, but I . . . asked that she be spared. They will build a glass tomb for her so that anyone who likes can see the proof of her defeat. And make sure she still sleeps."

I have an urge to reach across the table and put my hand over hers, which I squelch before remembering that I'm not a dying girl or a hero anymore. I put my hand over hers. "So how did you end up here? Wherever here is."

Eva's hand turns palm-up under mine. Her neck is now a definite shade of coral. "I didn't feel I should linger long in the castle. Red and her parents seemed grateful, but their friends didn't seem especially fond of witches or queens, so I left. And I found a little house waiting for me in the woods, just like there always is." Her smile this time looks like hard work. "So I suppose I shall rot away in a little hut, after all. It's better than being tortured to death."

I can hear the compromise in her voice, the same mediocre deal I cut in my own world. She's not dead, but she's still nameless and powerless, still trapped at the margins of a story that doesn't belong to her. Not a happy ending, but then, she's not the main character.

I find myself grasping desperately for alternatives. A voice that sounds very much like my therapist says, *Bargaining again?* I ignore it. "What if—maybe you could . . ." My eyes fall to the table, where she's arranged a glittering jigsaw of mirror shards. She's fit them all carefully back into the battered silver frame, with a single gap left for a missing piece. "You could come back to my world. With me. The mirror still works—"

Eva's fingers tighten around mine, but her voice is wistful. "And who would I be in your world?"

"I don't know, nobody in particular I guess?"

"Here I'd hoped to be somebody, one day. Isn't that silly?"

I want to shake her. "I didn't mean literally nobody, just like, not magical or royal or whatever. You could be a chemist or a fortuneteller or something, anything you wanted. I'd help."

She sighs in a way that reminds me forcibly of Dr. Bastille. "I know. Thank you." She slides her hand gently away from mine. "But I heard what Zellandine told you. I can't go with you, and you can't stay here without causing great harm." Her voice lowers. "We can't keep running from our stories forever."

"No." I don't know whether I'm agreeing or disagreeing with her. My lips feel numb.

Eva rises slowly from the table and takes a book from the shelf. The cover is worn red cloth, with a purplish stain on the back. "This was here when I arrived, somehow. It belongs back in your world, I suppose." She tries to say it casually, but I see the way her thumb moves along the spine.

I reach for the book with a feeling of profound unreality, flipping through the pages because that's what you do when someone hands you a book and you don't know what to say. Rackham's art flutters past like tangled shadows: branches and ball gowns, towers and thorns, dozens of dark tales told so many times they came true.

I think of Dr. Bastille saying tartly, *The existence of any story implies the existence of a storyteller.* I guess there must have been a first time each of these stories was told, somewhere in the way-back reaches of time, centuries before the Grimms ever tried to turn a profit on them. It was probably just some ordinary person whispering across a fire or carving pictures into whalebones or daubing mud on the walls of a cave, casually calling a new universe into existence.

It occurs to me with a sudden, slightly hysterical surge of hope that

I am a pretty ordinary person, myself. That the only thing stopping me from writing a new story is the fact that I'm bad at it, and dropped my creative writing class after three weeks rather than suffer a B+. I felt self-conscious and stupid every time I sat down to write, very aware that I was just making things up. But maybe every story is a lie until it isn't; maybe I'm not the one who has to tell it, anyway.

"Do you have a pen?" My voice sounds completely normal, as if my pulse is not double-timing in my throat, as if my whole heart isn't resting on the success or failure of this extremely sketchy plan.

Eva produces a trimmed feather and a pot of ink, looking at me as if faintly worried about mental stability. I turn to the very back of the book, past the afterword and the publisher's note about the typeface, past Rackham's final, curling vine. There are three extra pages at the end, entirely blank.

I set the quill to the page and write: *Once upon a time . . .*

And I swear, the universe listens. I feel it as a silent thrumming through the soles of my feet, the plucking of a string too vast to hear. The windows rattle in their frames.

I add another clumsy sentence or two about a princess who grew into a queen who became a villain and then, eventually, a hero. I spin the book to face Eva and slide it across the table. "Your turn."

She reads the page and her face goes tight and still. A muscle moves in her jaw. "I don't know what happens next."

I twirl the feather. "It's your story. You tell me."

I can't tell if she understands what I'm trying to do, or if she thinks the whole thing is some sort of inane therapy exercise, but when she takes the pen, her hand is shaking. She sits for a while, rolling the quill in her fingertips and staring at the page with a faint frown, before she begins to write.

It takes a lot longer than I expect it to. Eva pauses after every sentence to do some more staring and frowning. She blots out entire paragraphs and starts them over, often several times in a row. At one point she actually makes a motion as if she's going to ball the page up and toss it away like a novelist in a bad movie, before apparently recalling that she's writing in my favorite childhood book. She restrains herself to crossing out another paragraph.

I watch her, listening to the sound I can't really hear, hoping for a future that doesn't yet exist.

Night has fallen by the time she finishes. She doesn't set her pen down in triumph or anything, but I know the story is done because I feel it. The thrumming stops. The air changes. It's like someone has opened an invisible door and let in a breeze that smells like frost and fresh apples.

Eva gives a little sigh and un-hunches herself from the page.

"Looks good," I say over her shoulder, and the queen startles so badly she chokes. Apparently she hadn't noticed me getting up, rummaging for candles, asking three or four times if she was hungry, and eventually giving up and standing behind her. I thump her good and hard on the back. "Needs a title, though."

When Eva stops coughing, she flips back to the beginning of her story and runs her finger across the empty space above the words *once upon a time*. "I don't know what to call it." Her voice is hoarse and low. "I've never done this before."

I drag my chair around the table so I can sit catty-corner to her. "Well, it's your call, but the Grimms generally named their stories after the protagonist."

She goes still beside me. Only her eyes move, meeting mine. I assure myself that it's just the candles that make them look that way, bright and burning. Nobody's eyes are full of literal light; nobody's gaze actually smolders.

She writes a name without speaking.

I read the word, pretending not to notice the pair of watery tear drops blotting the page beside it. "You know I was just teasing when I called you that. You can choose any name you want."

"I have." Her tone might manage to be imperious, if there weren't tears in it. "How do we know if it . . . worked?"

I don't answer. I slide the last shard of mirror across the table, the one Prim plucked from my hair, and fit it neatly into the frame. Our faces look up at us from the surface, fissured and cracked, but exactly as we are: a skinny, sharp-chinned woman in a dirty T-shirt and a hard, hungry queen with a surprising number of freckles.

The only difference is what's behind us. There are no whitewashed walls in the mirror. It's distant and blurred, but I think I see a rich, rolling landscape, a stone shape that might be a castle. A new story, unfolding around us in all directions.

I take Eva's hand and place it gently on the mirror's surface. Her fingers fall through the glass as if it's an open window.

She doesn't drag me into the space between worlds this time. She looks at me with a question in her eyes, and I shrug. "One more time can't hurt, can it?"

Eva smiles. We fall together into the vast nowhere, where my imaginary body fights for air that doesn't exist, where the only real thing is the heat of her hand holding tight to mine.

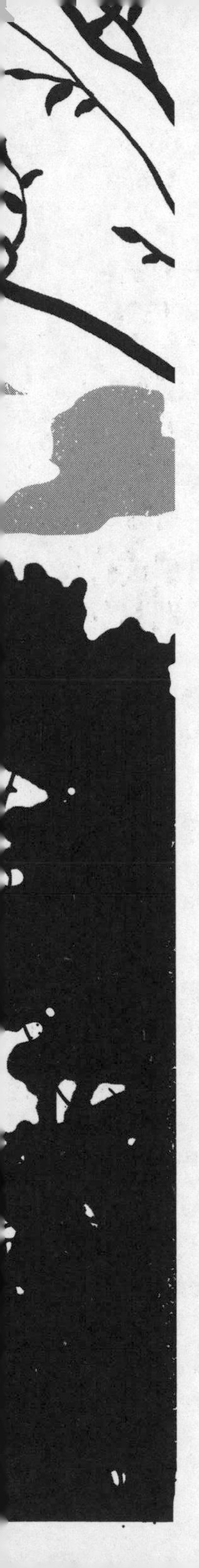

11

THIS IS, DEPENDING on how you count it, either my forty-ninth or fiftieth happily ever after, but I don't mind. It turns out I'm not quite sick of them yet.

It shouldn't be daylight for hours, but somehow we've arrived at that perfect moment just after dawn, when the air rushes away from the horizon and lays tall grasses low. The sunlight transforms the frost into dew and the dew into mist, which coils catlike around our skirts. There are trees surrounding us again, but they aren't dark or tangled. They stand in long, neat lines, their branches spreading low. An orchard, at dawn.

Eva is turning in a slow, wary circle, as if she's waiting for someone to leap out from behind a tree and shout, "Seize her!" No one does. Instead, the mist parts to reveal a pale stone castle standing on a distant hill. It's not very big or grand—in castle terms, it might even be called modest—and there's a shabbiness to it that suggests empty halls and unclaimed thrones. But it's enough for Eva, I can tell. Her mouth falls open as she looks at it.

A throne of one's own. A happily ever after fit for a queen. I have to remind myself forcefully that I'm not a queen or even a princess, and this story doesn't belong to me.

I expect Eva to stride straight for the castle, but she turns back to me. Her smile is wide and young, almost giddy. There are no convenient candles to blame for the bright blaze of her eyes. "It's better than I imagined."

I grab my own elbows so I don't do anything stupid, like fling myself at her. "Yeah, it's not bad." It takes a moment to unglue my tongue from the roof of my mouth. "It suits you."

A little wariness creeps back across her face. Her tone turns haughty, the way it does when she's uncertain. "Do you think it might suit you, as well?"

"I mean, sure." I find it easier to speak to her if I close my eyes. "But you know I can't stay."

"Because of the harm it would do to the universe." There's a flattering amount of grief in her voice.

"Yeah, and because Charm would murder me." And Prim would hide the body, and my parents would testify in court that I deserved it. "There are these people, back in my world, who need me."

"Still playing the hero." A note of bitterness this time.

"No, I need them too. It's just—they're my story. And I can't keep running away from them." I scrape together enough guts to open my eyes and find Eva looking at me with whatever the opposite of pity is—admiration, maybe, or compassion. I dig my fingertips into my elbows.

"So anyway. Enjoy your happily ever after."

Her lips curve in an expression too sad to be called a smile. "You know, I don't think I believe in those."

I raise my eyebrows at the bucolic perfection surrounding us, a Cézanne painting come to life. "Could've fooled me."

Eva takes a step nearer and hands me the red-bound book of fairy tales. "The last line was the hardest to get right. I tried to write it in the usual way, but it gave me goosebumps. It felt like a promise that couldn't be kept, a story that couldn't end."

I flip to the last page of my book, no longer blank. Her hand must have stopped shaking by then, because the last three words are firm and smooth on the page: *She lived happily.* The period is an emphatic black circle.

And then I'm on the sudden, embarrassing verge of tears. Maybe because I've gone a really long time without eating or sleeping and my nerves are shot. Maybe because I've fallen pretty hard for the (former) villain and don't want to leave her. Maybe because it never occurred to me that it could be enough just to *live*, as happily as you can, for as long as you have.

There are more wet splotches on the page now, distorting Eva's neat handwriting. She's gracious enough not to mention it.

I hear the soft tread of her bare feet, then the rustle of leaves, like she's plucked something from a branch. When she returns, she stands close enough that I can see the hem of her shift, the grass-stained ends of her toes. If I had the nerve to look up, her face would be inches away from mine. I don't look up.

"So. I will stay, and you will go home, and both of us will live happily." Eva's voice is light and easy. I nod at my book and cry a little harder.

She reaches for my hand and turns it palm up. She places something smooth and round in it: an apple. The skin is a glassy, poisonous red that only exists in fairy tales.

My laugh is watery. "Old habits, huh?" I scrub my face on my own shoulder. "Will I fall into an endless sleeping death if I take a bite?"

Eva's breath stirs my hair. "If you did, I know someone who would kiss you back to life."

On this, both our stories agree: a girl in an accursed sleep is woken by her true love. It's a strange point of plot convergence, a resonance that makes my skin prickle. I elect to ignore it; it feels too much like hope.

Instead, I look up at Eva and raise the apple to my lips. She watches my teeth pop through the skin and her eyes go suddenly wide and dark, as if she's just solved some very complex equation.

I'd like to say something seductive and clever, which maybe raises the chances of this scene ending with us making out, but what I say is, "You know there's no kiss in the Grimms' version, right? Snow White just barfs up a chunk of apple."

A cool finger touches my chin, tilts my head upward until I'm looking straight into the black satin of Eva's eyes. "This is my story, and I'll tell it how I like." If we were in a sexier sort of romance, I might call the tone of her voice a *purr*; I might note that her finger is still curled beneath my chin, that if I stood on my tiptoes our lips would touch.

"Uh." I swallow. The apple is sharp in my throat. "I don't actually have to leave right this second. I mean, I told Prim I'd come back, and I meant it, but I didn't give her like, a specific date and time—"

I don't finish the sentence, because the queen kisses me, and I kiss her back. I don't even have to stand on tiptoes, because she bends to meet me.

It's technically our third kiss, I guess, but the first two barely count. They were conducted under stressful conditions and interrupted by trips through the multiverse or attempts on our lives. Nothing interrupts us this time. We stand at the crossroads of our stories, in a kingdom of two, kissing in the rising light of a new world.

We do a lot more than kiss, actually, but that's between the queen and me.

Later—like, *much* later, not that I'm bragging—we leave the orchard and wander over the hills, into the castle. We drift through the halls without speaking, our hands clasped, our steps unhurried. But eventually I find a staircase that circles upward, and a round room waiting at the top of the tallest tower.

Eva kisses me once more, a brief heat against my cheek. "Thank you," she whispers, and slips something round and smooth into my left hand.

"We have apples in Ohio, you know."

"Good," she says. "Then you can save this one for the very end." She says it lightly, but I can see that vast equation in her eyes again. I guess evil queens can't help but scheme.

Eva holds her magic mirror to face me. I just stand there for a minute, looking at her, trying hard to convince myself that this is enough, that I'm content. My reflection in the mirror doesn't buy it; my face is pale and sharp, fractured with grief.

At least this time, when I touch the mirror and fall into the space between worlds, I'm not running away or rushing to anyone's rescue. I'm not looking for a new once upon a time or hoping, secretly and shamefully, for my happily ever after. This time I'm just trying to live. Happily.

❁ ❁ ❁

I OPEN MY eyes when my feet touch cold tile. I'm standing in Charm and Prim's tiny bathroom, looking at my own face in their medicine cabinet mirror. I can hear small, domestic sounds through the door: the hum of a vacuum, the clink of a spoon.

I can't make myself open the door just yet, so I study the apple in my hand. It's that same slick, unlikely red, but this one isn't unblemished. It looks like someone has pushed their fingernail through the skin, again and again, writing a message into the white flesh:

BITE ME

I smile, a little painfully, and then Eva's voice echoes in my skull: *I know someone who would kiss you back to life*, and *for the very end*. I stop smiling. My heartbeat sounds uneven, very far away. I wonder, distantly, why I'm so surprised. When you save someone, sometimes they save you right back.

I don't know if it would actually work. I don't know if Eva would wait for me that long, or if her kiss could cure me, or if we would irrevocably break the rules of the universe. But what rules would we be breaking, really? An unlucky girl falls into a terrible sleep; her true love wakes her. That piece of the plot could belong to either of us, couldn't it? It feels like a loophole, a cheat code, a chance. It feels like hope.

My story will still end—every story does—but I no longer know when, or how, or where. All I know for sure is what happens next, and I find it's enough for me.

I set the apple carefully on the edge of the sink and clear my throat. "Hey, uh, guys?"

The vacuum goes silent. A muffled conversation follows ("Who the fuck was that?" "It sounded like—" "I will *flay* her.").

I raise my voice, smiling at my own face in the mirror. "I'm home."

ACKNOWLEDGMENTS

This is technically the third acknowledgments section I've written for these two stories; that is, in itself, a testament to the hard work, generosity, and talent of the people behind these books.

I am privileged to thank all the usual suspects: my agent, Kate McKean; my editors, Jonathan Strahan and Carl Engle-Laird; expert consultants Ace Tilton Ratcliffe and J. D. Myall; the cover artist, David Curtis, and the entire team at Tordotcom, including Greg Collins, Christine Foltzer, Matt Rusin, Oliver Dougherty, Isa Caban, Giselle Gonzalez, Megan Barnard, Eileen Lawrence, Amanda Melfi, Dakota Griffin, Jim Kapp, Sarah Reidy, Lauren Hougen, Rebecca Naimon, Michelle Li, Ardyce Alspach, Jeremy Pink, Kyle Avery, Cassie Gitkin, and everyone from Tor Ad/Promo; the occupants of the bunker, who suffered collectively through every draft; my friends, new and old; my mom, for lovingly and criminally copying all those Disney VHS tapes from Blockbuster; my dad, for patiently rewinding the tapes when the VCR ate them; my boys, for letting me read out loud to them for at least a little while longer; Nick, for keeping me fed, warm, entertained, mostly sane, and obnoxiously happy.

I wrote these novellas during the worst of the pandemic. In retrospect, it doesn't surprise me that I escaped into the stories of my childhood, running through the nostalgic, frustrating, goofy, gorgeous, cliché world of fairy tales. What surprised me, and continues to surprise me, is that so many of you ran with me.

Which makes *you* the last person I have to thank. Without you, this book literally wouldn't exist.

ABOUT THE AUTHOR

Elora Overbey

ALIX E. HARROW is the Hugo Award–winning author of *The Ten Thousand Doors of January*, *The Once and Future Witches*, and various short fiction. Her Fractured Fables series, beginning with the novella *A Spindle Splintered*, has been praised for its refreshing twist on familiar fairy tales. A former academic and adjunct, Harrow lives in Virginia with her husband and their two semi-feral kids.

alixeharrow.wixsite.com/author
Instagram: @alix.e.harrow